CHOSEN

"With each book in the series, not only have Stein's characters become stronger but so has her writing . . . hard-hitting urban fantasy with a hard-hitting female lead." —*Fresh Fiction*

"I walked away from the book with a lot of thoughts and questions as well, and cannot wait to see where Anna's adventures take her next . . . *Chosen* is an excellent book and probably the most enthralling book in the series thus far." —*Bitten by Books*

"From the opening chapter of this terrific series, Stein has sent her gutsy heroine on an uncharted journey filled with danger and bitter betrayal . . . In this pivotal but emotionally brutal book, skillful Stein reveals some critical answers and delivers some devastating blows. Like a fine wine, this series is improving with age. Brava!" —*Romantic Times* (4½ stars)

RETRIBUTION

"The fifth book in the exceptional first-person Anna Strong series is a powerful entry in an amazing saga." —*Romantic Times*

"Ms. Stein has a true gift in storytelling and continues to add exciting new elements to this well-built world. *Retribution* is an engrossing read with an action-packed story line and secondary characters that are every bit as intriguing as the heroine. This is a must-read for fans of the series!" —*Darque Reviews*

LEGACY

"Urban fantasy with true depth and flair!"
—*Romantic Times* (4½ stars)

"As riveting as the rest . . . one of my favorite urban fantasy series." —*Darque Reviews*

continued . . .

THE WATCHER

BLOOD DRIVE

"A really great series. Anna's strengths and weaknesses make for a very compelling character. Stein really puts you in [Anna's] head as she fumbles her way through a new life and the heart-breaking choices she will have to make. [Stein] also introduces new supernatural characters and gives a glimpse into a secret underground organization. This is a pretty cool urban fantasy series that will appeal to fans of Patricia Briggs's Mercy Thompson series."

—*Vampire Genre*

THE BECOMING

"This is a really, really good book. Anna is a great character, Stein's plotting is adventurous and original, and I think most of my readers would have a great time with *The Becoming*."

—Charlaine Harris, #1 *New York Times* bestselling author of the Sookie Stackhouse novels

"A cross between MaryJanice Davidson's Undead series starring Betsy Taylor, and Laurell K. Hamilton's Anita Blake series. [Anna's] a kick-butt bounty hunter—but vampires are a complete surprise to her. Full of interesting twists and turns that will leave readers guessing. *The Becoming* is a great addition to the TBR pile."

—*Romance Reviews Today*

"With plot twists, engaging characters and smart writing, this first installment in a new supernatural series has all the marks of a hit. Anna Strong lives up to her name: equally tenacious and vulnerable, she's a heroine with the charm, savvy and intelligence that fans of Laurell K. Hamilton and Kim Harrison will be happy to root for . . . If this debut novel is any indication, Stein has a fine career ahead of her."

—*Publishers Weekly*

"In an almost Hitchcockian way, this story keeps you guessing, with new twists and turns coming almost every page. Anna is well named, strong in ways she does not even know. There is a strong element of surprise to it . . . Even if you don't like vampire novels, you ought to give this one a shot."

—*Huntress Book Reviews*

"A wonderful new vampire book . . . that will keep you on the edge of your seat."

—*Fallen Angel Reviews*

Ace Books by Jeanne C. Stein

THE BECOMING
BLOOD DRIVE
THE WATCHER
LEGACY
RETRIBUTION
CHOSEN
CROSSROADS

CROSSROADS

JEANNE C. STEIN

ACE BOOKS, NEW YORK

THE BERKLEY PUBLISHING GROUP
Published by the Penguin Group
Penguin Group (USA) Inc.
375 Hudson Street, New York, New York 10014, USA
Penguin Group (Canada), 90 Eglinton Avenue East, Suite 700, Toronto, Ontario M4P 2Y3, Canada
(a division of Pearson Penguin Canada Inc.)
Penguin Books Ltd., 80 Strand, London WC2R 0RL, England
Penguin Group Ireland, 25 St. Stephen's Green, Dublin 2, Ireland (a division of Penguin Books Ltd.)
Penguin Group (Australia), 250 Camberwell Road, Camberwell, Victoria 3124, Australia
(a division of Pearson Australia Group Pty. Ltd.)
Penguin Books India Pvt. Ltd., 11 Community Centre, Panchsheel Park, New Delhi—110 017, India
Penguin Group (NZ), 67 Apollo Drive, Rosedale, Auckland 0632, New Zealand
(a division of Pearson New Zealand Ltd.)
Penguin Books (South Africa) (Pty.) Ltd., 24 Sturdee Avenue, Rosebank, Johannesburg 2196,
South Africa

Penguin Books Ltd., Registered Offices: 80 Strand, London WC2R 0RL, England

This is a work of fiction. Names, characters, places, and incidents either are the product of the author's imagination or are used fictitiously, and any resemblance to actual persons, living or dead, business establishments, events, or locales is entirely coincidental. The publisher does not have any control over and does not assume any responsibility for author or third-party websites or their content.

CROSSROADS

An Ace Book / published by arrangement with the author

PRINTING HISTORY
Ace mass-market edition / September 2011

Copyright © 2011 by Jeanne C. Stein.
Cover art by Cliff Nielsen.
Cover design by Judith Lagerman.
Interior text design by Kristin del Rosario.

ISBN: 978-0-441-02077-5

ACE
Ace Books are published by The Berkley Publishing Group,
a division of Penguin Group (USA) Inc.,
375 Hudson Street, New York, New York 10014.
ACE and the "A" design are trademarks of Penguin Group (USA) Inc.

PRINTED IN THE UNITED STATES OF AMERICA

10 9 8 7 6 5 4 3 2 1

For the support of my family and friends, I thank you.

For Phil—these last two books are as much yours as mine.

CHAPTER 1

IT'S NEVER A GOOD THING WHEN YOU'RE AWAK-
ened from a deep sleep by someone pounding on the
front door.

It's worse when you stumble downstairs and see it's a cop.

A cop you recognize.

My first impulse is to creep back upstairs and pretend
I'm not home. But I know this cop. He's probably already
gone around back and checked the garage. Both my Jag
and the Ford Crown Vic I use for work are parked inside.
He knows I'm home.

Crap.

I pull open the door.

"Detective Harris. What a surprise."

For a pain-in-the-ass cop, he's not bad looking. Five-ten—
probably one hundred eighty pounds. Dark hair touched at
the temples with gray. Square jaw, serious eyes. Beneath that
off-the-rack suit, a body I suspect is neither lean nor flabby.
Carries himself like he was once an athlete—a boxer, maybe.

Now he's a fortysomething man fighting middle-age spread and from the looks of it, winning the battle.

The suit tells me he's not here on a social visit.

He gives me the once-over. I'm barefoot, wearing a pair of running shorts and a tank top. As a vampire, I'm not bothered by the effects of ambient temperature so I could be wearing anything. Or the nothing I was wearing two seconds ago when I crawled out of bed.

A bed still occupied, by the way.

Harris purses his lips, glances away as if uncomfortable. "Sorry to disturb you so early. Would you like to run upstairs and put some clothes on? I can wait."

I pull the door open wider and motion him inside. He's the one who appeared at the door at seven a.m. on a Sunday morning. Unannounced. I'm not exposing anything more than the joggers he sees every day on the street. I wave away the suggestion. "I'd rather put the coffee on."

He follows me to the kitchen. He watches silently as I go about filling the coffeemaker, grinding beans, setting the machine to brew. He still hasn't said why he's here. We're not friends. Our paths have crossed a few times. Most recently, with the death a couple of months ago of the ex–police chief, Warren Williams, a vampire, too, though of course Harris doesn't know that.

Or that Williams was killed by another vampire.

Could it just be a few weeks? Seems like much longer. Williams' death set into motion a chain of events that changed my life.

Forever.

I've got my back to Harris and allow a smile. To a vampire, *forever* takes on a whole new meaning.

Harris clears his throat. I turn, grab two mugs and join him at the table.

He takes one of the mugs, says, "Thanks."

That's it?

I pause, waiting to see if he's going to tell me the reason for this early morning visit. The bell on the coffeemaker chimes before he does. I take cream from the fridge and sugar from the counter, set out spoons and pour us each a cup of coffee before plunking myself down on a chair across from him.

I take a sip, let the magic of caffeine awaken half-sleeping brain cells. Harris seems to be doing the same. He's avoiding my eyes now. Concentrating on the mug in his hand with far more attention than he needs to.

This is getting old.

"Did you have a reason for stopping by unannounced at seven a.m., Harris? Or was my place closer than Dunkin' Donuts?"

When he looks up, there is a strange expression on his face. And I've been on the receiving end of plenty of his expressions. Negative expressions, mostly. Anger, frustration, exasperation being the most common. This one is different. Hesitant. He's got something on his mind and he doesn't know how to bring it up.

That's certainly out of character.

I wish I could worm my way into his head the way I can with vampires. But Harris is human and there is no psychic connection between vampires and humans. A design flaw for sure.

Finally, whatever battle he's been fighting is resolved. He sits up in his chair and pushes the cup aside.

"I don't know why I'm coming to you with this," he says. "You always seem to be mixed up in cases you have no business being mixed up in. The child molester a while back, the murder investigation involving that model, the missing DEA agent. But you had the respect of Warren Williams, and he was a good man. You were one of the last people to see him alive."

My turn to fix my mug with a riveting gaze. Where is he going with this?

"I know his wife believes you had something to do with his death," Harris continues. "I don't. But we just got the last of the forensic reports from his car. We found something—"

He pauses, as if searching for the right word. After a moment, he shrugs. "Odd. We found something odd."

I wait, wondering. Williams was set on fire by another old-soul vampire. There would have been nothing left but ash.

Wouldn't there?

I compose the question carefully. "What could you have found? I thought the body was completely burned."

"So did we. At first." He pulls a sheet of paper from an inside jacket pocket and smoothes it open on the table. "But turns out, our CSI's found something. DNA. And what they learned about that DNA has us baffled."

To keep the shock from registering on my face, I hoist my coffee mug and take a long pull. I don't know much about DNA, but I do know about vampires. When a vampire is immolated, there's nothing left to run tests on. Williams was identified by his badge and wedding ring.

Finally, I lower the mug. "I don't understand." An understatement.

Harris raises his eyebrows. "Neither do I. When a body is burned at high temperature, like cremation, there's usually no testable nuclear DNA left. But in this case, three things were able to be determined by something called mitochondrial DNA found in a bone fragment fused on his ring. It was human. It was Williams'. It was over two hundred years old."

My hand tightens around the mug, a gesture not lost on Harris. He leans toward me.

"The FBI lab is asking questions. Questions I can't answer."

"And you think I can?"

Evidently Harris can't or won't answer that question, either.

My turn now to stall, my brain racing into overdrive, as I rearrange silverware, straighten the sugar bowl and creamer. I have no idea what I'm supposed to say to Harris. That Williams was indeed two hundred years old—a two-hundred-year-old vampire, to be exact—and he was killed by another vampire who was even older? That sitting across the table from him drinking coffee is yet another vampire? Not so old, but even stronger than either of them. One who had fought Williams many times and won. One who was kidnapped by Williams' killer, and in turn, killed the bastard when he tried to rape me.

I feel Harris watching, waiting. I throw out the only lame explanation I can think of. "Maybe there was someone else in the car."

Stupid.

Harris doesn't mock me, though. He simply says, "Someone two hundred years old?" A shake of the head. "The DNA belongs to Williams. There's no doubt about that. The comparison sample was taken from a hairbrush found in his locker at SDPD. The big question isn't *who* the DNA belongs to, but how it could be two hundred years old."

"And you're asking me, why? Ask the Feds. The lab must have made a mistake."

"Could be." Harris pushes away from the table. "They're running a second set of tests." He stands, lets a moment pass. Then, "I was sorry to hear about your boyfriend, Lance something?"

I look up. That's an abrupt change of subject. "I didn't know you knew Lance."

"I didn't. Just heard he was killed. I'm sorry for your loss."

Does he know more than he's letting on? Lance was a well-known model. He was also a vampire and the one who arranged for me to be kidnapped by his sire. A bitter betrayal that left a wound that still festers. I loved him.

It didn't stop me from killing him.

The laws that govern vampires are different from the laws that govern humans. To the real world, Lance was killed in an automobile accident. His cremated remains were sent to his family in South Africa. The family that knew him as an eighty-four-year-old under a different name. So far, no one's made the connection.

Still, when I meet Harris' eyes, I see the unspoken accusation.

Men I become involved with have a nasty habit of disappearing. Or dying.

And to Harris, Williams and Lance were prominent men in my life. His scrutiny raises feelings I don't want to acknowledge. Feelings of pain, treachery, betrayal.

Then, in what can only be described as epic bad timing, a male voice calls out from the head of the stairs. "Anna, what's going on down there? I thought you were coming right back up."

Harris' eyebrows leap. "New boyfriend? You don't waste much time."

Shit. Stephen was headed for the shower when I came

downstairs. I figured I would have gotten rid of Harris by now. I shrug.

"Does this new guy have a name?"

Why, so you can keep an eye out for an obit? I shrug again. "I don't think that's any of your business."

Which precipitates a staring contest.

Harris breaks eye contact first. "Okay. You're right. Your personal life is none of my business. Williams' death is. I know Williams was a good cop and a good leader. What I don't know is much about his private life. You were closer to him than most. If there's anything you can tell me to help clear this case, I'd appreciate the help."

He drains his cup. I wait. He starts for the door.

"His killer is still out there. Until he or she is caught, I'll be keeping a close eye on anyone who had contact with Williams during those last days."

The words are spoken casually enough, but the meaning is clear. I follow him to the door, eyes on his back, understanding.

He'll be keeping an eye on me.

I close the door and lean my head against it.

Great. Harris is never going to solve this case because there's nothing to solve. Does that mean I'm going to have him on my ass forever?

There's that word again. Forever. This time, I don't feel like smiling.

I trek back into the kitchen, refill my own coffee cup, grab an extra mug for Stephen and head upstairs.

He's on the phone.

Dressed.

I hold a mug out to him and he takes it, smiles a thanks, and keeps talking.

I plop down on the edge of the bed and watch him.

Stephen and I have been together for a little over a month. He's human, but after being thrown together on an astral plane, barely escaping with our lives, and killing a monster who followed us back to earth, a bond was formed. It seems silly for an immortal thirty-year-old to call someone a boyfriend, and "lover" sounds frivolous, but that's what he's become to me. Friend and lover.

I pick up the thread of his conversation and realize what I'm hearing.

He's leaving.

When he rings off, and looks at me, he knows I know.

"It's just a week," he says. "The network wants me to anchor the evening news while Katie is on assignment."

He says it like it's no big deal, like it's business as usual. But I see the excitement shining from his face. For a co-anchor and lead investigative reporter on the local circuit, it's a very big deal.

"Wow. So next week, I'll be seeing you on the evening news?"

He puts the mug on the bed stand and sits down beside me. "You could come with me."

I trace the angle of his jaw with my finger. "Tempting, but I imagine you'll be pretty busy."

He slips his arms around me and pulls me close. "I'm going to miss this."

I lay my head on his shoulder. "Me, too."

Damn it.

Me, too.

WITH STEPHEN GONE, I HAVE NO PLANS FOR THE DAY ahead. I eye the bed, wondering if I should crawl back under the covers.

There's an ache in my gut, though, and I know I've waited too long. It's been a month since I fed from the blood of the demon Stephen and I killed.

Two months since the first anniversary of my becoming when I assumed the mantle of the Chosen One. I've gone about my daily routine as if nothing had changed when in reality, everything has changed.

I move out to the deck off my bedroom and sink into a chaise. The sun is hot on my face. It feels good. I can almost feel my blood warming though I know that's an illusion. Only feeding and sex warm a vampire's blood.

And it's been hours since Stephen and I made love.

He would have let me feed from him, if I'd asked. He knows and accepts I'm a vampire. But sometimes I enjoy simple human coupling. Let's me enjoy the illusion that I'm normal if only for a little while.

I sip coffee. A few blocks away, the ocean sparkles under a flawless summer sky. I live in Mission Beach, near the boardwalk. I love it here. The sea is vibrant, alive. People drawn to it are vibrant and alive, too. Kids at play in the sand, surfers bobbing on the waves, sunbathers eschewing warnings of dire consequences to bake pale skin to a toasty brown. All share a common bond. They are human. They belong.

I drain my cup, rise to go inside. I'm feeling the effects of lack of blood. Like a diabetic without insulin, my body is slowing down, my mind becoming sluggish. I'd better call Culebra and make sure he can arrange a host to meet me at Beso de la Muerte. I can't afford to let myself become vulnerable—not anymore. Not to anyone.

CHAPTER 2

T HE GUY WAITING FOR ME IN CULEBRA'S BACK
room looks to be about thirty. He's lying naked on the
bed, his clothes folded neatly on a bedside chair. He has a
sheet thrown over the lower part of his body. He's lean,
muscular, with the arrogant good looks of a guy used to
having his way with women.

I hate that type.

He smiles when he sees me, a smile of relief and anticipation. I'm sure the relief is because I'm female (a host
never knows) and the anticipation that because I'm female,
sex will be a part of the deal.

I pull a wad of cash out of my purse and lay it on top of
his clothes. "I just want the blood," I tell him. "Whatever
you do while I'm feeding is up to you, but I don't intend to
participate."

"Are you sure?" The guy pushes the sheet off his hips.
He started without me.

If the size of his dick is supposed to impress me, my

reaction must be a bitter disappointment. I flutter fingers in a dismissive gesture. "Yeah, I'm sure. Face the wall, please."

"Don't you want to know my name?"

"No."

He grunts and rolls over. I position myself behind him, spoon style, and pull his head closer. My body vibrates from need and the heady sensation that comes from watching blood course through an artery just a kiss away. His hands are busy between his legs and he groans before I break through the skin.

Then I'm lost in my own sensations. His blood is sweet and clean, his fitness the result of good diet and exercise, not pills or needles. Not that it would matter. Vampires are immune from human drugs and disease. Only the taste differs, like drinking vinegar or wine, and I'm pleased with this vintage. The first mouthful brings intense pleasure, my body now tingling with something other than hunger. There's a fleeting moment when I am tempted to roll him over, to mount him, feel him inside me while I feed.

But I resist.

I've treated sex too cavalierly in the past. I want it to mean something from now on. Something more than just scratching a biological itch. Something like what I have with Stephen.

I already miss him.

For now, the blood has to be enough. It awakens every cell in my body. It revives and restores. My skin warms. A flush of heat floods my cheeks. My senses become needle sharp. The feel of the host's skin against my lips, the smell of his arousal, the quickness of his breath, I experience it all. His heartbeat. Steady, rhythmic, until he nears climax. Then his heart begins to race until it reaches a crescendo and his body tenses. He moans, grinds against me, one hand clutches the sheet, the other moves faster and with more urgency.

I keep feeding until the last shudder of release passes and he is quiet beside me. I use my tongue to seal the puncture wounds, watch as the marks fade. He does not speak or move. In a minute, his breathing becomes deep and regular, and I know.

He's fallen asleep.

"Was it as good for you as it was for me?" I ask the snoring host.

I close the door quietly on my way out.

WHEN I JOIN CULEBRA AT THE BAR, HE LOOKS PAST me toward the door to the back room. "Is he still alive?"

He hands me a bottle of Dos Equis with a lime wedge propped on the rim.

I squeeze the lime down into the bottle. "Why wouldn't he be?"

He takes another beer from a cooler under the bar and motions for me to follow him to a table. When we're both seated he answers, "You looked hungry when you walked in. How long has it been since you fed?"

I shrug. "A while."

He watches me drink. "It's been a while since we talked, too. Two months to be exact. I have a lot of questions."

I figured. One of the reasons I've stayed away.

Culebra picks that thought out of the ether. He frowns. "I thought I was your friend."

He shuts me out of his head. He's angry or disappointed. Maybe both. I can't tell. But the result is the same. I give in with a sigh. "Sorry. You are my friend. I should have been in touch sooner. I guess I figured Frey would have filled you in."

I glance around the bar. It's almost empty this early on a Sunday morning. There are a couple of vamps sitting with two human women. The snatches of thought I catch from the vamps are that they're well fed and well sexed and are looking for a way to leave gracefully without offending the female hosts. They may want a repeat performance down the line. The vibes the females give off tell me they wouldn't object. I watch them a few moments until Culebra is back in my head.

You're stalling.

I'm granted another reprieve when my host appears at the door. He grins at me with a look calculated to let anyone watching think I'd sucked more than his neck. I'm tempted to make a snarky remark but don't. I simply let him swagger over to the other table. The females greet him and in another moment, all five leave with a parting wave to Culebra.

We're now alone.

Culebra waves his bottle in the direction of the door. "I assume that look was a bit of bravado for the benefit of his friends."

I laugh. "You'll need to change those sheets."

The moment passes. "What did Frey tell you?"

"What you told him. The challenge. Lance. The way you handled Chael. Sounds like you did well for yourself."

Did I? What I didn't tell Frey, what I'm hiding from Culebra now, is that nothing was settled. Not really. There is a schism forming in the vampire world led by the leader of the Middle Eastern Tribe, a powerful old-soul vampire called Chael. I met his challenge at the counsel called to proclaim me the Chosen One, but it did nothing to lessen his desire to pursue his own course. A course designed to elevate vampires to the top of the food chain and relegate humans to nothing more than fodder, an expendable food source whose only existence would be to serve their vampire masters.

Culebra's voice breaks through my dark thoughts.

"What are you hiding from me, Anna?"

"Nothing." Everything.

His thoughts are like a laser, trying to bore into mine. *I know you better than that. What aren't you telling me?*

I raise the beer bottle to my lips, drain it. Rise. "Have to go, my friend. I'll be in touch soon."

Culebra doesn't answer. Like Harris eyed me earlier, I feel the heat of his gaze as I stand to leave.

"Wait."

I'm halfway to the door; I turn, pause.

"I have a message for you."

"Who would leave a message for me here?"

Culebra crosses to the bar, reaches behind it for a folded piece of paper. "Somebody who is afraid you wouldn't return his calls if he tried to reach you directly."

He holds the note out to me. As soon as I see the signature, I understand why he'd go through Culebra. He's right. I wouldn't have returned his calls.

The note is from Max.

I stare down at the note. Culebra feels my anger build.

Max is an ex-boyfriend. Human. Couldn't take off fast enough when he found out what I am, even though it's *because* of what I am that he's alive today. To make matters worse, he decided that sex with a vampire while acting as a host was a pretty damned good way to get his rocks off. So he comes here to enjoy fucking vampires. Anonymous vampires. It's me he doesn't want to fuck anymore.

My hand curls into a fist, crushing the note. "When did he leave this?"

Culebra avoids my gaze. "Today. I told him you were on your way."

"So the coward didn't wait to face me in person? Why would you take this? You know how I feel about Max and his new hobby."

Culebra holds up a hand. "Max hasn't come here to be a host for some time. Whatever he needed to get out of his system, he seems to have succeeded."

"You mean me, right? He needed to get me out of his system."

Culebra shakes his head. "Read the damn note, will you?"

I drag my eyes back to the note, open my hand, smooth the paper against my thigh. I can't imagine being interested in anything Max has to say to me. The bastard left without so much as a good-bye.

The handwriting is cramped, uneven. As if he wrote the note in a hurry.

Anna. I need your help. Call me. Max.

"Wow." I wave the note toward Culebra. "This makes me want to drop everything and ring him right up. He doesn't even say please. Christ. Why would I want to help him?"

Culebra lifts his shoulders. "It must be important."

"He didn't tell you?"

"Not exactly."

"Didn't tell you *what* exactly?"

"For Christ sake, call him, will you?" Culebra's irritation flares, radiates outward from his thoughts and burns into my head. *Don't be so goddamned stubborn.*

I don't even know if I still have his number. A last whining excuse.

Of course you still have his number. In your cell.

He's right. Not that I'll give him the satisfaction of telling him. Just like I won't give him the satisfaction of knowing deep down I want to call Max. Only to satisfy my curiosity. Only to find out how Max plans to grovel his way back into my good graces. Only to enjoy turning down whatever he wants.

His leaving was no laughing matter, but telling him to go to hell would be good for a laugh, not to mention my ego.

I turn my back on Culebra and stomp out, letting one thought drift back.

Fucking men.

CHAPTER 3

ON THE DRIVE BACK HOME I DEBATE WITH MYSELF. Do I want to call Max? It's been eight months since the last time we ran into each other in Beso de la Muerte. He was on the arm of a vampire, stinking of sex and blood. My stomach still roils at the memory.

Why the hell would I want to call Max? On the off chance that he wants to tell me what an ass he's been and to thank me at long last for saving his ass in Mexico?

Shit.

It irritates me to realize I'm curious. It irritates me to realize I want to know why he wants to talk to me.

It irritates the hell out of me to realize I know how long it's been since I've seen him without doing the math.

I'm sure Culebra knows more than he let on. Max is a drug enforcement agent. He spends half his life in Mexico and has used Culebra as an informant. Not in an official capacity. Culebra has a lot of contacts on both sides of the law and the border. He and Max have a quid pro quo arrangement. Culebra helps Max when he can and Max keeps quiet when he comes to Beso de la Muerte to ensure those under Culebra's protection are not hassled.

At least that's the way it worked when Max and I were together.

A lifetime ago.

My cell phone rings just as I'm pulling into the garage at the cottage. Caller ID shows it's my partner, David.

"Hey—"

"Where are you?" he asks, interrupting.

No greeting. "At home. Why?"

"Stay there. I'm on the way."

He's gone before I can comment on his abruptness or ask the reason behind it. He sounds angry, and I can't imagine why. Business has been going well. I've been playing nice with our new partner, Tracey, an ex-cop. She's proven herself good at the job and through her contacts, we've had more work than the three of us can handle. I've managed to stick around the last month. No unexpected trips out of town, no excuses for missing telephone calls or office duty.

So, what's his problem?

I let myself in through the back door and start a fresh pot of coffee. At least having just fed, my head is clear. No risk of snapping David's off, literally or figuratively, if he pisses me off.

Blood—the vampire equivalent of Valium.

The coffee is ready. I set the kitchen table for two and take a cup out to the living room to look through the Sunday paper while I wait. I'm no sooner settled onto the couch when the doorbell rings.

As soon as I answer the door, David storms his way past me. "Are you alone?"

"If you mean is Stephen here, no, he left."

He traipses into the kitchen.

"What the hell is wrong with you?" I shut the door and follow him. "Somebody stomp on your kitten?"

He ignores me. Pours a mug of coffee. Takes a drink. Stalling tactics, I assume, because his hand is shaking.

Then he turns.

David is a big guy. He played a decade of professional football before injuries sidelined him. But while he adjusted to life without constant pain, he found he missed the adrenaline rush too much to mire himself in a typical desk job. Bounty hunting was the perfect fit. It takes detective work to hunt a skip down, cunning and resourcefulness to trap him, physical strength to bring him in.

It takes the ability to make the hair on a skip's arms stand at attention when David skewers him with *the* look.

The "don't fuck with me because I'm not in the mood" one he's giving me now.

The only effect it's having on me, though, is the urge to punch him. Hard.

I push my palms against my thighs to keep from giving in to the urge. I like him. Most of the time. I stare up into his face, narrow my eyes and frown to mimic his hard-ass expression. "What the fuck is going on?"

"I could ask you the same question."

"Jesus, David." Exasperation is churning my stomach. "I don't know what you're talking about."

He slams the mug down on the counter. "I was in Horton Plaza this morning. Guess who I ran into?"

The urge is getting stronger and tougher to resist. If I slugged him, when he came to, maybe he'd start talking sense. But I'll give him one more chance. I temper my voice with reasonableness. "I wasn't there. How the hell should I know who you ran into?"

He leans toward me, jabs a finger at my face. "Judith Williams."

Uh-oh.

My face must betray the uneasiness that washes over me. Like catching your kid with her hand in the candy dish, David pounces. "You remember Judith Williams, right? Wife of the police chief who died last month? Well, I didn't. I didn't think I even knew her. Then I ran into her this morning and her face looked so familiar. She caught me looking at her and guess what she said to me? That I looked pretty good with clothes on. Too. Then she asked if I remembered the good time we had at that doctor's house in La Jolla. And if I'd kept in touch with the twins."

His scowl deepens. "Twins?" He shakes his head. "And all the time she's talking, she's laughing because she knows I haven't a fucking clue what she's talking about. Then she says, 'You didn't really buy that stupid story Anna told you about having an accident, did you? She knows what really happened. Ask her.'"

David draws a breath, lets it out with an angry hiss. "So, I'm asking. What happened to me? And what did Judith Williams have to do with it and who are the fucking twins?"

If I weren't so busy trying to come up with a logical answer, David's referral to the "fucking twins" would have made me laugh out loud. That happens to be exactly what they were. Judith Williams drugged David and kept him for three days during which time he not only had sex with a set of twins she was kind enough to provide for his enjoyment but with Judith herself and god only knows who else. It was certainly a novel way to handle a kidnap victim. But it worked. When I found David, he was having so much fun I had to bring the twins with us to get him to leave.

He didn't remember any of it, which is why I came up with the accident story. That and the fact that Judith Williams is a vampire and took David to ensure I'd show up to play my part in a ritual she thought would kill me.

Didn't quite work out the way she'd planned.

But she also told him that she was a vampire.

And that I was one, too. David's amnesia was a blessing.

Was a blessing.

Judith must be laughing her ass off now.

David takes a step closer. "Anna. I want an answer. I've had some crazy dreams since that 'accident.' Now I'm beginning to think they weren't dreams at all."

For the first time, his expression is more concerned than angry. "Was she saying that I had sex with her? And those two girls? Why would I do that? Why can't I remember?"

The reason for his reaction hits me. I should have guessed it sooner.

David is a Boy Scout.

David has a girlfriend.

If he knew he had sex with those women, his conscience would force him to tell his girlfriend. If he suspected he'd had *unprotected* sex with those women, as is probable considering his condition when I found him, he'd want to kill me for knowing and not telling him and risking his health as well as that of his girlfriend.

Frankly, it isn't something I'd thought about before now. Judith is a vampire, no problem there. But the girls are human.

What the hell do I tell him?

I pull out two chairs from the kitchen table, motion David into one of them, sit facing him in the other.

"Okay, David. I'm going to tell you what happened. First though, you have to know I didn't think of the consequences of keeping the truth from you until now."

His body tenses, his expression freezes as he watches me. "Go on."

The words tumble out. A sanitized semi-factual version of what really took place.

"You were drugged. Somebody took you and brought you to a house where you partied. All weekend. You must have had sex with Judith and those twins and maybe others. It took me two days to find you and when I did, you didn't want to leave. I did what I thought was best. Brought you home, let you sleep it off. When I went back to the place, to alert the police, everyone was gone. The place was clean. I'm guessing it was some kind of rave. Anyway, I should have told you the truth. I was afraid you'd go looking for the people responsible and do something stupid. And honestly, I didn't see Judith Williams or anyone I recognized so I haven't a clue who might have been there."

Silence. Is he buying it?

David leans toward me. "None of this makes sense. How did they get me? Why did they take *me*?"

"Maybe you stopped in a bar somewhere. Someone recognized you, thought a local celebrity would be fun to party with. They must have slipped something in your drink. Shit. I don't know."

I stop. David isn't listening. He's hardly breathing. He's so still, I wonder for an instant if he heard what I said. Does he realize the flaw in my story? Is he going to ask how *I* found him? Shit. What do I say to that?

There's a shift in the set of his jaw, a flicker of light in his eyes. He's remembering something. I know it in the way he's looking at me and I know what it is.

He's remembering what Judith Williams told him about me.

I jump up so fast, it makes David jump, too. My brain is twirling like a dervish, trying to formulate a response to what I suspect David is about to say.

He stands up, too. Looks me square in the eyes. "Those twins. They were students at SDSU. I remember that. And they gave me their phone numbers. Do you know what I did with them?"

"*That's* what you want to know?"

Part of me is so relieved, my knees are weak. The other part can't believe what he just asked.

"I tell you that you were drugged and brought to a stranger's house where you partied for two days and all you want to know is if I kept the telephone numbers of who you were partying with?"

He rubs a hand over his face. "No. I have plenty of other questions. Maybe the twins can provide answers. But first I have to find a way to break what I did to Miranda. We have to get tested for god only knows what."

Whoa. So not a good idea. "Why would you tell Miranda?"

That earns me an "are you crazy?" look. "Why do you think? Evidently, I had multiple sex partners during a weekend she thought I was recuperating from an accident. I have to tell her we should get tested for STDs and worse because if I was drugged up enough to have sex with strangers, it's a safe bet I was too drugged up to use protection. She's not going to understand. Fuck, *I* don't understand."

The Boy Scout is back. Just as I predicted. Luckily, I'm not a den mother. "Wait a minute. Get tested yourself first. There might be nothing to tell."

His expression tells me that argument is not going to fly. So I go with, "Think about it. If you tell her, she's most likely to break up with you. Or kill you. Or both. What's the worst that can happen if you wait?"

"And what excuses do I use for not having sex with her while I wait for test results?"

"Ever hear of using a condom?" It pops out. He's giving me the look again. "Then don't see her for a little while. Go to a private doctor or clinic and request a rush. Shouldn't take too long."

The hard look evaporates into one of desperation. "Shit, Anna. How could I have let this happen?"

"You didn't do anything. It was done to you. The best thing now is to do damage control. Take care of the things you can."

"No." David's hands curl into fists. "The best thing I can do now is find those twins and see what they can tell me about that night—or *nights* if what you tell me is true. Then I'll go after Judith Williams. If she's behind what happened, I'll press charges."

Another bad idea. "Do you think anyone will believe the wife of the former police chief—the recently *murdered* former police chief—is involved in drugs and sex parties? Shit. David, I have a hard time believing it and I dragged you out of that house."

"Then we'll go back to the house. You know where it is. There's bound to be evidence. And she admitted to me that she was there. That should count for something."

He's got the locked-jaw look of somebody hell-bent on action. "What about those telephone numbers?"

I can't believe this is happening. If he pursues this, I'm screwed.

"I threw them away." I threw them away all right, into a

drawer in my desk. I figured I'd follow up with the girls and see how much they remembered about their weekend at vampire central. I haven't gotten around to it. Now I think I'd better just burn the fucking things.

David is not happy at the answer. He blows out an impatient breath and slams a hand down on the table. "Then I guess that leaves Judith Williams, doesn't it?" He stands abruptly and takes his mug to the sink.

I follow, pat his arm and steer him to the door. "First things first, David. Take care of those tests. In the meantime, I'll call Detective Harris and see what he knows about raves being held in the area."

No reaction so I plow ahead. "And David, forget about Judith Williams. For now. She's too smart and too well connected to let herself become implicated in a crime. The fact that she said what she said today proves that. It's your word against hers and you can bet she won't repeat it again in front of witnesses."

David gives no indication whether he intends to follow my advice or not. He leaves looking as dejected now as he looked angry when he came in.

My fault. Why didn't it occur to me that there might be greater physical consequences to his sexcapades that weekend? All I was concerned about was his remembering that Judith told him we were both vampires. At least she didn't throw out that nugget when she saw him this morning.

I wonder why. What is the bitch up to now?

Fuck. Just when I thought I was at a point when I could look ahead for once, I get hit with three titanic reminders of my past. All compliments of humans in my life: Detective Harris, Max and David.

Well, can't do anything about Detective Harris and for all I know, David might be off chasing down his girlfriend in spite of our conversation. The only one I can do something about now is Max.

Should I call him?

I'm right back where I started.

I look around the cottage. Usually this place is my oasis of tranquillity. This morning it's been invaded by a suspicious detective, an angry business partner and, by way of a note, an ex I never intended to see again.

My life was never so complicated when I was human.

CHAPTER 4

I'VE BEEN SITTING ON THE BED STARING AT THE telephone in my hand for fifteen minutes. Max's number is up on the screen, just waiting for my finger to press Send. I'm not sure why I'm so hesitant. There's only one reason I'd call him, and the only thing I have to decide is the number of expletives to insert before I tell him to fuck off.

So what's the problem?

I suck it up and punch Send.

He picks up so fast, it takes me a second to realize he's on the line.

"Max?"

"Anna." There's relief in his voice. "Thanks for calling. I need to see you."

"Why?"

"I can't talk about it on the phone. Can I come in?"

My grip on the phone tightens. "What do you mean, come in? Where are you?"

"Outside. On the boardwalk."

I cross the bedroom to the deck, look toward the ocean. The boardwalk is crowded. It takes me a second to locate him. Max is leaning against the seawall, staring up toward the cottage. He waves when he sees me. But it's not a cheery wave and he's not smiling.

I'm not smiling, either. "What are you doing here? How did you know I'd call?"

"I didn't, but Culebra told me you'd picked up the note."

"Did he also tell you I don't want to talk to you?"

"Yes. I'm glad to see he was wrong."

"He wasn't wrong. There's only one reason I'd call you. To tell you to fuck off—"

"Anna, please." I see Max cup his hand around the phone. "If there was anyone else I could go to about this, I would. You are the only one who can help."

"Jesus, Max. Could you be any more dramatic? You sound like a druggie jonesing for a fix. God. Is that what this is about? You want me to bite you? You get tired of screwing anonymous vamps? You remembering what a good thing you threw away?"

"No. Anna." His words are short, clipped, his anger burning through even over the phone. "Everything isn't about *you*. I need you because I think I'm dealing with a vampire. A vicious vampire. And I don't know how to fight him. He's killing innocent people. I thought you'd want to help. Culebra thought you'd want to help. Guess we were both wrong."

He snaps his cell phone shut, ending the conversation before I can respond. He doesn't look my way again, but heads up the boardwalk toward the parking lot. He shoulders are drawn up, his strides long, fast, stiff with fury.

Shit. A vampire? It takes me about a heartbeat to decide. I'm probably going to regret this but I'm down the stairs, have grabbed up my purse and keys and reached the end of the boardwalk before he does.

Max isn't startled when I appear in front of him like a genie sprung from a bottle. He knows what I can do. But he doesn't look relieved or pleased, either. He stares down at me from his six-foot-three-inch vantage point and waits for me to speak first.

"What do you mean you're *dealing* with a vampire?"

His shoulders hunch up even more. The lines of his face draw down, as if weighted. He looks tired. He looks stressed. The Max I knew—the one with lively blue eyes, a quick smile and sun-burnished Latino good looks—has been swallowed up by this sallow-faced, sober, weary doppelganger.

"Are you sure you want to hear this? Or are you waiting for another opportunity to tell me what a screwup I've been?"

I close the distance between us and jab a finger into his chest. "Oh, I'm sure there will be plenty of opportunities to do that. Right now, I want to know what you meant on the telephone."

He looks around. "Let's walk. I don't want to risk being overheard."

The boardwalk teems with people. Skateboarders, cyclists, Rollerbladers, joggers. If we walk here, we'll spend most of our time dodging incoming. I'm not going to invite him to the cottage, either. I don't want him invading my personal space. I've had enough of that today.

"Let's cross to the bay side."

He doesn't object. Neither of us speaks until we've crossed Mission and head for the sidewalk that runs along the harbor. Here the view spans the San Diego skyline on one side, row on row of condos and apartments on the other. There's a marina and a small park. We head for the benches in the middle of the park. We choose the one that faces a playground. The water is at our backs and we have a clear view of the sidewalk. It's much quieter here.

"So talk."

Max looks toward the sidewalk, eyes restlessly scanning the faces of the people moving at a Sunday-afternoon, warm-summer's-day pace. I look, too. But I know I'm not seeing the same things he is. He's looking at them with cop eyes.

"I've been working a joint task force with the Mexican border patrol," he says at last. "Drugs mostly. But in the last few weeks, we've been finding something else on our patrols. Bodies drained of blood. Entire families killed and dumped in the desert. No clue as to who is doing it. At first we thought it was some local drug lord's new and vicious way to intimidate."

"But now?"

"The victims all had their throats slashed. But there's never any blood at the scene. None. The tox screens we've run always come back negative for drugs. They're not addicts or dealers. The victims have no connection to local law enforcement, either, always a favorite target of the cartel. We've traced some of the victims to places in Latin America and as far south as Ecuador. A hell of a long way to transport bodies just to dump them. They're from poor families. If they were carrying anything of value on them, it's gone by the time we find them. All that's left are the clothes on their backs."

Max pauses, draws a breath. He hasn't looked at me since we sat down on the bench. He does now. "I think we're dealing with a coyote. I think he takes money from these people to get them across the border. Then he kills and dumps them within sight of the border. The bastard probably lets them know how close they are before he kills them."

It doesn't take much of a leap to know where Max is heading with this. "You think this coyote is a vampire."

"I do. The slash marks are clumsy. Because the bodies are found in Mexico, we haven't been able to do anything but drug sampling. But I'd be willing to bet if we could do the autopsies here, we'd find something under those slashes."

He would. When I worked as a Watcher, I used the technique myself. A vampire can erase puncture wounds from a live donor, but not a dead one. Slashing the throat is a way to hide the fact that a body has been sucked dry.

Confirming that Max is right about this and how I know that he's right is not something I want to share. I already know what he thinks of me. "What do you want from me?"

"There's a pattern to the killings. We find the bodies on our patrols on Tuesday mornings. Always in roughly the same location."

"If you know this, you don't need me. Set a trap."

"We did. Last week. The guy slipped past us as if he was invisible. But not before leaving us another victim. A young girl. You have to realize, Anna, our emphasis is on stopping the drug trade. Not human trafficking. We don't have the resources to conduct another undercover op. That's why I'm here. To ask you to come with me tomorrow night. If I'm right, the only way we're going to stop him is by fighting fire with fire."

I snort. "You mean vampire with vampire."

Max's mouth tightens. "This isn't a joking matter."

"Do I look like I'm joking?"

His expression shifts, softens. "Sorry. I know I'm asking a lot. I don't know what else to do. If we don't stop him, he'll go on killing. He likes it. He's found an easy food source. And he takes money from victims desperate to make a new life."

He stops, draws a breath. "Culebra told me you're some sort of uber-vamp now. Well, I need an uber-vamp. I can't think of another way to stop him."

Uber-vamp. Yeah. That's me, all right. Head of the thirteen vampire tribes. Only thing is, except for a few extra abilities, I don't feel any different than I did before. The only thing that's changed is that I have another uber-vamp, Chael, gunning for me.

I push the thought out of my head. I can probably help Max. I'm stronger than other vamps. The question is, do I want to?

Stupid question. I choose my words carefully.

"I'll do it. But not for you. I'll do it because a vamp who acts like this is a rogue, a threat to all vampires. Sooner or later, what he's doing will come to the attention of vampire hunters. Then none of us will be safe."

Max lets his relief show in a tiny gesture of gratitude. He holds out a hand.

I let my feelings show by standing up and taking a step out of reach. Max is still an asshole in my book. "Where shall I meet you?"

He stands, too, lets his hands fall to his sides. "The border crossing at San Ysidro. Tomorrow night. Ten o'clock."

I nod. Max stares at me a minute, waiting I suppose for the ice to melt. It doesn't, and finally, Max walks away.

For the first time, I notice.

He's not limping anymore.

At least one wound has healed.

When I get back to the cottage, there's no one waiting

for me, no urgent voice mails announcing yet another crisis. I decide to push everything that happened this morning
out of mind and do what I originally intended to do this
Sunday afternoon. Curl up with a bottle of wine and watch
a *Dead Like Me* marathon on the Syfy channel.

Only in my original plan, Stephen was supposed to be
curled up on the couch with me.

I pour myself a nice big glass of Merlot and fire up the
TV. The first time I saw this series I was human. Amazing
how one's perspective can change. Now not only does the
title seem ironic, but a story about a grim reaper? Reapers
have it easy. From where I sit, being a reaper is a hell of a
lot easier than being a vampire.

CHAPTER 5

I PLANNED TO BEAT EVERYONE INTO THE OFFICE ON Monday morning. Check telephone messages, the calendar, pull notices from the fax and, if no jobs presented themselves, sneak away before David showed up.

Well, I did beat David.

But not our other partner, Tracey.

She's already at work behind the desk, pencil in hand, scanning fugitive posters hot off the fax. She's sitting in David's seat and looks up when I come in.

She's pretty in a "don't fuck with me" kind of way. Big eyes, big smile she can switch to a just-as-big scowl. She uses both to her advantage. She wears very little makeup, and I've never seen her long auburn hair in anything but a ponytail. She's wearing a Chargers sweatshirt with the sleeves pushed to her elbows. I can't see anything else, but I'd be willing to bet there are jeans on those long legs under the desk. She and I could share the same work wardrobe if she wasn't four inches taller.

"Heard from David?" I ask, plopping into my chair.

She nods. "He's not coming in today unless we need him. Personal business."

My shoulders relax. I can imagine what that "personal business" is. Not many doctor's offices or clinics open on Sunday.

I pick up one of the flyers she's already set aside. "Anything for us?"

Tracey puts the rest of the flyers down, lays her pencil on the desk. "Not in this stuff. But I have something if you're willing to help me with it."

I look up. "Go on."

"It's not a paying gig."

I lift my shoulders in a "so what?" gesture.

She presses her lips together. Her expression says she's not sure now how to proceed.

Unusual for Tracey. Speaking her mind has never been a problem.

I sit and wait for her to decide. I'm in no hurry. And if I end up with the day off, so much the better. I'll go see Culebra. I have a bone to pick with him. My instincts were right. He knew what Max wanted. So why didn't he simply tell me? It would have saved all three of us—

"My sister is in trouble."

Tracey's voice cuts into my head, pulling me back from my irritation with Culebra and into the present. "Your sister?"

Tracey releases a breath. "She filed a restraining order against her ex. So far, he's evaded being served. I told her I'd do it. I need backup."

Coming from Tracey, this is surprising. She's an ex-cop who got hurt single-handedly taking down an armed bank robber. She didn't get shot. She got hurt tackling the guy who outweighed her by a good hundred pounds. Saved a room full of hostages but the back injury developed into spinal nerve injury and she was forced to retire from the force.

Hardly bothers her now. And I've seen her in action. That she thinks she needs backup to serve papers must mean this guy is one mean son of a bitch.

She's watching me and from the look on her face, reads my expression as clearly as if I'd spoken it aloud.

"He is," she says. "He's been in jail three times for spousal abuse and always gets away with a slap on the wrist. He's got money and a good lawyer on his side. My sister has me. I want to get this son of a bitch out of her life. If he violates a restraining order, it won't be so easy for him to beat the rap. But he has to be served first."

"Do you know where to find him?"

"I do. He follows my sister the minute she leaves the house for work. He hangs around the parking lot outside, always in sight, then follows her home. He won't let a stranger approach him, but he knows me. He'll think I'm there to warn him to stay away. Again. But this time . . ." Her eyes flick away briefly, settle back on mine. "I'll make sure he takes those papers."

I have no doubt. "So what do you need me for?"

Tracey lets a tiny smile touch the corners of her mouth. "He's been making threats. Tells my sister if she doesn't come back to him, he'll kill her. He has a weapon. He's never showed it to me, but Miriam says she's seen it. Something he picked up at a gun show. Miriam doesn't know about guns, it's evidently a rifle of some sort. But she's scared."

Tracey stands up, pulls the sweatshirt over her head. She has a T-shirt on underneath, and a .38 police special in a holster on her belt. "If the bastard tries anything, I want a witness."

My kind of girl.

This is exactly the kind of diversion I need.

I unlock a desk drawer and pull out my own .38.

"So, when do we leave?"

CHAPTER 6

TURNS OUT TRACEY'S SISTER, MIRIAM, WORKS AS A manager in a Ralphs supermarket. It's the anchor store in a strip mall on University in North Park, flanked on either side by smaller shops, a Vitamin Cottage, a Rite Aid. Miriam isn't due to work for thirty minutes. Tracey spies a Starbucks on the corner. I accept her offer of coffee and she walks away to get it while I wait in the car.

I look around the parking lot. Ralphs is open twenty-four hours. It's seven thirty in the morning and there are half dozen cars parked close to the entrance. Tracey and I checked to make sure Miriam's ex didn't beat her to work this morning, but his car is not among them. Neither is Miriam's.

At seven forty-five, Miriam pulls in. I recognize her by the picture Tracey showed me. She's early. I glance in the rearview mirror, toward the coffee shop, but don't see Tracey. No matter. I turn my attention back to Miriam.

She resembles her sister, same hair color, same eyes and

mouth. They are both thin. The difference is in their height. Tracey is five-nine, Miriam, five-two, if that. A gazelle and a greyhound. They carry themselves the same way. With confidence. Miriam walks straight into the store, not looking right or left. She knows Tracey is coming today and she knows her ex will be close behind, but her bearing is unflinching.

I watch the entrance to the parking lot. No cars pull in for five minutes after Miriam's and the one that finally does is driven by a gray-haired senior in a big SUV who heads for a handicapped space by the door.

I see Tracey now, starting toward me from the coffee shop. At the same time, the unmistakable crack of a rifle echoes across the parking lot.

It's muffled.

It came from inside the store.

I jump out of the car and run toward the store entrance. In one motion, I've unbuttoned my jacket and drawn my .38 revolver. I flatten myself beside the big, glass doors and peek around to look inside.

It's early enough that the store isn't filled with midday shoppers. Still, there's chaos inside. The two dozen or so people I see are flinging themselves behind checkout counters, store displays, a pyramid of canned goods—anything that can provide cover.

Then there's only one person left standing. His back is to me. He's dressed in a duster and black jeans. He moves to my left, out of my line of sight, but I catch a glimpse of the rifle before he disappears from sight. An AK-47. The weapon of choice for every fucking punk these days.

Tracey is suddenly at my side. "What's going on?" She's pulled her weapon, too.

I shake my head. "A robbery?"

She pulls a cell phone from her pocket.

A voice from inside. "Miriam. I know you're here. Come out or the next time I shoot, it won't be in the air."

Tracey's fingers freeze on the buttons. "Jesus. When did he get here? Weren't you watching? Didn't you see him drive in?"

Her voice is sharp with recrimination, but I understand. It's her sister. I place a hand on her arm.

"He must have already been inside. But I did see Miriam arrive. She was early." I gesture to her Tracey's phone. "Make the call." Then, "Is there a back way in?"

Tracey nods, phone at her ear. "An office door."

"If Miriam is in the office, try to get her out the back."

She nods and disappears around the corner, talking to the dispatcher as she goes. I maneuver for a look inside. Someone is approaching the shooter. A man. He's wearing a suit and tie with a little nametag pinned over the jacket pocket. His hands are in the air and he's talking quietly.

I can hear every word.

"Abe, you remember me. I'm Steve Robinson, Miriam's boss. Please put the gun down. You don't want to hurt anyone. I know it. Miriam knows it, too. But she's scared. She won't come out."

He's talking in a calm, steady voice. He's got guts, I'll give him that. At the same time, I know Abe is here on a mission. I could easily use vampire speed and strength to take him down, but in front of all these witnesses?

"Come on, Abe, give me the gun and it will be over. You haven't hurt anyone yet. We can talk it out."

Abe is quiet and still. It gives the manager the impression that he's getting through to him. He takes a step closer.

"No!" The word rips out of me at the same time Abe raises the assault rifle. He fires a burst that slams the manager back against a checkout counter. I see the gaping chest wound, smell the blood as it explodes out of his back, and I know.

Miriam's boss is dead before he hits the ground.

I step out, fire at the broad of Abe's back. I squeeze off every fucking round and pull back. I know the shots hit the mark but Abe doesn't go all the way down. He's knocked to his knees, staggers back to his feet, whirls toward me.

He's wearing a full torso vest.

He sprays a burst in my direction, shattering the door and sending glass flying into the parking lot. Instinctively, I duck and step back behind the door. In the distance, a siren shrieks. Reinforcements.

Abe hears it, too, and moves deeper into the store, yelling Miriam's name.

There's a service counter about ten yards inside the door. I pull a speed loader from the pocket of my jacket, reload. I could be at that counter and over before Abe could take another step. But there are too many eyes on me now after that exchange of fire. I suck in a breath and sprint toward the counter, feeling like I'm moving in slow motion.

I dive over and startle two female employees, pressed like frightened rabbits against the counter. They look up at me with eyes round with fear. I place a finger to my lips, push up to squint over the counter.

Abe is heading toward the back of the store. He stops at the office door, tries the lock. When it doesn't yield, he kicks at it and screams, "Come out, Miriam. If you don't, I'll kill everyone in this store. The blood will be on your hands."

One of the women beside me grabs my arm. "He's crazy. You've got to stop him. You're a cop or something, aren't you?"

I shake myself free of her grasp. I fall in the "or something" category. But she's right. Fuck restraint. I can't give that maniac the chance to kill someone else. Before she can say anything else, I'm up and over the counter.

I have a decision. I could break his neck. But how would I explain getting to him faster than is humanly possible and then using strength that is humanly improbable? No. I can explain one much easier than the other so I tap him on the shoulder and let him spin toward me. He has a heartbeat to look surprised. Then I fire. It takes only one shot. To the bridge of his nose. Abe collapses like a deflated balloon, leaving bits of his head plastered against the office door like a macabre Halloween decoration.

There's blood. Lots of it. Pooling around his head. He fell faceup and there's only a small rose blooming on his face. The pool is coming from the exit wound. Still pumping from a heart that hasn't gotten the message yet.

The smell. When I look down, I realize I'm splattered with blood, too. My clothes, my hands. I want to lick at it. Instead, I set my jaw and tense every muscle to keep the vampire in check.

It's a good thing I fed yesterday.

THERE IS A REASON I CHOSE TO BECOME A BOUNTY hunter and not a cop. I'm reminded of it in the minutes that follow. Cops appear from everywhere. I'm ordered to drop my gun, put my hands behind my head, kiss the ground.

I do what any sane person in that situation should do.

Obey.

My gun is kicked aside, my hands secured behind my back.

I can hear the same thing happening to Tracey behind

the closed office door. In a second, she's led out and pushed to the floor beside me.

Miriam is hysterical. She's yelling at the cops that it was her sister and I who saved her. Soon the two women who were hiding behind the counter join us and add to the din.

It takes six cops, a couple of detectives and two hours to sort out the story, check that Tracey and I are fugitive apprehension officers and are indeed licensed to carry. Tracey still has the temporary restraining order in her pocket, which adds credence.

By the time our hands are freed, Miriam has gone into shock. Tracey is told she can take her home. I'm told I can accompany a detective downtown to give yet another statement.

The wheels of bureaucracy creak round and round.

Tracey stops to thank me, but I wave it aside.

"Take care of your sister. Stay with her for as long as she needs you. David and I can handle everything at the office."

She smiles. "Maybe we should consider adding process server to our curriculum vitae."

"Might liven things up."

She glances down at the corpse of her ex-brother-in-law. I think if no one was watching, she'd kick the bastard. Instead she walks stiffly away and moves off to join her sister.

At the same time she's leaving, another familiar face is approaching through the throng of cops gathered around the door. He heads straight for me.

Shit. Detective Harris. I was hoping to avoid having to repeat the story yet again. I release a breath, huff, "What took you so long?"

Harris looks at me with raised eyebrows. "I heard what

happened. Knew there couldn't possibly be more than one Anna Strong." He walks over to the body. The medical examiner is off to one side making notes. He and Harris nod to each other. Then Harris kneels down for a closer look. "Nice shot."

"Couldn't miss. We were nose to nose."

"Heard that, too. How'd you pull that off?" He stands again and aims his squint-eyed Dirty Harry cop stare right at me. "A guy with an AK-47 and you manage to close the distance between a counter fifty feet away and the shooter without drawing fire. What are you, faster than a speeding bullet?"

It's grown quiet around us. The two women who were hiding behind the counter look away when they see me turning in their direction. What did they tell the police?

The truth, most likely. I am faster than a speeding bullet.

What can I tell the police? The same thing I've said three times before.

I raise my shoulders. "You know how it is when the adrenaline is pumping. People do things they couldn't do in normal circumstances."

Harris lets a beat go by. "You give a statement?"

"To every fucking cop you see. I'm still invited to headquarters. Anything you can do about that?"

Harris motions to one of the other detectives. "You need anything else from Ms. Strong?"

The detective looks at his notes. "Nah. Nothing now. She can go."

Harris turns back to me; a half smile touches his mouth. "And I know where to find you if we need anything else, don't I?"

I'm tempted to crack wise and suggest that he remember

the donuts the next time he drops by. But he's helping me get out of here. Best not to press my luck. I nod my thanks and turn to go.

He stops me with a hand on my arm. "Are you all right? Do you need a ride home?"

Those are the questions he's asking. He wants to know something else. A normal human being who just killed someone would be showing some emotion. He wants to know why I'm not.

I could fake it. Probably should. Instead, I tell him the truth. "He killed an innocent man. He would have killed Tracey's sister. What would you have done in my place?"

Harris allows a rare, real, honest-to-God smile. His only answer. Then, "I'll see you get your gun back as soon as forensics is finished with it."

"I appreciate it." I start for the door. Harris stops me again and jerks a thumb toward the back.

"Better go out that way. There's a shitload of reporters waiting out front."

He saved me again. That's three times now. If this keeps out, I might start to like the man.

Suddenly I'm glad Stephen is out of town. He's one reporter I would have a hard time shaking.

CHAPTER 7

THIS IS NOT THE WAY I INTENDED TO SPEND THE day. I keep seeing Harris' expression when he asked me if I was all right. It haunts me all the way back to the cottage. He's forming an opinion about me I neither welcome nor like. It's as if he's trying to get into my head. Trying to work a puzzle with missing pieces.

I recognize the look. I'll bet right now he's going over every detail of every time our paths have crossed. Maybe it's because of Williams. Maybe it's because, like he said yesterday, I end up involved in cases I have no reason to be.

Maybe it's because of the body count.

For the first time, I miss Williams. At least when he was chief, I had a buffer shielding me from the prying eyes of a human police force.

I have messages waiting for me on both my landline and cell phone. The local press picked up the story of the "Supermarket Shoot-out" and want interviews. I delete all ten of them. Curse the fact that they were able to get my unlisted numbers, then smile at the irony in that. I wonder how many people I've tracked down who've cursed me the same way?

An eleventh message is from Stephen. He caught the story as it came over the wire. When I call him back, his phone goes right to voice mail. I assure him that I'm all right, promise that we'll talk soon.

The last message is from Max. He heard what happened, too. He asks if I'm okay and if I still plan to meet him tonight. I return that call. Get his voice mail, tell him yes, I'm okay and yes, I'll see him as planned. I also ask him to bring an extra weapon. I'm sure I won't have my gun back for a few days. If we're dealing with a vampire, I won't really need a gun. But though a bullet won't stop a vampire, it can slow one down.

IT'S A CLEAR, QUIET, MOONLESS NIGHT. MAX AND I have tramped across two miles of barren desert. We're both dressed in dark camo, ski masks covering our faces. He dons night vision goggles. I don't need them. The creatures of the desert are as clear to me in the inky blackness as they would be in the brightest sunlight. I see more than Max ever can, down to the tiniest scurrying insects he crushes underfoot as we trudge onward.

I hear more, too. The faraway cry of a bird of prey. The squeal of a rabbit as the jaws of a coyote snap closed around its neck. The pebbles pushed aside in the wake of a slithering snake.

Then something else.

I touch Max's arm. Signal him to stop. Point off to the north.

Too far away for him to see, there's a dim shadow against the inky darkness. Moving toward us.

Max doesn't question me. We seek cover behind the sloping bank of an arroyo, dry as dust in the summer heat. And hunker down to wait.

The shadow draws closer, divides into three. I probe, careful to keep my own presence hidden. The unmistakable psychic pattern of a vampire comes back like the blip on radar. At least one of them is vampire.

Then a feeling I've come to recognize swamps my senses. Revulsion. Rage. Bloodlust so powerful the vampire within bursts from its human cocoon with the gnashing of teeth.

Evil approaches.

Max seems to detect the change. He leans away from me, an involuntary, instinctive reaction to danger. "What's wrong?"

I strip the ski mask from my face, let it fall to the ground. It takes effort to speak, to form words and force them through a throat that wants to howl. "Stay away from me. No matter what happens."

I don't wait for his reply. I leap over the embankment and head out to meet the monster.

CHAPTER 8

S HE SENSES MY APPROACH.

She.

Max's coyote.

We're still a mile away from each other, but she picks up the rage. I close the distance in seconds.

Then we're face-to-face.

The vampire and the man and woman at her side. They are stunned by my sudden appearance, by my vampire face. They are young, maybe twenty, dressed in dark jeans and hoodies that are tattered and stained. They each carry a small satchel. They cringe away, look to their guide.

I look at her, too. She has the smooth, unlined face of a very young woman. Dark skinned, dark hair and eyes that tilt up at the corners. Exotic. Latino or Middle Eastern?

I point to the humans. *Let them go.*

The vampire tilts her head to one side, studying me. Physically, we are evenly matched. She is weighing her options.

You have no options.

She is cloaking her thoughts. Then, abruptly, she says, *Perhaps you are right. These two are of no consequence.*

Do they speak English?

A nod.

I drag my eyes away from her, motion to the couple. "The border is three miles straight ahead. There is a tear in the fence. You can make it on your own."

I am trying very hard to sound human. Even to my own ears, my voice is rough. It comes from my gut, not my vocal cords. A growl.

The humans are mesmerized. They can't look away from my eyes.

The vampire raises a hand, strokes the hair of the woman. *They want to stay with me.*

She has not shown her true nature. The woman steps behind her for protection. The vampire laughs.

The fury in me builds. I realize her intention. Her mouth opens, her teeth gnash. She reaches behind to pull the woman forward.

I have her neck before she can grab the woman. I pull her away and spin her around, showing the cowering couple the true face of their savior.

They jump back, mouths open in astonishment.

The vampire laughs again. I force her to her knees. Reach into the pocket of her jacket. Pull a wad of bills from inside. Toss it to the man.

"Take your money. Go. Now."

This time, there is no hesitation. They circle around us in a wide arc, uncomprehending, fearful the creatures might change their minds. Then they're off, running across the desert floor.

I hold the vampire on the ground until the rustle of

their clothes, the sound of their footsteps is a distant echo.

You could have let me keep the money.

She is not afraid.

Why?

Do you know who I am?

Everyone of our race knows who you are.

Then you know I can't let you go.

Still no reaction. Her mind is closed. Mine is not. *Do you think because you are not resisting I will spare you?*

I think you will spare me because I have something to offer you.

I pull her to her feet. She faces me squarely. We are the same height. Her dark eyes have changed back, she still holds the vampire in check. She wears jeans and a blouse that skims her shoulders, a denim jacket. Her hair is tied back from her face with a scarf. She looks about twenty-five. Her thoughts are much older, much darker.

The creature before me radiates malevolence. She has killed for a hundred years. She has a taste for it. Lust for blood oozes from her pores like the foul smell of rotting meat. My instinct to kill her now and quickly battles with a desire to learn what a being like this thinks she can offer me.

See? You are curious.

I backhand her across the face. She flies fifty feet and lands on a barrel cactus.

She struggles to her feet. *Damn, bitch. That hurt.*

I'm at her side with my hands around her throat before she can finish whining.

She still has not released the beast. I can feel her fury building. She wants to. What is holding her back?

I have killed vampires before. Vampires more powerful

than this sniveling female. It can be done many ways. This one, however, deserves to die slowly. The same way she has killed the helpless humans she's lured to this place with a promise of a new life. She will feel her life ebb away drop by drop until there is nothing left but an empty husk.

I am done with you.

For the first time, something besides sarcasm and confidence flickers in the depths of her eyes. Fear is there, too. She pulls away, her hands on my arms as she tries to break my grip. Her struggles are fruitless.

But I have something you want. Information I am willing to offer in return for my life.

You have recklessly taken human life. Left bodies to be discovered—

No one of importance. No one who will be missed. I have incited no threat against us. Why should it matter to you that I thin the ranks of the miserable? I do them a service, ending their pathetic lives.

Her attitude is like a red-hot poker in my gut. It is the attitude of many of our kind. Something I came to realize in my first meeting with the heads of the vampire clans. It is the attitude that holds mortals in the same class as the beasts.

I tighten my grip until I feel my fingers sink into her flesh. *Do you ask these "miserable" if they want to die? Give them a choice? You kill for sport. You take their money. Worse, you offer hope, then snatch it away. You are an animal. You deserve the same fate as those you toy with, the ones you consider unimportant. I am here to exact vengeance.*

Then what Chael says about you is true.

The name makes me draw back a tiny step, to look into her eyes. *What does Chael have to do with you?*

She takes advantage of the momentary distraction to draw herself up. *Chael says you think more of mortals than you do your own kind. I see he is right.* Her words drip acid. *Well, be warned. You may soon find yourself alone. There are many of us who are tired of hiding. The tide is rising.*

So this is why you are here? Chael sent you to deliver a warning? He has made a grievous mistake if he thinks killing innocents is the way to gain my support for his cause.

She shakes her head. *I am not here to gain your support. Chael told me there would be only one thing to tempt you away from the path you have chosen. Kill me now and you will never know how to achieve what it is your heart desires.*

And how do you know what my heart desires? How does Chael?

It is obvious. You wish to return the gift of immortality, to become human again.

I make a guttural sound in my throat—half snort, half snarl. *You think you can forestall the inevitable with this foolish talk? The only reason you are not dead already is that I want to make sure the humans are safely away before I end your miserable existence. They have been traumatized enough.*

I may not be so easy to kill.

Finally. The beast is unleashed. Her right hand dips into her jacket. Lightning fast. She pulls out a small stake and lunges for my chest.

I am faster. A half turn and the stake strikes a rib. I wrest the weapon from her hand, toss it away.

She locks her arms around me, intent on bending me backward, her snapping jaws seek my throat.

It takes very little effort to break her grip. Our positions reverse. For a fleeting moment, I have a glimpse into her head. Hate boils in her blood, turns her thoughts red with rage.

And Chael is there, too. His whispered entreaties that she should seek me out. Tempt me with the secret.

Chael is there.

Who is this female to Chael?

What is the secret?

No matter.

The bloodlust burns too strong to pull back now. Nothing is more important than the hunger. I tear at her jugular. Her blood, hot and delicious, fills my mouth, my senses. She squirms and pounds at my chest with her fists. The blood from my chest wound seems to mingle with her own blood as the one flows out and the other flows in.

She is strong. Her will to live not easily extinguished. She is kicking at me, her hands frantically seeking anything to use against me.

Too late I feel her fingers close around the gun clipped to my belt. She fires it without drawing it out of the holster. The roar of the gunshot rips the quiet fabric of the night. A bullet pierces my side. Convulsively, I snap her arm at the elbow.

We both scream in pain.

The bullet moves inside me, scorching a path through muscle and sinew before it explodes out. It does not penetrate organ or impact bone.

It does not stop me from tearing again at her neck.

She is getting weaker. I tighten my hold, lock my jaws. Her blood is no longer thick, but thinning out as the last drops are consumed. She no longer fights. She is no longer capable of shielding her thoughts. The atrocities she's committed, the victims she's tortured, the senseless agony she's inflicted. All threaten from the dark. There is no thought of loved ones or family. Like her victims, she has lived most of her second life alone. Only fear is left. And dread for what comes next.

I drain the last of her blood, feel the shudder as her soul leaves the body, feel my hatred ebb with the final flickering spark of her life.

She has died like her victims, alone and afraid.

It is just.

The metamorphosis begins the instant the soul leaves the body. The young woman I held in my grasp is an old, withered shell by the time she hits the ground. It is the way. Drained of blood, the vampire body reverts physically to its mortal counterpart. I stand looking down at an old lady well past her one hundredth birthday.

My metamorphosis begins, too. The human Anna comes back, slowly, reluctantly.

Slowly. Infusion of blood temporarily warms a body that is even now returning to its natural state. The warmth fades too quickly.

Reluctantly. With the return to human form comes rational thought. I will not forget what I have done.

Twice.

I have killed. Two monsters. One mortal, one not.

I have no regrets. They both deserved to die. I only wish killing didn't come so easily.

With rational thought comes something else—awareness of the pain that racks my side. I was right. A gunshot can slow a vampire down. Especially one from the big .45 Max brought for me. Slowly, carefully, I draw myself up, stretch gingerly, willing the healing process to move more quickly, to numb this ache.

"Anna!" Max's voice. "Where are you?"

I rouse myself and step over the vampire's body. I realize I never learned her name. Does it matter? Not now.

Max is fifty yards out, moving toward me at a run.

"Here."

I let him find me. He has his gun in his hand and he is breathing hard. When he sees the crumpled remains on the ground, he turns to me, startled, bewildered.

"Who is that?"

"Your coyote."

He kneels for a closer look. "She's an old woman. How could she possibly—"

"What you're looking at are her mortal remains. You were right in suspecting a vampire was behind the attacks. She was with a couple when I found her. I let them go."

"I know." Max holsters his gun. "I saw them run by."

"Did they make it?"

"From what I could see."

"Good."

Max switches his gaze from the corpse to me. For the first time, he sees the blood soaking my shirt, on my thighs.

"You're hurt?"

"No." Not much anyway. He couldn't have brought a .22? I don't think I'll tell him I let myself get shot with his gun. "It looks worse than it is."

He nods. Luckily, he knows how it is with vampires.

"What should we do with that?" He points to the thing on the ground.

"Bury it."

Max swings his flashlight in an arc. "I didn't bring a shovel. What can we use?"

I spy a flat piece of rock and a long, sturdy branch kiln dried by the sun. I retrieve them. "It will take work, but we can use these."

I hand him the branch to begin scraping away sand and follow after, scooping out a hole with the rock. My side screams in protest but within fifteen minutes, we have a hole big enough and deep enough to cover the corpse. I grab her by the arm to throw her in.

"She's really dead, right?" Max asks.

"You mean is she going to rise up in three days and come after us?" I prod at the body with my foot. "No. She's gone."

The remains land in the hole with the brittle thud of desiccated flesh and bone.

We set to work, shoveling the sand back in, tamping it down with our feet, setting a layer of rock and debris over the grave. To protect it from scavengers.

A flashback. Another vampire corpse. Another grave dug in the desert. Another pair of hands working beside mine.

Lance.

A shudder racks my body.

Max's shoulder is so close to mine, he feels my body jerk. He pauses. "Are you sure you're all right?"

The vampire answers from the darkest place in my soul. "It's nothing. I just walked on someone's grave."

MAX RECOGNIZES ONE OF THE GUARDS AT THE BOR-der crossing. They exchange a few words in Spanish and he waves us through. It's good because I'm not sure I want to try to explain the rust-colored stains covering my clothes.

Max takes me back to my car. He watches me climb gingerly out of the passenger side. "Can you drive?"

I massage my side. The scrape caused by the stake is healed. The path the bullet tore through my side is healed.

Now it's just the skin pulling tight as it regenerates over the holes that makes me wince when I move.

"Yeah. I'm a little stiff but by the time I get home, I'll be fine."

I pull his gun and holster free from my belt. "Here. Maybe next time you can bring a cannon."

Max grins and watches as I get into my car and crank the engine before he motions for me to roll down the window.

"Thanks, Anna. You did good tonight. I owe you one."

Okay, here's my chance to tell him what I planned to tell him. To go fuck himself. To never call me again. To go to one of his vampire whores the next time he needs help.

What am I waiting for?

Max is leaning toward the window, smiling. He looks more like the Max I remembered. Superman, defending truth, justice and the American way . . .

Shit.

I smile back.

And drive away.

CHAPTER 9

S LEEP IS A WONDERFUL RESTORATIVE.

Except for one occasion when a dream proved to be prophetic, my dreams are of human things. My parents, my brother, my niece, my life before the becoming. I'm always happy in my dreams. I'm always human.

When I awake this morning, the glow of having spent time with those I love lingers.

Then confusion as I try to zero in on my surroundings. This isn't my bed. This isn't my room. The impersonal, artificial coziness of a hotel room with its heavy blackout curtains, disinfectant smell and sterile, generic furniture comes sharply into focus as I look around.

The reason I'm here floods back, replacing peace with aggravation. It was two a.m. when I arrived back at the cottage. They were waiting for me. TV reporters from every local station. All wanting to interview the *hero* of the Ralphs supermarket shooting.

The hero. Me.

Luckily, I spied the reporters perched like vultures on the seawall in front of my place before they spotted me. I've been down this path before and Williams' recriminations came back to haunt me. I did it again. I exposed my true nature to mortals. That time, my predicament was self-made. This time, I had no choice.

I drove to a nearby motel and checked in under a false name. It's useful to have a couple of bogus licenses at times like these—illegal as hell but useful. Also useful to keep an extra jacket in the car. The camos I'm wearing are dust covered and bloodstained. I pulled on an old jacket to cover the worst of it and paid cash for a single night. The guy at the desk looked at me with raised eyebrows but took my money.

Once settled in the room, I reviewed my options. I need to have a story ready in case I get ambushed by the press tomorrow.

I think I can use the adrenaline story I told Harris. If a mother can lift a car off a baby, why couldn't a woman cross fifty feet of floor and get the drop on a gunman in the blink of an eye?

And by tomorrow, the story may have been relegated from the front page to the police blotter. Who knows what might happen during the night?

Satisfied with the story, I hadn't bothered to get undressed, just threw myself across the bed. No reason to get undressed when you have no clean clothes to change into. It was amazing how quickly I fell asleep.

So now it's a quick face wash, a call down to the front desk to let them know I'm checking out and I'm headed for home.

I can't wait to get home, take a shower. Forget about the events of the last twenty-four hours.

I park on Mission Boulevard and hoof it into the cottage, using the alley in back. I could have pulled right into my garage. If there are any reporters still around, they are keeping a very low profile. Once inside, I don't check voice mail, don't turn on my cell. I want only to get into a hot shower and clean clothes. Enjoy a cup of my own coffee on my own deck.

It's what I want.

What I find when I step into the living room scuttles those plans.

He's sitting on my couch, feet up on the coffee table, looking for all the world like he belongs.

He's even helped himself to coffee and is reading my paper.

Son of a bitch.

It's Chael.

CHAPTER 10

T HE LAST TIME I SAW CHAEL, HEAD OF THE MIDDLE
Eastern Vampire Tribe, it was exactly two months ago
today. He was dressed in Savile Row then. Today it's Ro-
deo Drive. He's in dark slacks and a cream-colored polo
shirt, leather loafers on stocking-less feet.

He looks up when I enter, radiates no concern that I've
jumped into full vampire mode. He lays the paper down,
rises slowly, hands outstretched placatingly. He is slight of
stature, dark-skinned, with sharp features and hard eyes.
When he stands, we are eye to eye.

He waits for me to speak first, hands still outstretched as
if to show he has come unarmed.

We are vampire. We are never unarmed.

Teeth gritted, I open my thoughts. He speaks no English,
but we can communicate the way of all vampires, telepathically. *You have violated my privacy. How did you get in?*

A shrug. *It was not difficult. The glass door off your
bedroom was unlocked.*

Stupid of me. I often leave that slider open. Too high for a human to access but not a vampire.

Is an unlocked door considered an invitation to trespass in your country?

Chael lifts his palms in a gesture that admits he overstepped, but he offers no apology.

Why are you here?

Uninvited, he sits back down, picks up the newspaper and scans the front page. *You have been busy. Interfering in mortal affairs again. One eyewitness says that you "flew" over a counter and across the floor to shoot a man armed with a rifle. They are calling it a miracle. I call it an inexcusable display from one who is bent on keeping our existence a secret.*

So, you read English now?

A deprecating shrug. *I had someone translate the story for me.*

I'll bet. Irritation pokes at me. I growl, *The last time I checked, I didn't answer to you. And what concern is this of yours? You are a long way from your home territory.*

It is the concern of all vampire when their true nature has been exposed. What do you plan to do to rectify this violation?

I close down the conduit between us. What I plan to do is none of his business. I know faddish human nature. This will pass as soon as something more interesting comes along to capture the imagination of the public. A baseball team will reach the playoffs, a movie star will be arrested for consorting with a fifteen-year-old. Mortal attention span is short.

You have no plan, do you? Chael shakes his head. *As the Chosen One, you are proving once again how immature and ill prepared you are to lead a superior race.*

This again. My temper rises as the real reason for this visit suddenly strikes me. He is not here because of what happened yesterday at the supermarket. He couldn't have known about it until this morning.

He is here because of what happened last night in the desert. The rogue was his vampire.

Enough posturing, Chael. You care nothing for human concerns. You are here because I killed your whore.

A cold light flashes in his eyes, a hint of a smile touches his mouth. *She was a whore. But a useful one. She had influence over the vampire community in our part of the world.*

So why did you send her here? Why did you let her indulge her sick game?

He looks surprised at the question. *To get your attention, of course. I knew of your history with your own whoremonger, the mortal, Max. I knew he would come to you when it became obvious a vampire was committing the killings. I knew you'd kill her in turn.*

An elaborate charade. What if Max hadn't called me or I had refused to help?

Then the killings would have gone on until you had no choice but to get involved. You and that highly developed sense of responsibility toward mortals. It isn't in you to let bodies pile up in your own backyard.

So I met her and killed her. What was the point?

A miscalculation. I thought you'd at least hear her out before you killed her. I know you did not.

Shit. He was there. Why didn't I pick up on that?

For some reason, Chael doesn't unleash the beast in me. I sense he's evil, but I don't get the gut reaction to his presence that I have with others—both human and supernaturals. I don't understand it. I wish it wasn't so. I should have known that he was waiting inside for me before I opened the door. I should have known that he was out in the desert last night.

I didn't.

Chael is silent, calm, waiting for me to process what he suspects but cannot read because he has no access to my thoughts. I study him the way he is studying me. He is not inclined to comment or offer an explanation. Perhaps he doesn't understand, either, but he must know he has the advantage. Which is very likely why he took the chance of coming into my home.

My jaw clenches in frustration. *What do you want?*

Chael has placed the newspaper back on the coffee table, folding it neatly, squaring the corners so that it lies against the table's edge. He looks up at me, a real smile lighting his face and softening the hard glint in black eyes. For the first time, I glimpse the human twenty-year-old he must have been when he was turned.

I am here to solve your problems, Anna Strong. I am here to grant your heart's desire.

A snort of bitter amusement greets his proposal. *Oh? And you presume to know my heart's desire?*

I knew it the moment I first learned of you. And everything you have done since the beginning confirms my belief. I know how you can achieve your dream. I know how you can unburden yourself of all the problems in your life.

He gets to his feet, begins pacing as he talks. *That incident with your business partner? I can make it so his memory is truly wiped clean. You and he can once again become the friends you were, sharing more than the shallow relationship you have now. Detective Harris will find you much less interesting when he realizes there is nothing special about you. He will move on to more important*

*cases; Williams will finally be put to rest. You may even
wish to pursue a relationship with Max. He still cares for
you in spite of his bravado. All will be as it was before the
gift was thrust upon you. The gift you yourself have said
you neither sought nor wanted.*

How do you propose to work this miracle?

There is a way. I can show you.

And if I refuse your offer?

Chael lifts his shoulders in a gesture of resignation.
*Then your life becomes a nightmare. All who know you
will turn their backs on you. You will be hounded by Harris, who already suspects you are not what you seem. The
Revengers will target you. Even your family in France
will—*

Before he completes the sentence, I attack. He has no
time to react; in an eyeblink I have him on the ground, my
teeth at his neck. *Never threaten my family.*

He shudders under the ferocity of my attack. He is wise
enough to grow very still, to resist the urge to fight. His
hands are limp at his side, his eyes closed, his mind closes
in on itself like petals of a flower fold with the departing
sun. He becomes as motionless and devoid of all discern-
able life as a rock.

I want to make the illusion a reality. What would happen if I were to kill the head of one of the Thirteen Tribes?
I run my tongue along the base of his jaw. How would his
blood taste? What power does his blood possess? Would I
be held accountable even though he broke into my home
and threatened my family?

His pulse throbs, his blood sings under a millimeter of
skin so delicate, so easily broken. I need only close my
jaws, right here, grind my teeth to loose the flow. So
easy . . .

Chael opens his mind. *If you kill me, you'll never be able to go back. I am the only one who knows the secret.*

I draw back, a hairbreadth, my mouth still in reach of the prize. *If you have something to say, say it.*

Chael releases a breath. *I know the way. You think it not possible. You are wrong. I can show you.*

You speak in riddles.

Then I'll speak plainly. There is a way for you to become mortal again.

CHAPTER 11

CHAEL FEELS THE INVOLUNTARY SPIKE OF INTEREST that seeps through my thoughts at his words. He smiles. *Ah, I have your attention. Will you let me up now? Please.*

I don't trust Chael. It goes against every instinct to allow him to get back on his feet.

Still, it's what I do. Roughly, jerking him up by the collar of his shirt, teeth and fists ready, body poised to pounce again if I detect any aggression.

Why am I doing this? The little voice in the back of my head says it's stupid. It has to be a trick. There is no way to go back. No way to become human again.

Is there?

It's that tiny crumb of doubt that allows Chael a reprieve.

I step away from him. He straightens his shirt, brushes invisible dirt from his slacks. My clothes are grubby but the jacket conceals the worst of the dirt and blood. This affectation is merely for show. As is his comment, *I hope your sartorial taste was better as a mortal than it is now. You are filthy.*

Sarcasm? You try my patience, Chael.

A snort. *Is that irony? I imagine you try the patience of most who know you.*

My fists clench, my jaw and shoulders tighten. Every nerve in my body cries out to bring this arrogant bastard to his knees.

My inner voice comes again. Patience, Anna. There will be time. After he spins his fairy tale. Consequences be damned.

Speak.

He finishes his symbolic tidying by running both hands through jet-black hair, smoothing it behind his ears.

You're ready to listen?

I'm ready to rip your head off your scrawny neck if you don't get on with it.

He clucks his tongue. *No wonder you are bereft of friends.* He resumes his place on the couch. He starts to put his feet back on the coffee table, but the snarl that erupts from my throat stops him. He shakes his head and settles back against the cushions instead.

There is a shaman. He lives here in your American Southwest. He has the power to restore life. He can bring the dead back from the grave. He can restore mortality to the undead.

Impossible.

He stares at me, bemused. *That is your reply? Impossible? You have no questions for me? You are not curious why I would come here risking my well-being with a fabricated tale? What would I accomplish with such a foolish act?*

Chael, I have no idea why you do what you do. I do

know that you hate me. I can only guess you have prepared a trap. One you think I'll be foolish enough to fall into. One you think will rid you of me once and for all. You are wrong on both counts.

He doesn't react the way I expect—with vehement denial and heated recrimination. Rather he lifts his elegant shoulders. *You are right. It would benefit me greatly if you no longer held the position of Chosen One. A position you neither deserve nor understand. But if I wished only to remove you, it could be done in a much more direct way. I could have you killed.*

This is the Chael I recognize. The smile that I force to my lips is cold and menacing. *You could try.*

And I would succeed. You are strong. But you have not faced an army of determined vampires. We would lose some, maybe many, but eventually we would prevail. You are not invincible. If the Chosen One were invincible, there would have been only one down through the ages, would there not?

His bluntness strikes a chord. No one has yet been able to answer the questions I've asked myself since learning of my dubious distinction as the head of the Thirteen Vampire Tribes.

How and why was I chosen? What became of those before me?

My hesitation gives Chael the opportunity to push on. *You have wondered about that yourself, haven't you? Many of us have.* His tone is bitter. *If we could figure out the mystery, discover the source who predetermines our path, the master who makes us slaves to such as you, the fate of the world would be far different.*

You mean you would move against this master and take over yourself?

I would not be averse to such a situation.

But you can't do it alone, can you? That is what stops you. You don't have the backing of the others.

Chael snaps his fingers, dismissing my question with a derisive laugh. *Too many are bound up in the superstition. Like mortals cling to their archaic religions, they cling to a ritual that is illogical and irrational and has no relevance today. But in the right circumstance—*

The circumstance of my unseating, for instance?

His eyes flash. He actually allows the thought *or your death* to come through, but it is tempered by a smile.

A smile I don't return.

So that is why you come to me with this story? You dare not kill me, but if I become mortal, the thorn from your paw is removed in a way that cannot reflect ill on you. You will have done me no harm. You cannot be held responsible for the deposing of a Chosen One who returns to human life.

His self-satisfied smile widens. This time I return the smile with a cold one of my own. Crossing the distance between us, I bend so close, he has to cringe back to look up at me.

Your hypothesis has one severe flaw, Chael. You can't be sure you will be chosen to take my place. I'm assuming that is your goal if you wish to see the world remade in your twisted image.

My goal is of no concern to you. I am only here to offer you a gift. Not to debate what might happen if you choose to accept it.

I can't believe Chael doesn't see the irony in that statement. If I accepted this "gift," and a new Chosen One is swayed by Chael's vision, or even worse, Chael assumes the title himself, life as we know it for mortals is over.

They become as cattle, relegated to gulags, existing only to serve their vampire masters.

Except for one small detail. *I* know the plan. Even as a human, I might be able to fight it.

But I'm getting ahead of myself. What he proposes is not possible; planning countermeasures, ridiculous.

Chael cannot read these thoughts. He watches my face, suspicious of a mind suddenly as impenetrable as the steel in my gaze.

I turn away from him, moving to the other side of the room, putting distance between us as if that will help me sort conflicted emotions. To be human again. To be with my family. To love anyone I wish. To stop hiding what I am. To be free of the hunger.

It isn't possible? Is it?

Feelings I've relegated to the past well up, swamping my senses, radiating though the barrier between us and giving Chael the opening he seeks.

You are tempted. I feel it. You can't hide the passion. You want what once was. I will tell you what I know. Then it is up to you.

I face him. Shutting down the fierce longing that betrayed me takes such effort, my body shakes. But my thoughts are cold, clinical when I open my mind.

Tell me.

Chael now finds it difficult to control his own eagerness—excitement that I am asking, anticipation of all that he hopes to come burns from his eyes. He can't suppress his passion any more than I could.

He lives among the Navajo. A shaman.

And how do I find him?

Ah. That is easy. You ask your shape-shifter friend, Daniel Frey.

How would he know of this miracle worker?

He does not know him. But he knows where to find him. With his son.

I remember well the first time I learned that Daniel Frey had a son. Frey was preparing me for what I would face at the assembly of the Thirteen Tribes. He dropped the nugget that he had a son as casually as one would shake a pebble from a shoe. After recovering from the shock of such a startling revelation, it took some wheedling to get any information at all about this unexpected and stunning news. The little I got was sketchy at best.

The kid was four.

He lived with his Navajo mother in Monument Valley.

Frey didn't see him very often—to protect his identity as the one to inherit Frey's mantle as Keeper of Secrets when the time comes.

That Chael knows of him is not reassuring.

How do you know about Frey's son?

I try to keep the alarm from my tone, but Chael picks up on it. *I mean the child no harm. The Keeper of Secrets is an important and revered position that benefits all supernaturals.*

Even if I were to believe Chael's words, a question still remains. What happens to those supernaturals, vampire or not, who do not share Chael's vision for his new world order? I have no doubt he would exterminate them as ruthlessly as he vowed to exterminate any creature who will not bend to his will.

Once again, Chael watches me, his piercing eyes and laser-like mind trying to rend the barrier I've erected between us. I know whatever I decide, the first thing I have to do is get Frey's child to safety.

Chael stirs, irritated that I have shut myself off from him. I open my mind.

You have delivered your message. Now get out.

Suspicion darkens his thoughts. *What are you going to do?*

You will know when I'm ready. How do I get in touch with you?

He brightens. *I am staying with an old friend of yours, Judith Williams. You can reach me at her home.*

Judith Williams? It figures. And it explains a lot. I'm sure she took great pleasure in reading Chael the newspaper article that detailed what happened in the supermarket. I'm also sure she provided her own editorial comments along the way. Did she mention the game she played with David on Sunday?

Another whore. I wonder what her husband, whom you claimed to be a friend, would think of your alliance.

Chael inspects his fingernails. *He would not approve. To either my plan or my fucking his wife. She has been set free under my tutelage. A willing and talented student.*

I'll bet. Do you plan to dispose of her when you are through with her education?

Now he meets my eyes. *No. When the time comes, I expect you will do that for me.*

Chael's last sardonic remark touches a nerve. He doesn't expect a reply. I don't give him one. He knows the truth. If she gave me cause, I would kill Judith Williams without a second thought. But I will not do it at Chael's bidding.

I cross to the front door, unlock it, hold it open. *Give Judith a message for me. Tell her to leave David alone. If she speaks to him again, her days as your playmate may be over sooner than you expect.*

Chael departs without response, his bearing regal, a Middle Eastern prince whose fiefdom is comprised not of land but of control over thousands of the most powerful creatures on earth.

I watch him walk down the sidewalk to Mission Boulevard. A discreet black Mercedes pulls up at his approach, a rear door opens from the inside. As he climbs in, Judith Williams' pale face stares back at me.

I wonder if she knows she's consorting with death.

CHAPTER 12

I'VE JUST STEPPED OUT OF THE SHOWER WHEN I hear the trill of my cell phone from downstairs.

I choose not to answer it. The way the last couple of days have gone, it can't be anything good. If it's Stephen, he'll leave a message.

Besides, the person I need to talk to right now is Daniel Frey. To tell him of my conversation with Chael and to warn him that the existence of his son is not the well-kept secret he thought it was.

And to broach the subject of the shaman.

To become human again.

The idea fills me with excitement. At the same time, the logical part of my brain screams to put on the brakes. Nothing Chael says can be trusted.

I towel dry my hair, slip into clean clothes and start downstairs.

Then I remember—and retrace my steps to shut and bolt the slider. Of course, any vampire worth his fangs could break that door without breaking a sweat, but may as well not make it too easy.

The message light on my kitchen phone is flashing. My cell phone is chirping. Shit. Whoever is trying to get in touch with me is persistent to say the least.

I ignore the landline and reluctantly pull up the cell's voice mail messages. There are three. The first from a cautiously optimistic David. Test results were negative for STDs and preliminary HIV screenings though those tests have to be repeated in six months. At least he can have sex now. With protection, of course. He's decided not to spill his guts to Miranda.

And, "Oh, by the way, glad you and Tracey are okay. Nice plug for the business."

Plug for the business? I suspect that might have something to do with the newspaper article Chael was reading this morning. Either the reporter connected my name to our business or Tracey mentioned it.

Doesn't matter. The important thing is there is no need to call David back.

The second is from Tracey: checking in to thank me again and to warn me about the press interest in the story. She and her sister were hounded until she finally gave in and arranged a press conference scheduled for this afternoon. Did I want to participate? Might get the hounds off my trail.

This is easy. I send Tracey a text—

Go ahead w/o me. Tell the reporters I've left town.

A finger jab on Send and it's on its way.
The last from Harris. A simple, "Call me."
A finger jab on Delete and that's on its way, too, to the

great voice mail landfill in the sky. If Harris really wanted to *talk* to me, he'd be on my doorstep. There is precedent.

Then I'm on my way out the door. I debate calling Frey first to let him know I'm coming, but he's teaching summer school and if I time it right, I'll catch him before class starts.

IT'S AN ODD FEELING, WALKING ON THE CAMPUS where my mother was principal until her resignation a few months ago. Eerie because of the quiet. There are only a handful of classes offered during summer session; budget cutbacks trimmed all but the essentials. Frey's English Lit class is offered because of demand. He's such a popular teacher, even six classes a day during the regular school year can't accommodate all the students who want to take it.

It's not quite eight, but as I suspected, Frey is already on campus, cloistered in his cubbyhole of an office at the front of the room.

Memories flood back as I watch him. He isn't aware of my presence, his back half turned to the door as he pores over papers on his desk, a pencil in one hand, a mug in the other. It was at that desk I first learned that Frey was a shape-shifter and exactly what that meant. I hadn't been a vampire very long and everything about my new existence was frighteningly exotic, including the knowledge that creatures like Frey, a panther in his other shape, and like me, walk among mortals undetected. I soon learned though, that while there is plenty of evil in the world, Frey is one of the good guys.

He should be able to sense my presence. Like Culebra, he should be able to read my thoughts and I, his. But I broke our psychic connection when I attacked him months ago. I thought he was an enemy. I was wrong. Now the link that binds us is more human than supernatural—it's friendship.

I tilt my head, study him. Frey is handsome, forty-something, his dark hair touched on the sides with gray. He has a quality about him—trustworthy, strong. Must be that square jaw, those serious dark eyes. It's no wonder he's so popular with his students. I imagine he has to fend off at least one serious crush a semester. And not only from female students. I wonder how his girlfriend Layla handles the competition.

Chael's face swims to the surface of my consciousness, chasing away such mundane musings and bringing me sharply back to the reason for this visit.

I walk up behind Frey and tap his shoulder. I should have made more noise. He is so startled he jumps to his feet, sending the chair flying and a stream of coffee sloshing over the sides of the mug and onto the desk. When he sees me, those serious dark eyes flash with anger.

"Jesus, Anna. Where did you come from?"

"So much for catlike reflexes." I grab up a bunch of napkins piled beside the coffeemaker on his bookcase and use them to sop up the mess on the desk. "What were you working on with such concentration?"

He pushes my hand away and takes over clean up. "Final exam essays. One of which"—he holds up an ink-blurred, coffee-stained page—"is ruined. Now what?"

"That lucky kid gets an A."

Frey shoots me a look of exasperation, but the anger soon passes and a smile cracks the shell of irritation. He tosses the napkins into a trash can near the office door and comes around the desk.

"Wondered when you'd drop in." He peers into my face. "Are you all right?"

My back stiffens. Why does everyone keep asking me that?

Frey sees the reaction. "Got asked that a lot lately, huh?"

"Too damned many times."

He leans back against the filing cabinet. "Well, maybe if you didn't shut yourself off from your friends, we wouldn't have to ask."

There is a sharp edge to his tone. I deserve it. He's right. Two months ago, he put his own life on hold to help me prepare to meet my destiny. Except for a brief phone call to let him know I survived, we haven't spoken since.

I try to make light of the situation. "I figured after being cloistered with me for three days, you'd be happy not to hear from me for awhile. I'm sure Layla was."

Frey's expression changes, aggravation to a look I recognize. I wince. "Uh-oh. What's up? Trouble in paradise?"

His eyes slide away.

Guilt wiggles its niggling little fingers. "Because of me?"

Frey moves again, back to his chair behind his desk. "We're taking a break."

"Because of me." No question this time.

"Because of a lot of things."

Vague. Shit.

"I'm sorry, Frey."

He meets my eyes this time. "Nothing for you to be sorry about. We both did what needed to be done. If Layla can't accept our friendship . . ."

He leaves the sentence unfinished, words fading away like smoke in a breeze.

His eyes, though, are sad, and I know in spite of what he

said, I am the reason for their breakup. I don't know what to say or do. I never liked Layla, but he obviously did.

I wish I were more like my mother. She would know how to comfort him. I lack those instincts. A physical threat I know how to handle. An emotional hurt, my head swims with indecision. I can only stand here like a fucking idiot and stare.

"Well," I say in a stammering attempt to jump-start the conversation. "There is a reason I'm here. I have something I need to discuss with you."

He glances behind me into the classroom and checks his watch. "The bell is going to ring in ten minutes. Can it wait until after class?"

For the first time I'm aware of shuffling feet outside the office door. Students are filing into the room. "Sure. I'll wait for you in the parking lot. We can go to the cottage."

He picks up a pair of glasses from the desk and waggles them at me. "No need to wait. I'll meet you there. I drive now."

The only carryover between Frey's physical and metaphysical selves is the feline inability to distinguish a broad spectrum of colors. Made driving difficult. Layla (also a feline shape-shifter) came up with a special lens that corrects the defect.

I acknowledge the glasses with nod. At least he has something to show for the broken relationship. Something other than a broken heart.

CHAPTER 13

F REY IS AT MY DOOR EXACTLY AN HOUR AND A HALF later. I have coffee brewing and a couple of hamburgers in the microwave. I picked them up on the way home. Panthers are, after all, carnivores.

I set them on the kitchen table.

Frey eyes the burger. "Thanks. I'm starved."

I take the seat opposite him and watch as he eats. Makes my salivary glands jump into overdrive. I do miss a good burger. And chocolate.

But I'm stalling.

Frey seems to know it. He wipes his mouth with a napkin and looks at me over his coffee mug. "So. What's up?"

Now that he's here and asking, I'm not sure how to begin.

"It's about your son."

Frey lowers the mug, alarm tightening the lines around his mouth. "What about my son?"

"I thought no one knew of his existence."

"No one does. Outside of this room."

I push at his plate. "I met someone this morning who does."

The alarm in Frey's expression escalates. His hands crush the napkin into a ball. "Who?"

When I tell him of Chael, who he is and how he orchestrated the challenge that resulted in Lance's death, the alarm becomes fear. "Why would he talk to you about my son? Was he threatening him? Threatening you?"

"No. Not at all. In fact, he said he meant your son no harm. He said the Keeper of the Secrets was a revered position in the supernatural community. I think he was sincere." As sincere as Chael was capable of being anyway.

"So then why mention him?"

Here's the tricky part. I tell Frey about our conversation. About the shaman who could supposedly restore a vampire to mortal state. About how this miracle worker lived on the same reservation as Frey's son.

When I finish, Frey is quiet. He's slouched against the back of the chair, eyes downcast, as if trying to distance himself from me. I don't blame him. I seem to bring nothing but trouble.

I let a moment pass and another and when his silence presses on, I break it with, "A shaman who can restore mortality. Is such a thing possible?"

He raises his eyes. "Does it matter?"

"Truthfully, I'm not sure."

Frey looks up. "Then what do you want to do?"

"I think we should go to the village. Check on your son."

"I thought you said you believed that Chael meant him no harm?"

"I did. I do. Still—"

"You don't completely trust him, do you?"

"No."

Icy resolve narrows Frey's eyes. "And you want to check this shaman out."

"Yes."

"When do you want to go?"

"When can you go?"

"Today was the last day of summer school. I have two weeks before I have to prepare for fall classes. How about tomorrow morning?"

"I can have the jet ready to go anytime you are."

He shakes his head. "We'll drive."

He's already risen from the table. I do, too. "Drive?"

"It's a beautiful part of the country. Ever been there?"

I shake my head.

"No time like the present to appreciate it."

"Do you want to drive or shall I?"

Frey slips the black-framed, amber-lensed glasses over his eyes. "I'll drive. See you in the morning."

I SPEND A RESTLESS NIGHT. PLEASANT THOUGHTS OF how my life would change if I became mortal again ricochet around in my head until I'm dizzy with it. Chief among them is the kind of life I could have with someone like Stephen. I could go with him on assignment and not risk someone noticing that I cast no reflection or don't seem to eat anything. I could visit my parents anytime I want. Take Trisha shopping and not have to avoid mirrors. Simple things. Little things.

But the responsibility I'd accepted as the Chosen One beats its own counterpoint. Chael would not offer a gift unless he was the one benefiting from it. And if he benefits from it, all those pleasant scenarios might become very short-lived. The world as we know it would cease to exist.

I glance at the clock.

Six a.m.

Obviously, sleep isn't in the cards for me.

I roll out of bed.

I'm strangely excited about this trip. Partly for the obvious reasons. Partly because I'm going to meet Frey's son and the mother of his child. Partly because for the first time in a year I'll actually have a say in what happens to me.

Frey said he had to stop by school this morning and turn in his grades so we should be on the road by ten. All I have to do is throw some clothes in a duffle and I'm ready to go. Living mostly in jeans and T-shirts makes packing a snap. I haul the duffle downstairs and leave it by the front door. Time for coffee.

Frey dropped a map by early last night. It's spread out on the kitchen table and I study it while waiting for the coffee. I've never been to Monument Valley. Our proposed route is marked with yellow highlighter. We'll start out on Highway 8—not the most scenic route, Frey explained, but the fastest. Counting gas and food stops, we should make it in fourteen or fifteen hours.

Frey is excited about the trip, too. I'm not sure how long it's been since he's seen his kid. He won't tell me, but I have a feeling it's been quite a while. And though he'd never admit it, the timing is perfect. This is just the diversion he needs to take his mind off Layla. For a few days at least.

The pesky sense that I'm to blame for Frey's breakup with Layla rushes back. I'd probably feel worse if I thought she was right for him. It irks me that during that long weekend he and I spent together, the weekend most likely re-

sponsible for Layla's leaving, Frey had been a faithful
monogamous partner.

She doesn't deserve him.

Probably something I should be careful about bringing
up on our road trip.

I refold the map, lay it on top of the duffle by the door
and return to the kitchen to fill a mug. I tick things off a
mental checklist—

David knows I'll be gone for a few days. He's fine with
it. He didn't mention trying to contact Judith Williams or
find the twins. Hopefully, he's so relieved to have passed
the first series of tests, and to be able to resume his sex life,
he's content to let it go for now. I was afraid to ask.

I talked with Stephen. Let him know I was going out of
town, too, for a couple of days. I tell him it's work, since I
don't want to go into details. His voice is full of the excitement of preparing for his first big network shot. I'm smiling when I ring off.

Tracey's sister is doing much better. I caught snippets of
the press conference on last night's news. Tracey was terrific. What witnesses *thought* they saw was explained by
adrenaline and hysteria. The bottom line—no charges.
Case closed.

There have been a couple of telephone calls left by reporters requesting interviews but as other more pressing
stories arise, mine will be quickly forgotten.

Harris hasn't called back again, either.

So far, so good.

Coffee mug drained, coffeepot emptied, counter wiped.
I'm ready to go. It's fifteen minutes to ten. I'm fidgeting
like a kid with a sugar rush. I want to get out of here before the next disaster strikes. Everything that's happened
in the last few days either started with a telephone call

or an uninvited guest. Here. In my home. It's a disturbing trend.

Gathering my stuff, I lock up and head for the street. Better to meet Frey out on Mission.

I realize standing on the curb that I have no idea what kind of vehicle Frey will be driving. I picture a sedan, white or maybe gray, four doors, medium size. Something sedate, befitting a schoolteacher in his forties who is just now taking to the streets on his own.

When the bright red Jeep Wrangler slides up to me, my first impulse is to wave it on. Then I peer inside. Frey is looking back at me. He has sunglasses on his face and a Padres baseball cap on his head. He's dressed in a pair of floral print board shorts and a navy blue tee with the Quiksilver Mountain and Wave logo on the front. He's got leather huaraches on bare feet. He looks very much at home behind the wheel of the Wrangler, and it takes me a second to adjust to this new surfer-dude image.

I toss my bag in the back beside his. "Wow." I slip into the front seat. "When you go native, you don't fool around."

He puts the Jeep in gear and pulls into traffic while I'm still adjusting the seat belt. When it clicks into place, I turn in the seat to look at him. "When did you get a Jeep?"

He works the gears smoothly, maneuvering through busy midmorning traffic as we head for the freeway on-ramp. "A week or so ago."

The top of the Jeep is open; only roll bars separate Frey and me from a glorious summer sky. A breeze ruffles my hair and I push it out of my eyes, wishing I had a cap like Frey's to tame it.

As if privy to my thoughts, he reaches behind his seat and without taking his eyes off the road, pulls out a second Padres cap. "Need this?"

I answer with a grin and coaxing breeze-blown strands behind my ears, I pull the cap down over my forehead.

Then I relax back in the seat. I knew Frey *could* drive, I just didn't know he could drive this well. He's always had a driver. Or that he would enjoy driving so much. He steals a sideways glance at me every once in a while, I think just to see if I notice. I do. I settle in to let him have his fun.

CHAPTER 14

THE HALFWAY POINT ON OUR TRIP WILL BE PHOE-nix. Anyone who has traveled this route will tell you, the drive from San Diego to Phoenix is duller than dull. Butt-numbing stretches with not a Mickey D's in sight. Miles of nondescript desert. Habitual road construction projects that slow traffic to a crawl. Tempers and radiators overheat with enough regularity to keep state troopers and a dozen tow-truck companies in business.

The halfway point on the halfway point is El Centro. There the reclaimed desert is dotted with farms and patches of green. From the road, it appears like an oasis in the distance. Since we know there won't be much after El Centro, we pull off to get Frey some food.

El Centro is one of California's great mysteries. That is to say, the mystery is why anyone chooses to live here. The summer is unbearably hot, the winter can be frigid. Main Street stretches relentlessly east to west across town. There are two border crossings here. For the last ten years or so, El Centro has been poised to become Southern California's most promising new commercial and industrial region.

At least according to the El Centro Chamber of Commerce. It must be getting tired of holding the pose. It hasn't happened yet. Picking lettuce and melons remains the mainstay of the economy.

We pull into a Carl's Jr. and Frey orders a huge quantity of food: three cheeseburgers, a couple of chicken sandwiches, a large fry, an apple turnover and, with a glance to me for confirmation, *two* Cokes. I listen in awe. Frey doesn't have an ounce of fat on his body. I guess his feline alter ego contributes to his metabolism. I've never heard of a fat panther, either.

I watch as he walks to the counter to pick up his order. He looks damn good in those shorts. Nice ass. Lean muscled thighs. He and I were lovers once. Long time ago. Wonder what will happen when he sees his ex? Now that he and Layla are broken up, maybe things will heat up again between him and the mother of his child.

As soon as I catch myself having *those* thoughts, I give myself a mental slap alongside the head. Keep your mind on the purpose of this trip. We're not here on a matchmaking expedition.

Being happy in one's love life tends to make a person wish the same for those around them.

Or is it the guilt I feel because I may have been responsible for Frey's breakup?

Frey and I have hardly exchanged two words since we left Mission Beach. The rush of the wind coupled with road noise in the open Jeep makes simple conversation difficult. It's hardly an uncomfortable silence. After the last couple of days, it's a relief not to be peppered with questions. For

Frey, I imagine thoughts of seeing his son are foremost in his mind.

But now, sitting at a Formica table with a watered-down Coke, being forced to watch Frey devour his burgers and chicken sandwiches, I have to do something to resist the urge to reach across and help myself to a handful of fries. I know the consequences of that. The memory of retching into the kitchen sink the first time I unwittingly ate real food after becoming vampire is vivid.

I take another sip of my Coke and break the silence. "Did you let your son know you were coming?"

Frey looks up, a tiny smear of catsup at the corner of his mouth. I want to lean over and lick it off—instead I use my napkin.

He grins and finishes the job, mopping his mouth with his own napkin. "No. Communication is iffy on the reservation."

"Will they be surprised?"

"Oh yeah. They'll be surprised."

His tone suggests not pleasantly.

It startles me into asking, "Is there a problem?"

He shakes his head, waiting until he's swallowed the last mouthful of sandwich to answer. "Not for me. My son's mother may not so be thrilled to see me."

There's definitely a story there. "Want to tell me why?"

"No."

"Did you and she have a bad breakup?"

"You sound like a reporter. Are you channeling your new boyfriend now?"

"Wait. How do you know—?"

"That you have a new boyfriend? Well, why else would you have disappeared from the radar for the last eight weeks?"

Whoa. There's a bitter ring to that last question. Softly, I say, "I didn't know about you and Layla breaking up."

"Maybe because you didn't call or drop by to see how I was doing. Not until you needed something."

He's right, of course. "I'm sorry."

A scowl darkens his face. He chomps into another sandwich, chews, swallows. Looks over at me again. "Let's talk about what you're going to do when you find this shaman."

A little of the edge has left his voice. I take that as a good sign and ask, "Do you think he exists?"

"I know he exists."

"You've heard of him?"

"Not before yesterday. But I did some research last night."

Excitement bubbles up. "What did you learn?"

He holds up a hand. "Don't get ahead of yourself. It wasn't much. Just that he is rumored to have the ability to bring the dead back to life. For obvious reasons, his existence is protected by the Navajo. It will be up to the tribal council to determine if you will be allowed to meet with him. This may be tricky, Anna. You may not get permission. And if you do, he may not be willing to speak with a vampire. I don't want you to be disappointed."

I twirl the straw in my Coke. I wish I'd known this before we started out. I'm sure Chael knew. But he wouldn't send me out here unless he thought there was a chance. Or is this another trick?

On the other hand, what's the worst that can happen? I can be pretty persuasive when I want to be.

Frey's sarcastic laugh pulls me back. "You should see your face. The expression tells me your thoughts are spinning like the hard drive on a computer. Sorting information. Weighing consequences. Wondering how far you'd have to go if you're turned down."

I squint up at him. "You think I'd resort to violence?"

"Did I say violence? I know how you operate. If you want something, you get it. What I don't know is what you want. You haven't talked about it."

I slurp up the rest of my Coke, stalling.

"You haven't made a decision yet, have you?" He pauses a heartbeat, frowning. "Whatever you decide, remember. Using magic exacts a price. And a thing like this takes magic—powerful magic. The bigger the magic, the bigger the price."

He says it as though I'm not aware that there's danger in challenging the natural way. I know it only too well. I still carry the mental image of Frey broken and near death, fighting to save Culebra from a witch's spell.

And yet, how natural was it that I became a vampire? How natural that I had to send my family off to protect them? That I have to distance myself from my friends?

No, the only natural thing is that I'd want to erase the last year of my life. I owe it to myself to find out if such a thing is possible.

CHAPTER 15

W E'RE BACK ON THE ROAD, BOTH OF US, I THINK,
happy not to talk. I don't know what Frey is thinking, but the things he said at the restaurant linger in my
mind. He's right. Since the ceremony acknowledging my
position as the Chosen, I haven't talked to him except to let
him know that I survived.

Why was that? Certainly not because I was ungrateful
for his help. I remember how close we came to making love
that weekend. I exercised restraint because of Layla. Because I didn't want him regretting the time he spent with
me or becoming resentful if it interfered with their relationship.

That's rich. They broke up anyway.

Something I'd have known if I'd bothered to call him.

Lifting a hand, I shield my eyes against the glare of the
midday sun, enjoying the warmth that penetrates my skin,
remembering the warmth that mortals feel from the inside out.

If I find a way to make things right for Frey, I will.

But first. Frey was right about something else, too. I don't know what I want from this shaman. If he's powerful enough to solve the riddle of life and death, maybe he can solve my riddle, too. How I was chosen and why. What it would mean if I relinquished the title.

How I can get Chael out of the picture.

Because before I could make any decision, I'd have to know the mortal world would be safe. No matter how much I want to become human again, I wouldn't put my desire ahead of the well-being of billions.

Another hour of desert boredom and we cross the Arizona border at Yuma. Right outside Casa Grande we leave Highway 8 and pick up I-17. Then it's on to and past Phoenix and finally, the monotonous scenery becomes interesting again. We're headed north, approaching the Verde Valley area, and for the first time, we're seeing more than brown dirt and scrub. Red rocks light a fiery landscape punctuated with the green of real trees. Alder, ash, cypress and a half dozen others I don't recognize. Bushes in hues that range from the lightest feathery green to brilliant emerald to cloud gray. Ocotillo and yucca raise thorny fingers to the sky. I'm mesmerized by the wonder of it all, my absorption broken only when a movement catches the corner of my eye.

Frey looks at his watch. "We're not going to make it before dark. Do you want to stop for the night in Flagstaff?"

I hadn't noticed how much time had passed. The sun is low on the horizon. The dark doesn't bother me so I volunteer to take over behind the wheel.

Frey looks at me as if I'd just suggested he become a vegetarian. "Do you know how to drive a stick?"

"How hard can it be? I've been watching you."

I can see by his horrified expression he's imagining scenarios where I strip his new baby's gears.

"I'm kidding. Of course I can drive a stick."

He isn't convinced so I add, "Look. I drive a ninety-thousand-dollar car. What'd you pay for this?"

Still no relaxing of the worry lines around his mouth. "How long until we reach the reservation?"

"Four hours."

"So let me take over for a while. You take a nap."

Frey pulls off the road so I think I've convinced him. Instead, he adjusts his seat back and stretches his legs. "We should both take a nap," he says. "Thirty minutes or so and we'll hit the road again."

I give him the evil eye. Jesus. What a baby. I adjust my seat, too, and stare into a cloudless, cerulean sky. Then it hits me, "Frey, are you stalling?"

His eyes are closed. He huffs out a breath. "That's a ridiculous assumption."

"Is it? You sounded like your ex will not be happy to see you. Could it be that you're a little skittish about seeing her, too?"

I'm teasing, but there's nothing amusing in the way he snaps back at me. "The roads we're going to travel once we get to the valley are not well marked or lit. And there's no moon tonight. It won't be easy navigating in the dark."

"You're joking, right? You have the vision of a cat. And I'm a vampire. My eyes are better than night-vision goggles."

He turns at that. "Jesus, Anna. Do you always have to argue? Thirty minutes. Is that too much to ask? Just close your eyes and shut up, will you?"

Wow. He *really* doesn't want me to drive his Jeep.

"Okay, okay. It's what you get for carb loading at that Carl's Jr. but I'm not sleepy. I'll just lay here and watch you sleep off that ten-thousand-calorie meal. It won't bother you, will it, if I stare at you while you nap?"

He doesn't answer. He's already asleep.

I humph an irritated breath. Stare around. Close my eyes.

Just for a minute.

CHAPTER 16

THE DREAMS COME IN DARK FLASHES. THE CHAOS of the last three days. Killing. The gunman in the store. The vampire in the desert. Always the blood is what stands out most vividly. Starkly, like a retouched photo where the background is shades of gray, but not the blood. It's crimson, fragrant, sweet—sexual in its allure. My body responds to the images and the first stirrings of arousal send heat rushing to warm my skin. I lose myself in the sensation, let the excitement build, yearn for release.

A hand on my shoulder. A voice.

I'm pulled from exquisite pleasure. Pulled unwillingly back into reality at the moment before climax. I react with frustration and anger, batting the hand away. "What the—?"

We're on the road. Frey glances over. "Jesus, Anna. You're moaning. Were you having a nightmare?"

Shit. I scrub a hand over my face, partly to recover

from the effects of the dream, partly to hide the embarrassment.

I struggle upright in the seat. I'm still groggy and disoriented. "How long have I been out?"

"Maybe three hours." He shoots me a look. "You weren't sleepy, huh?"

Three *hours*. It couldn't be.

He's still talking. "But you've been moaning and thrashing around on that seat for the last fifteen minutes. I was afraid you'd hang yourself in the seat belt. What were you dreaming about?"

If I told him the truth, that I was just about to have an orgasm and he interrupted not a nightmare, but a really, really good dream, I'm not sure who would be more mortified. Frey for mistaking moans of passion for groans of terror or me for admitting it. I decide to save Frey the humiliation.

"I can't remember what I was dreaming. You know how it is."

Frey doesn't take his eyes off the road. "Must have been awful."

There's an undertone of sarcasm that makes me swivel in the seat to search his face. Is he screwing with me? Is the only misinterpretation going on here mine? But it's dark in the Jeep and in profile, only a hint of a smile plays at the corner of his mouth. He's not giving anything away and I'm certainly not going to pursue the subject.

I turn my attention back to the road. The Jeep is bumping along and I realize we've left the paved highway. I remember Frey mentioning unpaved and unlit roads. He wasn't kidding.

There's no moon, either. But when I look up, the sky

seems closer than I've ever seen it, the stars so bright, I have to fight the impulse to reach up a hand and pluck one down. As I watch, one of them separates from the rest and tracks slowly across the sky, blinking at me as it goes.

My breath catches. "What is that? An airplane?"

Frey follows my pointing finger. "No, too high. It's a satellite. You don't see many of those in the city, do you?"

I watch until it disappears out of sight. "I've never seen *anything* like that."

Frey shoots me a sideways glance. "You have, you know. The night we went after Belinda Burke and stopped the demon raising. You don't remember?"

The memory floods back. Frey and I racing across the desert. Panther and vampire. The sky as brilliant and close as it is now. I nod. I remember.

Frey pulls the Jeep to a stop. "Put your seat back. Let's watch the show."

We both recline the seats once more, mesmerized by a sky that moves and shimmers as if it were alive. Within minutes, we see two shooting stars, one right after the other, meteors trailing bits of rock and dust that disintegrate into fiery balls when they hit the earth's atmosphere. The Milky Way, a soft blur of hazy white light, divides the sky. Constellations form patterns that I can actually distinguish. I feel like a kid, lost in awe and trembling with delight. It's so beautiful.

"Is it like this out here every night?"

I'm whispering. Somehow to speak out loud might break the spell.

Frey whispers, too. "Is it any wonder the Navajo consider this a sacred place?"

My heart pounds in my chest. Why have I never been here before? How could I not know of such wonders?

Frey turns toward me in the seat. "Wait until sunrise. This valley is one of the most breathtaking on earth."

I glance at the clock on the dashboard. It's almost four—and to the east, a faint line of pink blossoms on the horizon. Not an unbroken horizon. Jagged rock formations rise from the desert floor like the ghostly abodes of long dead gods. One rises straight and narrow to the sky. It towers over the rest like some giant navigational pylon aimed at the stars.

Frey follows my gaze. "That's called the Totem Pole. It's four hundred fifty feet high but only a few meters wide. It's one of the most photographed spots in the valley."

I glance over. "You know a lot about this place. How often do you come?"

"Not often." His tone is regretful. "I should come more."

"Why don't you? You obviously love it."

"It isn't a good idea for me to spend a lot of time in the valley."

He's answering my questions, but he may as well not be. The closeness we'd been experiencing shatters into a million hard, brittle pieces. "For god's sake, Frey, spill it. What keeps you away?"

When the silence lingers on too long, my temper flares. I reach over and punch him in the arm.

He yelps and grabs at his bicep. "What was that for?"

"For being a jerk. You know every fucking thing about me. Every bad thing that's happened, every man I've ever slept with, every body I've buried. And you won't share with me one single detail of your personal life? After all we've been through together? You're really beginning to piss me off."

Frey grips the steering wheel. "Why would you be interested now?"

His voice is rough, whether with suppressed anger or guilt I can't tell. It hardly matters. My own suppressed anger boils to the surface. I slam my seat back into its upright position. Jerk around to look down at him.

"I've had a bitch of a week. In the last three days I had Max, David and Harris in my face. Then Chael showed up. I'd like to think you have some appreciation for that since I came to you out of concern for your son.

"I'm sorry about Layla. I'm sorry I didn't call to check in with you sooner. I'm sorry if my life keeps screwing up yours. If I could change any of it, I would. Maybe that's what this trip is about. Maybe if things work out, I will be out of your life forever and you can go back to Layla. She won't have me to blame anymore for your problems and you can go back to your safe, stupid, boring existence."

When the tirade passes, I swivel away from him on the seat and wait for Frey to unload on me. He should. He has every right to. My body tenses, every muscle steeling itself to receive the verbal blow I deserve.

Nothing happens.

I steal a sideways glance. Frey is staring straight ahead, his knuckles still stiff on the steering wheel, his face pale.

Another moment passes. Then, slowly, he brings his seat to an upright position. He looks over at me. At first, his mouth is drawn in a tight line, his brow furrowed into deep, angry grooves. As I watch, though, his expression shifts. Like ice cream melting, the lines smooth, the mouth turns up instead of down. His shoulders start to shake.

Frey begins to laugh.

A laugh so hard it doubles him over.

A laugh so hard, tears run down his cheek.

A laugh so hard it casts a net that catches me up and

before I realize it, I'm laughing like an idiot right along with him. I can't say why. I don't really care why. Letting go is such a fucking relief.

Our laughter echoes across the still night air and bounces off the rock citadels around us. We're howling like moon-crazed wolves, lifting our faces to the sky. For the first time in weeks, I feel something loosening deep within me. A knot finally cut. A fist suddenly open.

I feel hopeful.

I recover my wits first. Wipe tears from my face. Slump on the seat, blinking in disbelief. "What just happened?"

Frey draws in a deep breath, lets it out slowly, shaking his head. "I don't have a fucking clue."

"Why did you start laughing?"

His face in profile, I see an eyebrow arch. "Well, my first impulse was to smack you. Then I started to think what would happen if I did. I got this image of the two of us wrestling in the dirt like something from *Monday Night Raw*. But you'd kick my butt and I'd be humiliated, and knowing you, I'd never hear the end of it."

"And *that* made you laugh?"

"I didn't say it made sense."

"I guess I should say thanks for not smacking me."

"And I should say thanks for not kicking my butt."

It's grown quiet all around us, the echoes of our manic laughter finally fading away. Frey and I retreat into our thoughts. I've spent more of the past year, my first as a vampire, in the company of this man. Yet I know so little about him.

I lower my head and look at him out of the corner of my eye so he won't catch me studying him. His eyes are still on the stars, his expression relaxed and unperturbed. He's a good guy. I wish he'd let me in even if I don't deserve it.

I make a vow to myself. I'll keep my friends closer from now on. Not just Frey, but Culebra, too.

I'll be the kind of good friend they've been to me—not just a friend when I need one, but a friend for all days.

And I make that vow to the bright glow of the morning star.

CHAPTER 17

FREY PUTS THE JEEP IN GEAR AND WE'RE BACK ON the road just as the sun makes its first appearance over the desert. Shafts of light flood the valley, painting inky silhouettes with shades of red. So far, I haven't seen any sign of human habitation. Or much of any habitation at all. A few ground squirrels and rodents. A hawk circling against an ever-brightening sky. Low-to-the-ground scrub brush and spindly yucca. A desolate but remarkable landscape.

After traveling for another thirty minutes, I ask Frey, "Where the hell does your son live?"

"Patience. We're almost there. The area we're traveling through is called Wildcat Trail. Not many people venture back here because this is private land. There are hogans and houses all around us, just so far off the trail, you won't see them unless you know where to look."

"Hogans?"

"Some Navajo still live as their ancestors did—in small, mud dwellings. They're called hogans."

A concept hard for me to grasp. I think of my own cottage. Could I give it up to live in a mud house? Even in this beautiful place? Could Frey? I think not. "Does your son live in a hogan?"

Frey laughs. "No. His mother is much too modern. She likes her creature comforts. She lived in Boston for a while. It's where we met."

His words trigger a memory. Frey lived in Boston before moving to San Diego. He was tracking a pedophile—the same one who abused my niece, Trish. It was how he and I met. How we learned to trust each other. Seems like a lifetime ago.

"You thinking about Trish?"

I blink over at him. "Can you read my mind again?"

"Not your mind. Your expression. You get a certain look when you're thinking of your family."

"Hmmmm." I refocus. "What was your ex doing in Boston?"

"She was spending the summer with a mutual friend. She went to Massachusetts to study at Amherst. Native American Studies. She's full-blood Navajo."

"Why did she move back to the reservation?"

Frey shifts in the seat, as if suddenly uncomfortable. His reaction prompts me to ask, "Did she leave because she got pregnant?"

He doesn't answer. He doesn't have to. The answer shows on his face. Guilt. Regret. Longing.

"Why didn't you go after her?" I ask softly.

"I did. She sent me away. Only after our son was born did she let me back into her life. And then only for visits.

Brief visits. I was an outsider in her world. She made it plain that I was unwelcome."

I want to keep Frey talking. This is the most information I've ever gotten from him about his past. But we're turning off the dirt road and heading for an outcropping of rocks in the distance. I don't know how Frey knew where to turn. There's not even a rutted trail to follow. He scans the terrain, searching for landmarks indistinguishable to me, but obviously as clear as street signs to him. He drives straight onward through hardscrabble dirt. I grab the sissy bar to keep from being bounced out of the Jeep. Clouds of dust billow in our wake like ragged coattails.

I don't disturb his concentration. For two reasons. I don't want to distract his driving and end up upside down in a heap. And secondly, I'm lost in my own head, filled with speculation about this woman who bore Frey's child. This woman . . . I can't believe I haven't thought to ask her name. No. If I'm honest, I know exactly why I haven't asked her name. A name takes her out of the realm of conjecture and makes her real.

The Jeep hits a deep rut, and I'm jerked back out of the fuzzy world of conjecture. Frey is pointing to the left. I follow his direction, and there in the distance, a trail of smoke like a white ribbon rises to the sky. It issues from what looks like a small, round dome. I feel an inexplicable thrill of anticipation.

"A hogan?"

He nods.

"It's so small."

"It doesn't need to be big. It's used mainly for shelter when the weather's bad and certain ceremonies. The Navajo spend most of their time outdoors."

"Where are the others?"

"Others?"

"Don't the Navajo live in villages?"

He shakes his head. "No villages. No towns."

"A lonely existence."

"Not if you're used to it. The Navajo have a special connection to the land."

He turns his attention back to driving and I turn mine back to the scenery. It's as if we are the only two people on earth and for the first time in my life, I *feel* the force of nature. The wind, the sky, the sun on my face. The contrast of red sand and tall rock formations bathed in the newly minted gold of daybreak swamps my senses, and yet, I fight to take it all in. A thousand years—ten thousand—years ago, this land was as I see it now. A taste of eternity. Of timelessness.

Of eternal life.

A tug of melancholy. This may be where I belong.

Here. With other ageless things.

Strands of early morning mist rise from the desert floor and twine around and through stone arches on their way to the clouds.

I follow with my eyes, watch as wisps break free, travel straight and sure to the heavens.

I wish my way were that clear.

A sound reaches us—haunting, melodic, rising and falling like feathers on the wind.

"Do you hear that, Frey?"

He just smiles and steers in the direction of the music.

The Jeep traverses around a series of low, flat outcroppings and there, ahead of us, a house rises as if born of the earth. A small, single story house made from logs the same color as the dirt and rocks with a roof of caramel-colored tile. A porch spans the front, facing due east, and on the porch steps sits a girl, a flute at her lips. The melody from the flute and the golden rays of a rising sun reflect off her like a halo, giving the scene a surreal quality.

Frey stops a few yards away and turns off the engine. The dust cloud that had been following us gusts away as if fanned by an invisible hand.

Frey makes no move to get out or greet the girl, neither does she acknowledge our presence. She continues to play, the sweet song poetic in its simplicity.

Her skin glows in the sun. Her black hair hangs shiny and straight over her shoulders, framing brows drawn in concentration. Her full-lipped mouth is pursed over the flute, an expression of pure joy on her face. It's impossible to tell her age, she has a face that seems at once youthful and mature. But my impression is that she's young.

I sneak a look over at Frey. How old was she when she got pregnant, you dog?

She is dressed in a long-sleeved full cotton shirt, a velvet skirt that covers her ankles, a pair of leather moccasins on her feet. She wears no jewelry but a belt that looks as if it is made of carved black onyx, small rectangles linked together by silver, cinches her waist.

The setting, the way she's dressed, the ethereal quality of the music, all seem to belong to another time. If it was a hogan instead of a house, I'd imagine her a Navajo princess paying tribute to the sun god with her playing. The idea makes gooseflesh race up my arms.

When she finishes the song, when she lowers the flute, only then does Frey open his door and jump out.

The girl flashes a huge grin, whoops, and runs to meet him. She wraps her arms around his neck and her legs around his waist. She peppers his face with kisses. She's laughing and talking all at the same time, her bunched-up skirt showing a lot of leg.

I turn away in embarrassment. So much for the image of the stoic Native American. And so much for Frey's apprehension that she would not be happy to see him. If she were any happier, I'd have to cover my eyes.

Frey is laughing, too, though turning his face this way and that, as if trying to avoid those persistent lips. He is also making an attempt to set her back on her feet. An attempt she resists by tightening her arms around his neck and her legs around his waist.

The banging of a screen door behind us makes me jump. I turn to see another woman standing on the porch steps.

"Mary Yellow Bird! What the hell do you think you're doing?"

Her sharp voice brings the joyful reunion to an abrupt end. The girl sighs and releases her hold on Frey, jumping down and turning with a sweep of her long skirt.

"Don't get your panties in a bunch. I was just saying hello."

"I could see what you were saying," the newcomer snaps. "Get inside. Give John-John his breakfast."

The girl stomps by with a scowl and disappears into the house. Frey and the woman on the steps stare at each other. She has the same coloring as the other, the same sculpted facial lines, is a few inches taller, a few pounds heavier, several years older. Her hair is drawn back in a bun, a tricky configuration adorned with ribbons and beads. She is dressed in jeans and a Western shirt, a bandanna tied around her neck.

She crosses her arms over her chest and taps one booted foot. Rings of turquoise and silver adorn two fingers of both hands, flashing as they catch the sunlight. She is wearing earrings of turquoise, too, long strands that almost touch the collar of her shirt.

Her expression is in startling contrast to the exuberant greeting of the other.

This woman is not so happy to see Frey.

This must be Frey's ex.

CHAPTER 18

T HE STANDOFF GOES ON. IT'S OBVIOUS NEITHER
Frey nor the woman is willing to be the first to break
the silence. I feel like an intruder. An invisible one, maybe,
since she hasn't paid me the slightest bit of attention, but an
intruder nonetheless.

Should I say something? I find myself shifting impatiently
from one foot to the other. I try to distract myself by perusing
the surroundings. The yard around the house is bare dirt, the
only greenery a couple of scraggly desert junipers on each
side of the porch. There's a carport on the south side, a tarp
strung between four poles sheltering a battered GMC truck. I
can see one pole of a clothesline in the back of the house and
hear sheets flapping in the breeze. Still farther back, a corral
with an open, rough-hewn wooden shed. Three horses nibble
at something in a long feeder that spans the back of the
lean-to. I also hear the hum of a generator. Since I see no
overhead electrical wires, I assume that's how they get their
power. Frey did say his ex liked her creature comforts.

But how much comfort can a generator provide? It's just after daybreak and the temperature is rising faster than the sun.

Which is another reason to break this stupid stalemate. I take a step toward the woman.

"*Yá'át'ééh.*"

She blinks and looks at me as if I'd just sprung fully formed from the earth.

"*Yá'át'ééh,*" I repeat. It's the only Native American greeting I know. I heard it in the movie *Midnight Run.* The way she's eyeing me makes me think maybe it doesn't mean hello. Maybe it really means fuck you and the horse you rode in on. Martin Brest's idea of a joke.

Finally the lock on that tight jaw breaks, and she relaxes enough to smile. She comes down the porch steps, extending her hand.

"I'm sorry. I don't mean to be rude. I'm Sarah. We don't get many visitors out here." She shoots Frey a pointed look. "Especially unannounced."

Her hand is warm and rough. When she feels how cold mine is, she tries to hide her reaction, but I see it. She draws back just an inch, her breath catches. She wants to pull her hand free but composes herself not to. I let go first. Step away to increase her comfort zone.

I look over at Frey. I wish we still had the psychic connection because I could swear with that one moment of contact, Sarah recognized me for what I am.

Her next words confirm my suspicion.

She rounds on Frey. "You bring a vampire here? To your son's home? Are you crazy?"

Frey's face pales. "Anna is a friend. She means no harm."

"Vampires always mean harm. It is their nature. They are predators like the wolf or the snake or—"

"The panther?"

The freeze descends once again. Was this what caused the breakup? Sarah found out what Frey was? I always thought Native Americans accepted that there were humans whose spirit transcended the normal. Maybe accepting and being bound to one of those spirits, though, are two entirely different things.

She must have found out the truth about Frey being a shape-shifter after becoming pregnant.

I'm glad I wasn't around for *that* conversation.

"Daddy!"

The screen door bangs once again and a small child flies down the steps like a miniature whirlwind and into Frey's arms. Frey scoops him up and dances around in a circle. They speak in Navajo, their pleasure at seeing each other so genuine, so unaffected, I almost join them just to be a part of it. If I didn't feel Sarah's eyes boring into my back, I might have. But her glare is as obvious a warning to Frey as it is to me. She doesn't want me anywhere near her son. Mama bear has her claws out.

Frey either doesn't notice or doesn't care. He stops dancing long enough to bring the boy over to me. "John-John," he says in English, "this is my friend, Anna."

I still feel the heat of Sarah's angry glower, but I smile anyway. "Very nice to meet you."

He sticks out a chubby hand. "Nice to meet you, too." His English is perfect. His round, cherub face aglow. He has his mother's coloring, but he has Frey's eyes and mouth.

I touch his fingers and give a nod. Before I can say anything else, Sarah has swooped down on us. She takes the boy from Frey and calls out to Mary. When Mary joins us, Sarah barks something in Navajo and puts the boy in her arms.

Mary responds, her tone and expression tells me she is arguing with Sarah, but she's quickly cut off.

"Take him inside." Sarah speaks in English this time. "Don't argue."

Frey's face betrays his disappointment. He waits until Mary is back inside before bracing Sarah. "You have no right to keep my son from me."

"And you have no right to show up and demand an audience. We agreed. I would bring John-John to you when the time was right."

"We agreed?" Frey snaps back. "No. *You* agreed. If you think I'm going to wait until he's nine or ten to forge a relationship with my own son, you're crazy. He'll have forgotten me by then or, worse, think I've abandoned him. Reservation kids have enough trouble without adding insecurity to the mix."

Angry color floods Sarah's face. "Don't you dare criticize our life here. Our son is far better off with people who love and can protect him than he would be with you, exposed to things like that."

She finishes by jabbing a thumb in my direction.

A *thing*? Until now, I've listened to their vitriolic exchange as an interested and intrigued voyeur. Even found it mildly humorous, being of a somewhat twisted nature. But now she's dragging me into the fight. My backbone stiffens. I open my mouth to spew an angry rebuttal, but Frey cuts me off.

"You don't know Anna. And you don't know me. You ran away before giving me a chance to prove that I could take care of you—both. If I had to pick now between you and Anna to protect our son, Anna would win. No contest."

He takes a step toward her, and I half expect him to

thrust an angry finger into her chest to emphasize each word as he continues. Instead, he balls his hands into fists and presses them into his side, his voice shaking with rage. "She has the best heart of anyone I know. She's risked her life more than once to save mine. She's fighting even now to save your ass and you don't even know it. So, yeah, I'd pick Anna over you any day. I just wish John-John was her son instead of yours."

My stomach gives a jolt. I don't know who is more shocked by Frey's outburst, Frey, Sarah or I. Of course, the reason for being shocked is different for each of us. Sarah looks as if she's been sucker punched. Frey looks as if he can't believe what he just said. I'm so flabbergasted, my mouth falls open with an astonished gasp. The three of us stand still as statues each waiting for the other to speak first. I won't be of any help. Frey's last words twirl around in my head like sticky threads of cotton candy, completely confounding rational thought.

It's Mary who breaks the stalemate.

She's standing on the porch, glaring down at Sarah and Frey, her eyes blazing with fury. "Are you two crazy? Don't you realize John-John can hear you? He's in his room crying his eyes out because his mommy and daddy are fighting over him. What's the matter with you?"

Sarah releases a breath, her shoulders slump. Her face reflects regret and bitterness. "I'll go to him in a minute, Mary."

"You should *both* go to him. Now."

Sarah looks up at Frey, gives a small nod of capitulation. The two of them move into the house, each careful to keep their distance as if any physical contact might precipitate another verbal explosion.

Mary comes down the steps to join me. "Can you be-lieve those two?"

I shake my head. I'm still a little thunderstruck by what transpired.

Mary motions toward the porch. "Let's get out of the sun."

I follow her up the steps and we plop our butts down on a couple of old canvas chairs set back in the shadows.

"Want anything to drink?"

I finally find my voice. "No. Thanks."

She eyes me under a fringe of bangs. "So what are you to Frey?"

"What are *you* to Sarah?"

"Sister."

"Friend."

"Well, at least one of us is telling the truth."

I sit up a little straighter. "I'm telling the truth, too. Frey and I are friends."

"A friend that he wishes was the mother of his child."

So she heard that. "He didn't mean it." Did he? Of course he didn't. I'm vampire.

"Well, he said it." Mary fixes me with a penetrating stare. "Are you really a vampire?"

She heard that, too. "Yes."

"Cool."

My turn to stare. "You're not repulsed like Sarah?"

"Shit, no. Sarah is being overprotective."

"Seems more like paranoid."

Mary shrugs. "She has her reasons. But if Frey trusts you, I do, too."

I look around. The area is beautiful, true, but it's lonely. Too lonely for the average—

"How old are you?" I ask.

"Nineteen."

"And you live here?"

It comes out far more disparagingly than I mean it to. I backtrack quickly. "It's just you are so young and—"

Mary laughs and brushes the air with a hand. "It's okay. No. I don't live here year round. I attend college in Phoenix. I'm here for the summer. Helping Sarah with John-John and as she likes to put it, reconnecting with my roots. I won't stay here after I graduate, though. The atmosphere on the rez is too claustrophobic."

"But it isn't for Sarah?"

"Not since she had John-John. It's like she feels safe here."

"Safe? From what?"

For the first time, Mary's expression becomes guarded. Her shoulders draw up a little, her posture stiffens. "You should ask her."

I don't want to risk Mary shutting down. I scour my brain for something to get us back on the friendly track we were before. A whiff of horse drifts up from the corral. "I noticed you have horses. You ride a lot?"

Mary's shoulders relax. "Yes. It's one of the reasons I don't mind spending summers here. Do you ride?"

"Me?" I laugh. "No. Never been on a horse."

"Well, we'll have to remedy that. I'll take you out this afternoon if you'd like."

We'll have to see what the horse says about that. The last time I was close to a horse, it shied away from me with a baring of teeth and flattening of ears. I think it sensed the beast. But I don't want to call attention to that side of my nature, so I pause to compose a noncommittal reply. Before I come up with anything, the door opens behind us.

Sarah is back.

CHAPTER 19

SARAH DOESN'T LOOK PARTICULARLY HAPPY TO SEE me sitting on her porch, even less happy to see me chatting up her little sister like we're a couple of school chums. But surprisingly, she doesn't lash out. She has car keys in her hand. When she speaks it's with a decidedly resigned air.

"Mary, you and I are going up to the lodge."

Mary raises her eyebrows. "John-John?"

"He's staying." She has pointedly refrained from looking at me. Now she does. "Frey says I can trust you. He'd better be right."

She doesn't wait for me to spout reassurances. She tromps down the porch steps and heads for the truck. Mary gives me a thumbs-up and follows.

Sarah pulls away, her grim face pointed straight ahead, both hands gripping the wheel. I half expect the truck to come roaring back and Sarah to wave a wreath of garlic and a stake at me so I wait until even the dust from their abrupt departure has dissipated before figuring it's safe to go inside.

The house is cool and dark. The front door opens to a living area painted stark white. The walls are hung with blankets of intricate design woven in primary colors—red, blue, green, yellow. The furniture is leather, big, built more for comfort than style, kid scuffed. A couch and two over-stuffed side chairs cluster around a rectangular table that looks homemade. It's wood, juniper maybe, and polished to a high sheen. Coloring books and crayons and children's games and books are scattered over its surface. In the corner, a loom with a half-finished blanket. The pattern is diamond shaped, strands of yarn trailing to the floor.

In my mind's eye I picture Sarah weaving while John-John colors close by.

It's an image that invokes a strange heaviness in my chest.

A lovely image.

A hint of sandalwood mingles with the aroma of freshly baked bread and the earthy smells of juniper and desert sage.

This is a house that is well loved—again I feel a pang—and it's a house filled with people who love each other. Frey may be the kid's father, but we are intruders.

Maybe I shouldn't have brought Frey. I could have come alone. Made sure his son was safe and found the shaman on my own. Chael knew the location.

Why do I always drag Frey into things that threaten his well-being? I accuse Chael of not doing his homework—I should have done mine. Forced Frey to tell me the story of his son's birth back when I first learned he had a son. But I was too consumed in my own drama, and now look . . .

Should have, could have, would have.

Makes no difference. The damage is done.

From down a short hall, I hear Frey's quiet voice. He's talking to John-John. I don't know whether to join them or not. Guilt at being the cause of the kid's sadness makes me want to flee.

Until I hear the giggle.

John-John's giggle.

I tiptoe toward the sound. There are four doors, two on each side of the hall. The first on the left and right are bedrooms, probably Sarah's and Mary's judging from the vanities and flowered wallpapers. The third door leads to a bathroom. The last is John-John's.

Frey is sitting on the edge of the bed, John-John on his lap. They are looking through a picture book. John-John points to a page and Frey recites in English followed by John-John in Navajo. When Frey attempts the Navajo translation, it sends John-John into squeals of laughter.

At that moment I know. It was selfishness on my part to want Frey with me on this journey, but it was selfishness on Sarah's part to keep him from his son. I'm glad we're here.

John-John looks up and sees me standing in the doorway. I start to duck away, but Frey calls me back.

"Come on in, Anna. John-John is helping me with my Navajo."

"Are you sure I'm not intruding?"

John-John wiggles off Frey's lap and comes to the door to grab my hand. "Would you like to learn Navajo?" he asks. "I could teach you."

At first, I'm unsure whether to let him touch me. But John-John already has my hand in his little fist. He seems not to notice that my hand has no warmth. At least there's no violent physical reaction the way there was with Sarah. I let him lead me to the bed and hoist him back on Frey's lap, settling myself next to them. "No, no. I'll just listen to you and your daddy. Will that be all right?"

He nods and picks up the book and the two of them take up where they left off, John-John's head bent over the pages and Frey's arms tight around his son.

It's been a long time since I've been around a four-year-old. I'd forgotten how much warmth their little bodies exude or how they smell of clean earth and talcum powder. I snuggle closer just to share in some of that warmth and breathe more deeply of his scent.

Frey and John-John go back to their lesson. I look around John-John's room—very much a boy's room with racing cars and Legos and curtains patterned with galloping horses. A bookcase has three shelves of books and one of pictures. I see only one of Frey. John-John was still a babe in arms when it was taken. I recognize where it was taken, here on the front porch. Did Sarah leave Boston when she found out she was pregnant or right after the baby was born? Did Frey know she was returning to the reservation? Or did she leave without a word, forcing him to track them on his own?

What happened to make her take John-John away from Frey? He's one of the most honorable men I know. And one of the most loving. I can't think of any justification for Sarah's actions. Not when it's so obvious that Frey loves his son.

A child needs both his parents.

I listen to Frey and his son talk and laugh, feeling very much the outsider. This is a relationship that I'll never have—the relationship of parent and child. It's a relationship I never thought I wanted—even before becoming vampire. So why do I feel this sudden emptiness? What has changed?

John-John's sweet laugh makes the answer clear.

Everything.

I hear Chael in my head, echoing my thoughts. All I have to do is choose to become human again and the possibility of having what Frey and his son have becomes real.

I misjudged Chael.

He dangled the right carrot. He'd done his homework after all, the tricky bastard.

CHAPTER 20

AFTER TEN MINUTES OR SO, JOHN-JOHN YAWNS and rubs his eyes. Frey takes the book from his hand and lays him down on the bed.

John-John looks up at him with eyes suddenly wide with worry. "You'll be here when I wake up, won't you, *Azhé'é*?"

Frey brushes a fringe of raven hair back from John-John's forehead. "I will, *Shiye*."

John-John curls up and Frey pulls a blanket from the foot of the bed and snugs it around his little body. Within seconds, the kid is asleep.

I wish it was that easy for adults.

We tiptoe out and Frey closes the door behind us. I follow him through the living room to the kitchen. It looks like something from the fifties—turquoise refrigerator and stove, Formica table with a patterned top that looks like cracked ice, four upholstered leatherette chairs with chrome legs. The countertops are empty and spotless. The white lace curtains in the window are starched and ironed. Even the linoleum on the floor sparkles.

"Wow. Sarah is some housekeeper."

Anal, is what I'm thinking. But Frey's place is the same way, so I play nice.

He's crossed to the refrigerator, opens it and withdraws a couple of bottles of water. He motions with the bottles to the table and I take a seat.

After we've both washed the dust out of our throats, I say, "He's really cute."

Frey smiles and nods.

"And smart, too."

"Whew. Much smarter than I was at that age. Speaks and reads Navajo and English. At four."

"Who teaches him?"

"Sarah, mostly. But when Mary isn't here, he goes to a preschool on the rez while Sarah is at work."

"Where does she work?"

"At Goulding's Lodge. She's a tour guide."

That must be the lodge she spoke of when she took off with Mary. "How long do you think she'll be gone?"

"She has a half-day tour lined up so it'll be a while."

"How did you ever convince her to leave John-John with us?"

"Wasn't easy." Frey shakes his head. "I had to promise not to leave you alone with him. And to tell her why you've come—to seek out the shaman who can restore human life."

"Does she know about him?"

"All Navajo know *of* him. But she's never seen him and she has no knowledge of anyone here ever seeking him out. She thinks he's so reclusive, being granted an audience is next to impossible. If he isn't dead."

"Dead? Great." Still, why would Chael send me here if the shaman was dead?

I look up to find Frey studying me. "What do we do next? How do we arrange to meet the tribal elders?"

"Sarah will make the contact for us."

"Sarah? Why would she do that?"

Frey snorts. "Easy. The quicker we meet with the elders, the quicker we get the hell out of here."

There's a lull while Frey and I retreat into our own thoughts. There's so much I want to know about Frey and Sarah and that cute little guy asleep in the bedroom. I'm not sure how to broach the subject, so I just ask bluntly, "Why did Sarah run away?"

Frey looks at me with weary eyes, as if he's been expecting the question. He pushes away from the table. "Let's go outside. If John-John wakes up, I don't want him to overhear. He's had enough of that today."

We go to the front porch, Frey closing the front door carefully behind us, and take a seat on the porch steps.

"Sarah was studying to be a teacher. She wanted to get her degree, come back to the reservation and teach at the Indian school. She was proud of her heritage, proud of her blood. When we met, at a party, we were attracted to each other right off. The Navajo say we were struck by the thunderbolt." He grimaces and smiles as if it suddenly self-conscious. "I can't believe I said that out loud. Go ahead. Laugh. I know how stupid and immature that sounds."

"Stupid? No. If anything, it sounds very romantic." What I don't add is that I think it happened to me, too. With Stephen.

Frey pats my arm. "Be careful what you wish for. She told me her plans. She knew mine. I never had any illusion that I could be content on a reservation—I'd spent a couple of summers volunteering on a Chappiquiddic reservation—just as she could never imagine being content anywhere else. We came to the mutual agreement that we would enjoy our time for the two months she was in Boston. When the new semester started, we'd go our separate ways. When summer rolled around again, if I wanted to get in touch, I'd do it."

"But she got pregnant."

"She got pregnant. We'd taken precautions, but you know how that goes." He pressed fingertips against his eyes. "At first she wanted to get rid of the baby. Frankly, I didn't protest. But to the Navajo, life is sacred. When it came down to doing it, she couldn't bring herself to have an abortion. That was when I knew I had to tell her the truth about me."

"The truth about being a shifter? Or the truth about being a Keeper?"

"Both."

"I imagine she didn't mind the Keeper part so much."

Frey's short laugh is humorless and bitter. "No. The Navajo have their own traditions passed down from generation to generation. My position of Keeper of the Secrets is not so different from that of a medicine man or shaman. We are both responsible for the accumulated knowledge of our people. With the Navajo, the knowledge is passed on verbally. With us, the supernatural community, it's passed on in written works. She understood that. Even admired it, I think."

"But as a Navajo, isn't another of those traditions belief in shape-shifters? I don't understand why she would have such a dramatic reaction."

Frey turns his face away, looks out over the yard and beyond. I follow his gaze. This is a landscape as foreign to a San Diegan as the dark side of the moon. Beautiful in its color and dramatic scope but lonely and unwelcoming to those who don't belong. I understand how Frey knew he couldn't spend his life here.

He releases a long breath. "It's different. I'm not Navajo. My ability to shift is not a gift from the gods, it's a genetic trick of nature. Or at least that's how Sarah sees it. And the possibility that I could pass that gene onto our child, that he might have no choice but to undergo a painful and danger-ous transformation every month in order to survive was too much for her. She hated me for keeping such a huge secret."

"But you didn't intend to have a child together. It was an accident."

"An accident that never would have happened had she known what I was. She's made that very clear."

"Is John-John a shifter?"

"There's a fifty-fifty chance he will be. We won't know until he reaches puberty."

"Ah. That's what Sarah meant when she said she would bring him to you when the time was right."

Frey nods. "As if I'd wait that long. We're going to have to work something out. I won't be a stranger to my own kid."

My thoughts turn to John-John. When I became vam-pire, the life I knew as a mortal ceased to exist. I had to learn to control the animal side of me so I could cling to the human side. I wasn't ready to give up my family and friends so it was a constant balancing act. I handled it because I was an adult. What happens to a child who learns at nine or ten that he's not like everybody else? Those years are difficult enough. This isn't just bad skin or raging hor-mones. This is learning you're fucking supernatural. I can't imagine the trauma.

"I know this is none of my business, Frey. But don't you think you should start preparing John-John? Just in case?"

He shoots me one of those "duh" looks. "Any thoughts how we might do that? Should I start showing him picture books of animals and say, 'Oh, by the way, you may turn into that bear one day. But don't worry about it. It might not happen at all and if it does, it won't happen for a few years yet.'"

His sarcasm doesn't faze me. I throw it right back at him. "So, smart-ass, is that how you learned you were a shape-shifter?"

"It wasn't the same. Both my parents were shifters. There was never any doubt that I'd be one, too. They prepared me because it was a part of our everyday life. It's not a part of John-John's."

"It's not something you can ignore, either. Sarah must realize that."

"She doesn't want to think about it. Which is why she's hiding out here. If she doesn't have to see me, she can pretend I don't exist and John-John is just a normal kid who will someday inherit the mantle of Keeper. It's all she can handle."

Another mystery solved—Mary's comment about Sarah feeling safe here. Safe meaning away from Frey and the constant reminder that John-John may inherit more from his father than a title.

I wish I could offer Frey some words of wisdom, but I've got nothing. I'm not sure how I'd handle the situation if I were in his place. The only thing I do know is I wouldn't be a drop-in visitor in my kid's life, no matter how much resistance I faced.

After a moment, I ask, "So what do we do now?"

Frey sweeps a hand to encompass the scenery. "When

John-John wakes up from his nap, we'll take a ride. Sarah made arrangements for us to stay overnight not far from here. We'll drive out and drop our stuff off."

I didn't think before now that we would need a place to stay. Stupid, considering Sarah's small house and the animosity between her and Frey. Obviously, we couldn't stay with them.

I lean back against the porch step and drain the water bottle. Well, we've made it this far. Neither Frey nor I have answers to our respective questions, but being here is a start.

John-John must have awakened from his nap. Through the closed door we hear him calling out to his father in a voice that borders on panic. Frey and I rush in to find him running from room to room. When he sees Frey, he tumbles into his arms with a whoop of relief. "I thought you left."

Frey hugs him and rubs his back with a gentle hand. "I said I'd be here when you woke up. I wouldn't break a promise to you. Not ever."

Frey scoops him up and we go into the kitchen to prepare his lunch. Sarah left instructions, and I take a seat beside John-John while Frey assembles apple slices and something that looks like blue pudding. I raise an eyebrow.

"What's that?"

Frey spoons the stuff into a bowl. "Blue corn pudding—a Navajo specialty." He takes a mouthful himself and rolls his eyes. "Heaven. A concoction of blue cornmeal, grape juice and yogurt."

"Sounds—ah—healthy."

He passes a bowl to John-John. "Your mom told me this is your favorite."

John-John doesn't answer. He doesn't have to. He's already at work with his spoon, making quick work of the pudding.

His enthusiasm makes me laugh, though eating something with the consistency of smooth tapioca would not have worked for me when I was his age. I was a Cocoa Puffs fan. A taste treat, I have no doubt, John-John has not experienced. I'd be willing to bet there are no packaged cereals in Sarah's pristine cupboards.

John-John polishes off his apple slices, gulps a glass of milk and squirms in his chair with the impatience of a kid on a mission. "I'm done. Can we go now?"

Frey quirks quizzical eyebrows. "Go where?"

"I heard you talking to Anna. We're going for a ride, right?"

Frey and I exchange startled looks. How could he have heard our conversation through the closed door?

John-John points to his head. "I heard you here."

I close my eyes, afraid to look at Frey. If John-John can already pick up telepathic communication between vampires and shape-shifters, Frey does not have to wait years to confirm what just became obvious.

His son is a shifter.

CHAPTER 21

FREY SENDS JOHN-JOHN OFF TO BRUSH HIS TEETH. He doesn't speak first, so I do. "Could you read your folks' minds at that age?"

Frey's shoulders wilt. "No. I don't know what to make of this."

His expression, however, says he knows *exactly* what to make of it. "Maybe we're wrong. Maybe he heard us through the door."

Frey retreats into his own thoughts. As usual, I can only guess what he's doing. He's testing John-John's powers.

A little voice penetrates my head. *Almost done.*

Yikes. I broke the connection with the father, but John-John comes through loud and clear.

"We'd better be careful what we think," I whisper to Frey in a monumental understatement.

Frey rubs his hands over his face. Don't need any psychic connection to read what's behind that gesture. How the hell is he going to break *this* to Sarah?

John-John races back to join us, and we scrub the shock from our expressions and our thoughts. Frey lifts John-John onto his shoulders, and we head for the Jeep. It becomes obvious that John-John isn't aware that there's anything special about being able to read our thoughts and makes no effort to reach out to us on his own. Maybe if we're careful not to probe, he won't, either.

Frey turns the Jeep deeper into the valley. The Jeep fascinates John-John. He lifts his face and hands to the wind and squeals with delight. Each time we're jostled by a bump, his laugh rings out like the sweet peel of a bell. Soon it becomes a game, Frey swerving to hit small furrows in the dirt and John-John and I exaggerating our reactions by bouncing in the seats and screeching our laughing protest.

I can't remember having so much fun.

Finally, I manage to get John-John quieted down enough to ask, "Where are we going? I can't imagine there's a hotel all the way out here?"

Frey's eyes sparkle. "Who said we're going to a hotel?"

I get one of those uh-oh moments. What's Frey up to now? "If we're not staying in a hotel, where are we staying?"

"You'll see."

We're headed into a flat basin surrounded on all sides by red sandstone cliffs. Off in the distance I can see a small encampment of some kind. A hogan and what looks from here like a couple of low-slung concrete buildings spring from the level plane of barren desert like flora in an alien garden.

"Frey? That's not a campsite, is it? Because you know I don't sleep outside."

Frey chuckles. "Well, actually, I didn't know. And yes, it is a campsite. But don't worry. You won't be sleeping outside."

Not very reassuring. "I'm not a camper. I like real beds and sheets and a shower in a bathroom of my very own."

No response, just a smile that looks suspiciously smug. As we get closer, more details come into focus. I imagine the temperature is about 95 degrees; heat shimmers from the desert floor in undulating waves. There are only a handful of cars parked in a roped off area and no one at all in sight. The hogan I saw from the distance is bigger than the one we passed earlier and in front, a loom much like the one I saw at Sarah's sits deserted, a half-finished project baking under the August sun. The buildings are small, rectangular and marked with the familiar symbolic logos proclaiming them bathrooms.

Bathrooms barely big enough for a toilet or two. Just a toilet or two. If there's a shower in there, I'll eat some of that blue corn pudding and the consequences be damned.

"The place looks deserted." My tone is hopeful, suggesting it's time to turn around.

Frey pulls the Jeep behind a clump of brush and glances at his watch. "We're a little early. George will be here in a few minutes." He turns to John-John. "Want to get out and stretch your legs?"

Before I can follow up with any more questions, John-John has wiggled out of his seat belt and is holding out expectant arms to Frey. Frey jumps out of the Jeep, hefts his son to the ground and the kid is off.

He studiously avoids looking in my direction.

"Kid's got a lot of energy."

I'm gritting my teeth so hard, my jaw aches. "Where exactly are we sleeping tonight?"

Frey motions in a vague away. "There."

"There? Where? I'm telling you, I'm not going to sleep on the ground. I did that once on a rafting trip down the

Grand Canyon with my folks. We were told to put our sleeping bags perpendicular to the river so the critters coming down at night to drink wouldn't crawl into your bag. It was a nightmare."

One I'm not about to revisit.

Another vague arm wave. "No river, see?"

"Shit, Frey. I don't care. There's got to be a hotel around here. This is a major tourist attraction. What about the lodge where Sarah works? Why can't we stay there?"

Frey hesitates, directing his attention to his son, pretending John-John *needs* his attention when in reality, John-John is chasing a butterfly and oblivious to the two of us. Finally, he drags in a breath and blows out a reply. "Sarah doesn't want anyone but the elders to know we're here. She suggested we stay where we're least likely to attract attention. Not many people camp out in the summer. It's too hot."

"So what about the cars in the lot?"

"They belong to people taking tours. They'll be back soon and tonight, we'll have the camp to ourselves."

Oh great.

I plop down on the bumper of the Jeep, the acid of frustration and anger eating a hole in the pit of my stomach. I cast a look in John-John's direction and lower my voice to a whisper. "Are you going to let Sarah dictate every fucking detail of this trip?"

"Are you going to tell me that a hot-shit vampire is afraid to sleep in the dirt?" Frey is whispering, too.

So not fair. "Did I say I was afraid? I said I don't like it—not that I was afraid."

"Right."

John-John circles back toward us making me swallow the earthy response that had sprung to my lips. Having a kid around activates an internal censor I didn't even know I had.

He screeches to a stop in front of us. "Did you tell Anna that you were sleeping in the hogan tonight?"

Frey looks confused and then consternation furrows his brow.

John-John picked that out of his father's brain.

"The hogan?" I glance behind me. "We're sleeping in that?"

Frey lifts his shoulders. "It's not outside."

I tromp over for a closer look. The walls of the hogan rise about twelve feet from the desert floor. It looks like an igloo fashioned from red mud instead of ice. Its dome shape has only one door, a rectangular piece of heavy leather pulled back and secured with a rawhide cord. When I peek inside, I'm impressed in spite of not wanting to be. The walls and ceiling are interwoven branches of juniper. Beautiful in a primitive way. Then I look up. There's an open, square hole in the top. Just the thing to let in all sorts of unwelcome creeping, slithering or flying guests. No furniture, just a couple of sleeping bags and mats rolled up against one side and a woven rug covering the dirt floor.

No windows. No beds. No shower.

Shit.

When I turn around, Frey is right behind me. "What do you think?"

He doesn't want to know what I think. I cast a glance toward John-John, who doesn't seem to be interested in our conversation but still, I keep my voice low and a lid on what I might project telepathically. "I think you're nuts to want us to stay in a mud hut."

Frey bristles and gives me a little push inside. When we're standing out of the sun, he says, "Look around,

Anna. This is not a mud hut. The hogan is respected and cherished by the Navajo. In their creation stories, the first man and first woman built the original hogan to represent the universe and all things in it. It is more than a home. It is a sacred place to conduct ceremonies. It is built of and is harmonious with nature. It is eternal. You of all people should understand that."

His words carry the sting of reproach and for the first time, I see a spark in Frey I never saw before. "Do you have Navajo blood?"

He gives his head an impatient shake. "No. Do you think one has to be Navajo to appreciate their culture? I don't have vampire blood, either, and I get you pretty well. What's wrong with you? I never thought you'd be so narrow-minded. It's an honor to be invited to stay in a hogan. I even had the stupid notion you'd be excited to try something different. I never suspected a fucking shower was more important to you than the chance to connect with the earth and its people in a unique way."

Wow. I've just been verbally spanked and adding to the humiliation is the realization that I deserve it. His passion robs me of any snarky comeback I might throw back at him even if I could come up with anything. Right now, my immediate response is the desire to crawl through that hole in the hogan's ceiling and disappear.

I offer the only gesture of conciliation I can think of. An apology.

"I'm sorry. Really. I came off like a prima donna when you're here to do me a favor. I have no right to denigrate Navajo heritage. I didn't understand. It's no excuse. I do have a great deal of respect for Native Americans. If this is where we're to stay tonight, I'll do it gladly."

Frey's dark irritation shifts into something that looks

like dark skepticism. "Gladly? Don't push it, Anna. But apology accepted. I might have come off a tad strongly. Since John-John, I've learned a lot about the Navajo and their belief system. I respect them enormously, but I can't expect everyone to."

I'm saved from further chastisement by the sound of a vehicle approaching the campsite. Frey and I step outside.

"Here comes our host," Frey says.

In the distance, a plume of dust marks the return of a group of day-trippers. Frey calls John-John to his side, and we slip inside the cool interior of the hogan to wait out of sight.

I surreptitiously sneak another look around as we wait.

Okay. I can sleep in here. As long as there are no spiders hiding in the chinks of those log walls.

I really hate spiders.

CHAPTER 22

I T TAKES ABOUT TWENTY MINUTES FOR THE NAVAJO
guide to answer a spate of last-minute questions, accept
gratuities pressed on him by enthusiastic tourists and herd
them to their cars and off. Frey and John-John and I wait in
the hogan. Soon after we hear the echo of the last car heading
back for civilization, soft footfalls approach our hiding place.

"Hxida'ish hoghan yii, sida?"

"Here, brother." Frey steps out, John-John and I at his
heels. Frey and the Navajo embrace, talking quietly in the
language that sounds magical to my untrained ears. After
a moment, Frey turns in my direction.

"Anna, I'd like you to meet my very good friend, George
Long Whiskers."

I take a step forward, hesitantly because I'm unsure of
protocol. But I needn't have worried. Before I can acknowledge the introduction, John-John has scooted around my
legs and thrown himself into George's arms.

George laughs, lifts John-John into the air and spins

him around. He says something that sends John-John and his father into heartier gales of laughter. I hang back, feeling once more like the outsider I obviously am.

But it gives me a minute to size up George Long Whiskers. He's the same height as Frey, thicker through the middle. He's wearing a black leather vest over a long-sleeved white cotton shirt open at the neck but still warm weather attire for an August afternoon. He appears not to notice. No sweat beads his forehead, no telltale circles under his arm. He's got on jeans and scuffed boots and a bright red baseball cap. His hair is not black but light brown, and when he puts John-John back on the ground next to Frey and turns to me, I'm startled to see blue eyes under the brim of that baseball cap.

My reaction makes him grin as he puts out his hand. "Hey, Anna. Pleased to make your acquaintance. Never seen an albino Indian before, huh? Folks around here call me the white sheep of the family."

I'm not sure whether to take his hand or not, still leery of physical contact after Sarah's reaction. But a glance at Frey, who gives a subtle go-ahead motion with his head, and I return the handshake.

His grip is firm and dry and he doesn't yank away. He has a wide, warm smile and a face that makes it impossible to guess his age. Sculpted cheekbones, straight nose, complexion touched with color, but not as dark as Sarah's. An interesting genetic mix.

And not a long whisker in sight.

He seems to be sizing me up, too. "I like this one, Daniel," he says after a second.

"I like her, too," Frey says.

"Me, too," John-John pipes up.

"Glad it's unanimous." I reach down and muss John-John's hair.

George goes over to the loom and cuts off a length of yarn with a pocketknife. "Hey, John-John, how about you play with this while your dad and Anna and I talk."

A piece of yarn? I'm wondering what kind of reaction that suggestion is going to get when I'm surprised by the look of delight on the kid's face. He grabs it and squats down with his back against the wall of the hogan, ties a knot in the yarn and soon immerses himself into some kind of finger weaving.

Most four-year-olds I know would demand a wide-screen TV and a dinosaur manga cartoon marathon to hold their attention like that.

George leads us over to his vehicle—a converted bus, open on the top and sides, six rows of bench seats under a striped awning. Perfect for sightseeing. He waves Frey and I into the bus and we take seats facing each other. George on one side, Frey and I on the other.

Frey starts the conversation. "Did you talk to Sarah?"

George nods. "She is not happy that you are here. She worries how it will be for John-John when you leave again. And she sees Anna's presence as a threat."

"I'm a threat?" Bristling with indignation, I lean forward on the seat. "I'm not a threat to anyone. I'm here for one purpose. Once I've accomplished that purpose, I'll leave."

"It's not that easy, Anna," he says. His eyes regard me with frank appraisal. "You are vampire. By your nature you are a threat. There are many who would demand you leave our nation now. They will fight to prevent you from meeting with Sani."

"Sani?"

"That is the name we call the shaman. He is a holy man and his identity is a closely guarded secret among the elders. They are sworn to protect him. Sarah is going to talk to them tonight at council. But you should be prepared for disappointment."

I turn toward Frey. "Shouldn't I be there when she speaks with them? Plead my case."

George places a hand between Frey and me, his answer coming as quick as it is adamant. "No. In fact, Sarah will not make it known that you are here. She will address the council with the request from a friend who will come only if permission is granted. Bringing a vampire to a gathering of the *Dine'é* is foolhardy and dangerous. Sarah could be held responsible if something goes wrong."

"Goes wrong? What do you think? I'll go berserk and start attacking people?"

Frey tries to temper my rising indignation. "It's not you specifically," he says. "Traditionally the Navajo are morbidly afraid of the dead. They have no concept of life after death nor are deeds done in this life rewarded or punished. Mortal life is all. Death at an early age is viewed with dismay. You are young. You are the walking dead."

"But that's the reason I'm here. To see if it can be reversed. Surely that has to carry some weight with the elders."

Neither George nor Frey answers. I can see by their expressions, they do not expect I'll be granted an audience. Well, I'm not going to argue the point now. I'll wait and see what happens. Then I'll start arguing.

John-John skips over to us, the circle of yarn held between his two hands. "Look what I made."

We climb out of the bus and I squat down so I'm eye level with John-John. "Is that a cat's cradle?"

He giggles. "Watch." He lets go of the bottom string and like magic, two patterns form and when he pulls his hands apart, the patterns move away from each other. "The gate is opening."

I clap my hands. "That is wonderful, John-John. How long did it take you to come up with that?"

"Oh, I can make lots of things. Would you like to see more?"

But George lays a gentle hand on John-John's shoulder. "We have to go meet your mother now. You can show Anna more another time." He looks at Frey. "I have food for you in the bus. And blankets. Will the two of you be all right here tonight?"

We both nod, Frey more enthusiastically than I. John-John is reluctant to leave. He shadows Frey to the front of the bus where George hands down a cooler and blankets. Frey leans over and whispers in John-John's ear. He speaks in Navajo but whatever he tells the boy, John-John seems appeased by it. He lifts his arms to his father for a hug and climbs up to sit beside George.

Frey lifts a hand. *"Hágoónee'. Hazhó'ó nídeiyínóhkááh."*

John-John waves. George nods to us both and steers the bus out of the lot.

"What did you say to him?" I ask, John-John's little hand still waving to us from the open window as the bus pulls away.

"I told him to be safe going home."

We carry the food and blankets into the hogan. Frey busies himself setting out sandwiches and chips and settles cross-legged on the rug to eat.

"You look right at home."

He smiles up at me. "Don't know about that. But I do feel at peace. Being with John-John makes me realize how much I've missed him. I'm glad we made the trip."

I sit, too, back against the wall of the hogan, legs outstretched. There is a sense of peace. Maybe because it's so quiet. No city noises. No traffic. Not even a birdcall to shatter the stillness.

Odd.

I tilt my head, listening.

Frey frowns, puts down his sandwich. "What's wrong?"

"It's too quiet. We should be hearing birds or coyotes or *something* moving around outside. Why aren't we?"

I climb to my feet, take a step outside.

Movement in a clump of brush thirty feet from the hogan. It catches the corner of my eye and as I turn, something sharp pricks the skin of my forearm.

I jump and clap a hand over my arm. I scan the brush, then race toward it. Even with the speed of the vampire, whatever was there is gone. Not even a footprint or the echo of a footfall reaches my ears. I scan the distance. The only thing I see is a crow far off, solitary, silent, floating over the mesa. Then it, too, is gone.

Frey is suddenly beside me. "What happened? Your arm is bleeding."

We both look down and as we watch, a bump forms over something embedded just under the skin. Then the wound closes and the swelling disappears.

I wipe away the spot of blood. There's nothing left but a blush of red that fades as we watch.

"What the hell was that?" I ask. "Was I bitten by an insect?"

Frey's eyes scan the distance. He grabs my arm and pulls me back toward the hogan. "We need to get inside."

I feel the tension in his touch, let him lead me to the shelter of the hogan. "What's going on?"

He pulls the leather thong free and the rawhide door falls into place. Only then does he look at me. "I think it was a skinwalker. We need to get that charm out of your arm. Now."

CHAPTER 23

F REY PULLS A SMALL SWISS ARMY KNIFE FROM THE
pocket of his jeans. He reaches for my arm.

I jerk it out of reach. "What do you think you're doing?"

Frey isn't deterred. He snatches my arm in a strong,
solid grip. "I'll explain after I get the charm out of you.
Believe me, Anna, you don't want that thing inside you
very long."

I start to object, but he's already pierced my skin with
the very sharp point of a very small knife.

I yelp. Vampires are indestructible, but we feel pain just
like any mortal. I could free myself, but there's something
in Frey's expression that stops me. Anxiety. Worry. He's
afraid for me.

He digs around under the skin for what seems a long
time. I bite my lower lip to keep from squirming. "Damn,
Frey. That hurts."

No answer. No apology. Finally, he switches the knife
blade for tweezers—gotta love those army knives—digs

around some more and pulls something small and bloody out of my arm.

He holds it up. "Got it."

The wound on my arm is already closing. "What is it?" I ask, wiping residual blood on my jeans. "And why did you have to remove it? You know there are very few things that can kill me."

Frey mimics my action, wiping blood from the object until it's clean. Then he holds something small and round and white out to me.

He lays it on the palm of my hand. "It wouldn't kill you, not right away. That's a human bone bead dipped in bone dust. Causes heart failure in humans. Paralysis in supernaturals." He lets a beat go by. "In the case of a vampire, permanent paralysis. It would take you a long time to die."

The bead is tiny, white, seems harmless enough, though from what Frey just said, obviously isn't. "How did it get in me? I didn't hear a shot."

"It didn't come from a regular gun. It came from a blow-gun. Favorite weapon of the skinwalkers."

And now for the next question burning my brain. "What the hell is a skinwalker?"

Frey resumes his seat on the floor of the hogan, motions at me to join him. When we're both seated, he begins.

"The Navajo call them *yee naaldooshii*. It's a Navajo witch who practices curse magic. They can travel in animal form. Wolf, coyote, owl . . ."

"How about crow?"

He nods. "You saw a crow?"

"In the distance."

"Probably our culprit."

"Why would it attack me?"

"Don't know. I only know three people who know you're here—Sarah, Mary and John-John."

"And now, George."

Frey shakes his head. "George wouldn't say anything. He's been a friend for a long time."

"But you haven't brought a vampire to his home before. He may feel like Sarah."

Another adamant shake of the head. "George would never practice curse magic, let alone become a skinwalker. To do that, you have to desecrate the corpse of a loved one. I already told you how the Navajo fear the dead. I can't see him being a party to such a powerful taboo."

"But maybe his fear of me is even greater. Maybe this is his way of letting me know I'm not welcome on the reservation."

"It's not George." Frey's jaw is set, his mind made up.

I rub my hand over my arm. There's nothing left to show of the wound. "Then who?"

"Maybe we can get some answers from Sarah," Frey says. "We'll drive over first thing in the morning."

"Why not drive over right now? Wait for her to get back from the council."

Frey looks around, uneasy. "Best not to travel at night out here. Not with skinwalkers around."

I give him a do-you-hear-yourself look, complete with raised eyebrows and clucking tongue. "You are a shape-shifter. I'm a vampire. What's going to attack us?"

"Didn't you hear what I've been saying? Skinwalkers aren't afraid of us. One already hit you with a bone charm. It's just good luck that I recognized what it was and got it out of you in time."

"But now we're on to them. Nothing will get close enough to try again. We'll be in a vehicle with windows up and doors locked. Don't see how anything can possibly happen."

Frey presses the palms of his hands together. "No. Even if I was stupid enough to risk it, I won't risk drawing them to Sarah's. I won't put my son and his mother and aunt in danger."

He picks up the half-eaten sandwich and snaps off a bite, as if punctuating the end of the conversation. His concern is real. I capitulate to it with a sigh and look around the hogan. "What are we going to do all night? Don't even have a book to read."

"How about sleep?" Frey replies. "Haven't done much of that in the last few days."

"Will we be safe? What if they come back?"

"I don't think they will. They have no way of knowing I removed the charm. The logical thing would be for us to take off. To go for help. If we stay out of sight they should leave us alone."

I suppose Frey's thinking makes sense and he is right about one thing—we haven't gotten much sleep in the last twenty-four hours. I push the sleeping bags and mats out to the middle of the floor, work around Frey eating his picnic lunch and set things up. The sleeping bags appear to be new, at least, and of good quality. I stretch out, a test run.

"Not bad. Now if we could just cover that hole in the ceiling."

Frey looks up. "Why would you want to do that? You can see the stars."

Along with bats or flying insects or anything else that might wander in. But I know if I say that to Frey, I'll get another lecture about nature and being bigger and stronger than anything that could fit through that hole.

I roll over onto my side. Maybe if I don't look, I won't see. It's worth a try.

"Good night, Frey."

"*Danootch'ííl*, Anna."

THE SOUND OF THE WIND AWAKENS ME.

It's pitch-black in the hogan. If there's a moon out, it's doing nothing to penetrate the dark. Once my eyes have adjusted, I look at my watch.

Midnight.

I sit up to find Frey awake, too, staring hard at the door. The rawhide flap covering it moves to the wind gusts, billowing out and in as if blown by bellows fanning a fire.

I listen. The soft pad of bare feet approaching. I jump to my feet. Frey, startled, does, too.

"You heard it?" he whispers. "I thought it was my imagination."

Not imagination. Someone is walking around outside . . . someone or something.

The vampire erupts, bursting the fragile shell of humanity instinctively at the threat. I touch Frey's chest, growl, "Stay here."

Then I'm sliding out of the door, sticking close to the walls of the hogan, a shadow among shadows, a beast among beasts.

I see him, working his way around the hogan, slowly, carefully. Not barefoot. Moccasins on his feet. His smell is familiar. I draw the vampire back enough to appear human before I confront him. His back is to me.

"George?"

His shoulders twitch involuntarily and he whirls around. He releases a sharp breath. "Shit, Anna, you scared me."

"What are you doing here?"

Frey steps out. "What's wrong?"

I see now what prompts Frey's question. George's face is ashen in the dark, a pale specter, drawn and anxious. He's dressed in buckskin pants and tan vest. He shifts uneasily under Frey's intense stare.

Frey grabs his shoulders. "What's happened?"

George closes his eyes, inhales slowly. "It's Sarah."

"Sarah?"

George puts his hands on Frey's shoulders now, pulls him close. "*Sik is*, there's been an accident."

CHAPTER 24

F REY LETS HIS HANDS DROP TO HIS SIDES. "WHAT do you mean? What kind of accident?"

George tightens his grip on Frey's shoulders. "Sarah. And Mary. Coming back from the tribal council. Their truck went off the road. Sarah must have been driving too fast. It flipped. Neither was wearing a seat belt."

I watch Frey try to process what George is telling him. His body is so still, his face so expressionless, it scares me. I step closer, drop my voice to a hoarse whisper, asking the question I know Frey is afraid to ask. "What about John-John?"

Frey looks at me, drawing a shaky breath.

George never takes his eyes from Frey. "John-John wasn't with them. He's all right. Did you hear me? John-John is home with my wife."

Frey's stony expression finally breaks. I sense his pain. His jaw quivers, his eyes widen, brows draw together with the effort to keep from howling. His body shudders, racked with emotions he has no words to express.

I know what he's feeling. I've felt it myself.

I don't know how to console him. I do the only thing I can think of. I step between Frey and George and wrap my own arms around my friend's trembling body.

"What do we need to do?" I ask George, holding Frey tight, supporting him as he leans into me.

"The four who are to prepare the bodies are with them now. They are friends of Sarah's and will take care of the ritual bathing. Daniel will have to choose what items are to be buried with them and how they are to be dressed. He will also have to choose where they are to be buried."

From his answers, it is obvious the Navajo have very specific burial customs. No outside police. No funeral homes or embalming. "How long do we have?"

"Burial will take place four days from now. Do you wish to return to Sarah's? I will bring John-John to his father when he awakens. Daniel should be the one who breaks the news."

I nod that I understand. "I'll get him to Sarah's. Thank you."

George lifts his hand in silent salute and walks toward his car, parked next to the Jeep behind the hogan. Only when he's driven away and Frey and I are alone do I remember—I never found out what was decided at the council.

Right now, it doesn't seem important.

Frey doesn't say a word. Not when I get him settled in the Jeep, not when I return from packing our things out of the hogan. For once, I'm glad I'm not privy to his thoughts. The pain would be intolerable. He may not have been close to Sarah now, but she was John-John's mother and that alone is a powerful connection.

I manage to find my way from the hogan to Sarah's house—more vampire instinct and senses than anything else. I don't turn the Jeep's lights on; I can navigate far better in the dark by picking up our scent and watching for our tire tracks in the dirt.

How different retracing this path. John-John's laugh echoes in my head. Yesterday he was happy.

The house is dark when we pull up. This time, no welcoming flute to greet a new day. It's almost daybreak but the sky is leaden and heavy with impending rain.

I go in first, turn on lights. Not because we need light to see, but in an effort to chase away the gloom.

It doesn't work.

When Frey comes up the steps, I know he feels the same thing I do. The house has lost its spirit. The quiet, the emptiness press in on us.

Only John-John will be able to make it a place of life again. And I doubt that will happen for a while.

Frey sinks into the couch. Buries his face in his hands. But still no tears. No release.

I sit on the coffee table in front of him. "Can I get you anything? Coffee? Some food?"

He rouses a little, drops his hands, meets my eyes. "No. Thanks. Just sit here with me, will you, until John-John comes?"

I move next him. We sit there side by side, not touching, but closer in spirit than we've ever been.

After a while, Frey stirs. "At least John-John's home has been spared."

I swivel to look at him. "Spared? What do you mean?"

Frey's voice is husky, devoid of emotion. "It's the Navajo way. If Sarah and Mary had died at home, their parents would have most likely had the place burned to the ground."

"John-John's home?"

"The belief is that after death, one goes to the underworld. To protect against the deceased returning to the world of the living, no contact must be made with the body and that includes the place they died. The place would be destroyed."

I'm trying to process how such a belief could still be considered relevant in the twenty-first century when I'm hit with the implications of something else Frey said.

"Sarah and Mary—their parents live here on the reservation?"

Frey nods. "I only hope they allow me to take part in the burial. While we weren't married in the eyes of the state, when Sarah told them she was going to have a baby, they insisted we go through a traditional Navajo ceremony. In the eyes of the tribe, I am her husband. In their eyes, I deserted her and my son to live outside."

A worm of uneasiness twists in my gut. "What's going to happen to John-John? Will they insist he stay here with them? Will you allow it?"

Frey presses the palms of his hands against his eyes. "I can't think about that now. I can hardly bear the thought that I'm going to have to tell him his mother and aunt are gone. How am I going to do it?"

His voice breaks. I move to put my arms around his shoulders. I'm stopped mid-gesture by the sound of a car approaching. I feel Frey tense and draw in a breath.

George is here with John-John. I push up from the couch. "I'll let them in."

Frey doesn't answer or move. I hardly know John-John,

but my heart is as heavy as Frey's at how that little boy's life is about to change.

I don't wait for a knock but swing the door open.

It's not George coming up the porch steps. It's a man in a beige uniform, a gun on his hip. He's wearing a badge and the car parked in front of the house bears green and yellow stripes and emblazoned on the side *Navajo Nation Police*.

He is as startled to see me as I am by his unexpected presence. He sweeps a round-crowned, broad-brimmed hat from his head. "Ma'am. I'm here to see Daniel Frey. Is he in?"

I nod him inside. When he brushes past me, I get a whiff of citrus aftershave and the fresh scent of fabric softener. His uniform is crisp, ironed creases as sharp as a ruler. His gun leather creaks where he rests one hand on the holster. In the quiet of the house, it's like the rasp of a ghostly voice.

Frey has the same reaction I did. He stares a moment, then recovers and stands to greet the officer.

"I'm Tony Kayani. Officer with the Navajo Nation Police. I'm sorry for your loss."

Frey shakes his hand, gestures over Kayani's shoulder to me. "This is my friend, Anna Strong."

Kayani half turns, nods in my direction, turns his attention back to Frey. "Can we sit? I have a couple of questions to ask you."

Frey sits back down on the couch. Kayani takes one of the chairs across from him and I take the other.

Kayani takes a notebook from a breast pocket. But no pen. He rests the book on his knee. "I understand you arrived yesterday."

Frey nods.

"And that you have been estranged from your wife and son for some time."

"Yes."

"May I ask why you came back now?"

Involuntarily, my shoulders tighten. How is Frey going to answer that?

"I came to visit my son. As you noted, it's been a while since I've seen him. It was time."

"And what business did you have with the tribal council?"

Another involuntary shoulder twitch. How could he have known about that? Frey is quiet for a long moment. Maybe too long. Kayani leans toward him.

"Is there a reason you don't want to answer that question?"

Frey bristles at the tone. "Is there a reason you're asking it?"

Kayani smiles in a tight, determined way. "Sorry. I realize this is a difficult time. I also realize Sarah wasn't addressing the council on her own behalf, was she?"

He doesn't look at me. Perhaps he doesn't know, but the implication hangs heavy. In profile, Kayani reminds me of the picture on the old Buffalo nickel. Broad forehead, straight nose, tight lips turned down at the corner. His dark hair is short and brushed straight back. His greyhound-lean frame is as tightly strung as the close weave on Sarah's rugs. His posture and attitude suggest something more than a law officer's impartial inquiry into a tragic accident.

"Officer Kayani?"

He turns slowly, as if reluctant to look away from Frey.

"Did you attend the tribal council tonight?"

He shakes his head. "No. But I heard what happened."

"Can you tell us? We don't know any of the details except that Sarah and Mary had their accident on the way home."

He seems reluctant at first to answer. His jet black eyes bore into mine. But there's nothing accusatory in his gaze. It's more resentment that he has to talk to Frey and me. Hardly professional. He hasn't written anything in that little notebook still perched on his knee, either. It dawns on me that he's not here to shed light on the accident. In fact . . .

Before I can complete my thought, he says, "I don't know. Exactly. Nobody's talking. Sarah had a request of the elders. Whatever it was, it wasn't well received. She was asked to leave. She was pretty upset by all accounts."

His voice has lost the demanding "me cop/you suspect" staccato. His shoulders sag a little before he catches me studying him and recovers himself. Too late. He's not here on an official visit. He's here on a personal one.

If I had to guess, I'd bet Kayani had something going with Sarah.

Frey hasn't picked up on the same vibes that I have. At least he gives no indication that he has. Not surprising, since his main concern now is his son's grief.

Kayani is quiet for a long moment. He and Frey stare at each other but I suspect, for different reasons. Frey is waiting for more questions, Kayani sizing up the man he may see as having been his competition. For the first time, I wonder if Sarah still loved Frey. If, in spite of everything, she put off a life with anyone else because of it.

The sound of another car approaching draws us all back. Frey's eyes dart toward the door. Kayani stands up, as do I.

I touch Frey's hand. "I'll go."

This time, I wait for the knock. When I open the door,

George is there, holding John-John. There is a momentary flash of surprise in his eyes when he sees me. Then it's gone and all I see reflected there is sadness. He puts John-John down and the boy scoots around me, his arms out flung. It's not until I turn that I realize Kayani is behind me and it's to him that John-John runs. The surprise I saw in George's eyes becomes clear. He did not expect to see Kayani.

Kayani scoops John-John into his arms and stands up. I tense, wondering if he's going to say something about Sarah. They're talking in Navajo and from John-John's re-action, it's only friendly greetings being exchanged. Maybe Kayani caught the warning look on George's face or maybe he just didn't want to be the one to break the kid's heart.

One thing's for sure—Kayani is no stranger to John-John.

Kayani puts John-John down, nods to George and me, and leaves without a word. I shut the door behind him and we join Frey in the living room.

John-John has run to Frey, scrambled up on the couch to climb into this lap. He's chattering in Navajo until with a kid's intuition, he realizes something is wrong. Frey hasn't moved, not even to put his arms around John-John.

George taps my arm. "We should leave them."

I'm reluctant until I realize Frey is nodding at me, a tiny, subdued movement. "We'll be in the kitchen."

I can't think of anything else to do. I follow George like an automaton into the kitchen. We sit at the table—not across from each other but side to side. Harder to look at each other that way.

But it's harder still to turn off that acute vampire hearing and not listen to what's going on in the next room. I'm almost relieved when I succumb and find Frey and John-

John speaking in Navajo. I can't understand the words, but the emotion comes through in heartbreaking clarity. I think they are both crying.

I close my eyes and will my thoughts to center on something—anything—else.

I turn to George. "Who is Officer Kayani? What was he to Sarah?"

The abruptness of the question catches him off guard. He answers just as abruptly, without taking the time to censor his reply. "Kayani loves Sarah." He stops himself, draws in a breath. "He *loved* her."

"Did she love him?"

George looks away, toward the living room. "I think she did. In a way. He was good for John-John." His eyes slide my way. "A father he didn't have."

There is accusation in his tone. Accusation directed at me. "You think I kept Frey from Sarah and John-John?"

"Didn't you?"

"I didn't even know about them until recently."

"But you and Daniel—"

"There isn't any me and Daniel. We are friends. That's all."

George gives no indication what he's thinking. I get the feeling, though, that I haven't convinced him. I rub my hands over my face and ask wearily. "What happened last night, George?"

He looks at me with cold suspicion. "What kind of question is that? You know what happened."

"No. I don't mean the accident. I mean at the council."

A flash of satisfaction flares in his eyes. "You don't know, do you? Your request was turned down. All this"—he sweeps a hand around the room—"was for nothing."

George brusquely pushes himself away from the table

and stands up and away as if he needs to put distance between us. "You are unclean. Evil. A dead thing. I hope Daniel puts an end to you and stays here with his son where he belongs. I can't be here with you any longer. Tell Daniel I will see him at the burial."

He leaves without another word through the back door, back unyielding, long strides stiff yet brisk, determined to waste no time in getting away from me.

So much for the cordiality of our first meeting. Can't say I blame him, though.

I watch him leave. In spite of what Frey thinks, I am unconvinced he could not be the skinwalker who planted that bead in my arm. Even before he knew Sarah's request was turned down, he might have thought the quickest way to rid the tribe of my presence was to rid it of me. Maybe the surprise I saw in his eyes when I met him at the door was not because Kayani was here but because he didn't expect me to be.

I don't know what to do with myself. I still hear soft voices from the living room. I can't intrude on Frey's time with his son. I let myself quietly out the back door and find myself drifting down toward the corral in the back of the house.

The sun has risen over the horizon, not in a blaze like yesterday but in smeared shafts of light filtering through the clouds. The horses watch me approach with intense curiosity and nickering expectation. Feeding time. I wonder if they'll let me get close enough to feed them. Animals tend to react badly when they sense a predator. They do indeed start to shy away, but when I pick up a pitchfork and toss a couple of flakes of hay into the feeder, their natural defenses are overcome by another compulsion—the need to fill their bellies. I am ignored as they start to feed.

I climb up on the fence to watch. There are three horses. Small of build, sturdy and well cared for. Two are pintos, brown and white with dark manes and tails. One is a buckskin, golden coat shining, taller than the other two, dark mane and tail and four black hooves. I wonder which was Sarah's and which was John-John's. Did the third belong to Kayani?

I haven't been on a horse for a long time—since a long-ago birthday party and that wasn't really a horse at all but a pony. Mary's invitation springs to mind and the gloom deepens. We won't be taking that ride after all.

I close my eyes and let senses take over from emotion. The smell of the horses, warm, earthy, pungent; the smell of sage and mesquite and hot sand; the warmth of the sun where it touches my face; the sound of the horses crunching the fragrant hay; wind blowing softly through desert juniper; the sound of a fox slinking back to its den; the call of a crow circling overhead—

My eyes snap open.

A crow.

I jump down from the fence and scan the heavens. Against the horizon, a large black crow flaps glistening wings, flying due east away from me.

Shit. It could really be a crow.

Or it could be George off to spread the bad news that I'm still alive.

CHAPTER 25

I DON'T KNOW HOW LONG I STAY IN THAT POSITION, back against the fence, eyes on the sky. Partially it's because I'm still numb with what's happened, partially because I hear George's words repeat in my brain.

All this was for nothing.

He's right. Worse, what happened to Sarah and Mary is my fault. If I hadn't persuaded Frey to come, if I hadn't been so curious about a shaman I won't be allowed to meet, if I hadn't once more drawn Frey into my own private battle, John-John would still have a mom and an aunt.

How can Frey ever forgive me?

Movement from the house breaks through the pall of despair shrouding my thoughts and look I over to see Frey coming toward me.

He's alone.

"John-John?"

"Cried himself to sleep. He's on the couch. I don't want

to be gone long in case he wakes up, but I wanted to check on you." He looks around. "George left?"

Couldn't leave fast enough. I glance toward the sky then nod.

"Did he feed the horses?"

"No. I did."

"You did? Wouldn't have thought a city girl like you knew the business end of a pitchfork from a branding iron."

"Like you're the expert. How much time have you spent on the range, cowboy?"

He lets a tiny smile touch the corners of his mouth. "Touché." The smile is gone as quickly as it appeared. He leans back against the fence, resting a foot on the lower rail. Once again we're side by side, silent, weighed down by sadness that pulls at us the moment we let an unguarded thought slip through.

The sky should be light by now, the sun casting shadows across the burnished landscape. Instead, the clouds crowd thicker and lower until a light mist begins to fall.

I put a hand on Frey's arm, afraid if I don't say it now, I'll lose courage. "Frey, I'm sorry."

He straightens up, not meeting my eyes, pretending, I think, not to hear. "We'd better get inside."

We trudge back to the house. John-John is still asleep on the couch. I give Frey a gentle push toward his son. "Go. Be with him. I'll make coffee."

Frey settles himself on the couch, gently lifting John-John's head to rest on his lap. The boy stirs but doesn't waken. Frey rests his own head back against the cushions and closes his eyes, too. I leave them and head for the kitchen.

It shouldn't surprise me that Sarah has no coffee in the

house. Only various kinds of loose tea in glass canisters. I pick one up, feeling a tingle of irritation until I catch myself.

The woman is dead. I'm criticizing her because she doesn't have coffee in her own home.

She's dead because of me. She's dead because I let Chael influence me. She's dead because I didn't have the backbone to do what I should have the moment I saw him in my house.

And I'm irritated because she drinks tea.

My fingers tighten convulsively around the glass canister and with a crack that shatters the quiet, the canister breaks, sending shards of glass and tea as fragrant as sage across the kitchen floor. I glance down at my hand. Only the metal ring lock is left. It glistens with blood from the gash across my palm.

There's no pain and as I watch, the cut starts to heal. Skin tingles as it reknits over the gash, blood soaking down through the skin until it's reabsorbed. Soon there's nothing to show but a faint flush and then that's gone, too.

Why can't I perform that same magic on Sarah and Mary? What good is power if I can't use it on others?

I let the metal ring drop and look around for a broom. There's a closet beside the back door and in it, I find what I need. I sweep up the debris and deposit it into a trash can under the sink. I do it without thinking. I don't want to think. I want to turn the clock back and start over from Tuesday morning. I want to walk in on Chael and snap his neck before he has a chance to say a word. I am the Chosen One and I let myself be drawn in with his tale like a stupid child.

Why is this happening?

I close the closet door and sink into a kitchen chair. I'm

not prone to tears. Even as a child, crying seemed a sign of weakness. My brother never cried. I'd be damned if I would. But becoming vampire while making me stronger in so many ways pushes some emotions closer to the surface. There's a little boy in the next room who has no mother.

Because of me.

I feel the sting of tears. Swallow hard to fight them back, press fingertips against my eyes until the pain drives away the bitter urge to break down. It's a sign of weakness I don't deserve to indulge. I need to figure how to make things right.

Restless, I push myself from the table, cross to the sink, let my gaze fix on the view from the back window. Rain is falling in soft sheets, turning the landscape into an impressionistic blur of red and brown. The sound as it hits the tile roof beats a counterpoint to my efforts to sort through tangled emotions.

None of this makes sense. How could Sarah have had an accident traveling a road she traveled every day for years? What could possibly have happened at the council to throw her into such a tizzy she lost control of an old truck she must have driven for years? I know my own car so well, I can't imagine such a thing. Especially on familiar terrain. Was she distracted by something?

Jesus.

Could she have been distracted by something?

Frey didn't want to travel at night because of the skin-walkers.

But they have it in for me. Not for Sarah.

Right?

I must be crazy. No one would want Sarah dead just because she made a request of the council. What sense would that make? Once Sarah came back and told me the request was turned down, it would be logical to assume I'd soon be gone. And probably Frey, too.

No one had anything to gain by killing Sarah and her sister.

Did they?

I can't believe I hadn't thought of it before this minute.

There is someone who would not want me to leave quite so soon. Someone who is capable of killing to ensure I'd stick around and pursue the shaman on my own. Someone who doesn't want me to give up the idea of becoming mortal again.

Chael.

CHAPTER 26

A S SOON AS THE PIECES FALL INTO PLACE, I BANG my hand against the counter hard enough to make the set of canisters dance.

Chael is here. I'd be willing to bet on it. And I'd also be willing to bet he has forged some kind of alliance with the skinwalkers. He might already have known I wouldn't be granted an audience with the shaman. Getting rid of me with the bone charm would have served his purpose just as well. When that didn't work, he had to fall back on the original plan. Keep me around and hope I'd try to make contact on my own.

He'd know I wouldn't leave a grieving Frey.

Did he arrange the accident? Or did he cause it? It would be easy for him to appear in the path of a speeding car. To startle Sarah into swerving off the road. Without seat belts, the two would have been helpless in the rolling truck.

Did he watch it happen?

Rage rises like bile, harsh and sour in my throat. Something else for Chael to answer for the next time we meet.

But how do I find him? I have no allies here except Frey. George made his feelings about me clear.

Unless Kayani would be willing to help.

I remember the dark intensity of his gaze. I have the feeling he would want to avenge Sarah's death almost as much as I do. But how do I get in touch with him?

And do I tell Frey what I suspect?

I close my eyes and draw in a deep breath. Telling Frey confirms that the blame for Sarah's death rests squarely with me. Do I have the courage to do that? I tried in a very lame way when we were at the corral, but I admit I was relieved when he changed the subject and instead suggested we go inside. Now that I suspect Chael is behind the accident, there's no dancing around the truth.

There's a murmur of soft voices from the living room followed by Frey's appearance at the kitchen. John-John is in his arms, his head resting on Frey's shoulder.

"I think John-John should have something to eat. Will you check the refrigerator?"

I do, afraid to open my mouth for fear of breaking down. There is such a look of sadness on that little boy's face, I can hardly bear it. Wordlessly, I extract the container of pudding I recognized from yesterday and spoon a portion into a bowl I find in a cupboard over the stove. I take it to the table and Frey seats himself, still holding John-John, and tries to coax the boy into taking a few bites.

John-John buries his head in Frey's shoulder, pushing the spoon away. He mumbles something in Navajo and Frey lowers the spoon, his arms tightening around his son.

I've poured a small glass of milk and hold it out to Frey.

At least John-John accepts a few sips of milk before once more turning his face away.

Maybe if I left them alone?

I touch Frey's arm and motion toward the other room. He nods and I take my leave.

I start pacing. I wish now I'd taken a card from Kayani or asked how to contact him. If Chael is staying in the area, especially if he's staying on the reservation, there are not too many places that offer lodging. Chael with his dark Middle Eastern look would not have to worry about keeping a low profile. He'd blend in with the hundreds of tourists who flock to Monument Valley every summer. Perfect camouflage for a vampire intent on keeping an eye on me.

I wander from one end of the living room to another, absently taking in the pictures on the book case, the bits of rocks and feathers scattered here and there on end tables, John-John's toy horses and cars clustered under the coffee table. Touches that make a house a home.

Touches that made this house Sarah's home.

I return to the bookcase. Now I recognize some of the faces in the photos. Kayani with John-John on horseback. An older couple in full Native American garb. Sarah's parents? George with Sarah and Mary standing in front of a Jeep with the name of a tour company on the side.

Maybe that's where I should start.

I look around for an address book or a computer. There is neither in the living room. Should I ask Frey if it would be all right to look in Sarah's bedroom?

It's so quiet in the kitchen, I don't want to interrupt whatever is going on between father and son. I'll take my chances and if Frey gets angry with me for snooping, I'll take my lumps.

Sarah's bedroom is neat—bed made up, closet doors

closed, very little on the vanity except what one might expect—brush, comb, a few items of makeup. There is no desk. No computer in sight. I peek in the closet. Boots and shoes lined up against the back, clothes hung, shelves with carefully folded sweaters and scarves along one wall. The only thing out of place is a wicked-looking crossbow leaning against the back corner. A quiver holds both metal and wooden bolts.

I take a deep breath, close the door, and start opening drawers. Three in the dresser—underwear, jeans, jewelry. I try the nightstand. A Tony Hillerman paperback, a flashlight, a pad of paper and a pen and . . . condoms.

I shut the drawer quickly. That answers one question. Maybe Sarah wasn't in love with Kayani, but she was having sex with him.

No address book. No computer.

I shut the door to Sarah's room quietly behind me. I'm facing Mary's room. That door is open. There is a desk in this room. And a laptop computer. But is it Mary's or Sarah's?

My bet is on Mary. She's home from college . . . I catch myself with a grimace—*was* home from college—and would have wanted to keep in touch with her friends. When I take a closer look, I see it has a mobile web browser. But when I try to connect, there is no service. Too far away from cable or satellite access I guess. Mary must have taken the laptop with her to the lodge when she wanted to go online.

Are her friends wondering why they haven't heard from her? Are they concerned? No. It's too soon for concern. Most likely they assume she's enjoying her summer the way they're enjoying theirs. Who will be the one to break the news that Mary is gone?

I power the laptop down and leave it on the desk.

I open the top middle drawer. The usual array of home-office items. The drawers to the right are a file drawer and one other. It's in that one that I spy a small leather-bound address book.

I carry it with me to the living room and take a seat on the sofa.

Kayani's number is there, as is a number to the lodge. No addresses. I call Kayani's number first. Get an answering machine that has the ubiquitous generic message to leave a number after the beep. Obviously a home rather than work number since no reference is made to the Navajo police. I don't leave a message. When I call the lodge, I'm connected with an operator. I ask for the address and directions to the lodge, which are cheerfully given.

I sort them away in my head.

It looks like I'll be going after Chael first.

It's still quiet in the kitchen. I have Frey's keys but don't want to leave without letting him know. I swap the address book for a piece of paper and pen from the desk and scribble a hasty note. When I tiptoe into the kitchen, I find Frey and John-John both asleep at the table. I leave the note, kiss the top of Frey's head and tiptoe back out.

Frey's Jeep has everything, including a GPS system. The operator was kind enough to provide latitude and longitude and I plug it in: N 37 00 39 W 110 12.116.

I have no clue what it means, but the Jeep does. In less than a minute, I'm on my way.

I haven't gone more than a couple of miles before I pass another vehicle headed toward Sarah's. Through the driver's side window, I see gray hair and a pinched, hollow-cheeked profile. It's just a quick glance and the driver doesn't look over at me even though we're the only two cars on a deserted stretch of desert. But I'm pretty sure I recognize him from one of the pictures on Sarah's bookcase.

Sarah and Mary's father.

For a moment I wonder if I should go back. Then reason takes over. If he recognized what I was, it would be that much harder on Frey. Better to let them have this time alone.

Finding Chael and getting him out of our lives is more important than anything else.

My jaws ache with anticipation. I will take great pleasure in killing him.

CHAPTER 27

G OULDING'S LODGE IS LOCATED ABOUT TWENTY miles from U.S. 163. Not built exactly the way I would have imagined—nothing rustic here though its modern sand-colored stucco and red-tile roof do blend in against the backdrop of steep red cliffs. It's only eight and already the parking lot is full of cars, RVs and campers. Now that I'm here, I wonder how I'll find Chael. I doubt he's registered under his name.

There is one way.

A light mist is still falling, but it doesn't seem to be discouraging visitors from flocking to the lodge. I make my way past a motel, museum and gift shop to follow the crowd to the lobby. I find an out of the way corner and close my eyes.

I cloak my own thoughts while opening the conduit that will permit me to pick up on the unguarded thoughts of other supernaturals.

At first, I don't sense anything. The drone of mortal

voices makes it hard to concentrate. I try harder, filtering out ambient noise and the high-pitched wail of an unhappy baby. Then I get a psychic hit.

A voice from the far corner of the lobby. Then another. I make my way over, stand a few feet away and watch.

But it's not Chael. It's a family of shape-shifters. Two adults and a petulant teenage daughter. From Minnesota. They're arguing because the girl wants to call her boyfriend and her mother tells her there isn't time before the tour.

You're just saying that because you don't like Jack, the girl whines.

You're right, her mother snaps back. *I don't. He's a werewolf and can't be trusted.*

Shit. I tune out. Retreat back a few steps and try again. Chael has to be here. There aren't that many places to stay on the reservation. He would want to be close enough to enjoy the havoc he's created, to taste the pain.

"Anna Strong? What are you doing?"

The voice makes me jump—not only because it comes right at my elbow but because I was concentrating so hard on picking things out of the air, I didn't sense the physical approach of this very real human.

"Officer Kayani. You startled me."

He narrows his eyes. "What were you doing?"

How do I explain? "Just—people watching."

"With your eyes closed?"

Now would be a good time to change the subject. "You're in civilian clothes. Off duty?"

"Just. Stopped by for a cup of coffee before heading home. Care to join me?"

I nod and he motions me toward glass doors at the back of the lobby. I let him lead the way, still keeping the vampire radar on alert for a ping of recognition. All I get though is another nasal round of squabbling from the shape-shifters.

I give up with a sigh and turn my attention to Kayani. He's changed into tan chinos and a long-sleeved black shirt, untucked, and on his feet he's wearing leather sandals. He asks what I'd like. I order coffee, black, and when he's been handed the cups, he leads the way once again to a long deck spanning the length of the lodge.

It's not very crowded; the rain keeps most of the tourists inside. But the view from the deck is astounding. It's a panorama of ragged rock formations stretching unbroken for miles. Once again I feel the tug of immortality, a sense that I belong here. I cross the deck to stand by the railing, drawn by a force I don't understand.

Kayani joins me. "Wouldn't you rather sit in the back? Out of the rain."

Reluctantly, I nod and pull myself away. There is a sheltered area with a dozen café tables and chairs and Kayani picks one. We sit, but my eyes keep drifting back to the view.

"First time here?"

"Is it that obvious?"

Kayani smiles. "There is no place like this on earth. It has been inhabited by indigenous people since the beginning of time. A holy place. At least until silver was discovered in the 1800s. Then we Navajo were rounded up and driven out. It wasn't until the mid-1800s that we were allowed to return and 1884 before it was declared officially the Navajo's. This is our land by right, and we will never be driven out again."

He speaks as if I might be planning to make an attempt at it. "Those days are over."

He gives me a look that might be put into the "are you really that naive?" classification—brows lowered, lips drawn back into a frown.

Is he this touchy with all the tourists? Or is it because of my connection to Frey.

Regardless, I don't jump to the bait. Instead I sip coffee and let my gaze linger on the countryside, all the while deciding how best to broach the subject I intended to when I set out this morning. I don't know any way to do it but to speak directly. He'll respond one way or the other—be receptive and stay or get angry and leave.

I place the cup on the table, lace my hands together and lean in toward him. "I'm sorry for your loss. I know you and Sarah were close."

No response. No tightening of the shoulders or jaws. No sharp intake of breath. Is this stone face because he's Navajo or because he's a cop?

"The way you and John-John greeted each other made me suspect. And George confirmed it. I want you to know Frey was no threat to you and Sarah. He came here to see his son. That's all."

Kayani is watching me more closely now. Still, he lets nothing of his own feeling show. I wish I could penetrate his thoughts, figure out the best way to proceed. I can't. So I fumble onward.

"There was a second reason we came. Had nothing to do with Frey and everything to do with me. Sarah was speaking on my behalf before the council. You may already know it."

Finally, a response, a tiny nod of the head. I take that to mean "go on."

Now we tred on dangerous ground. Do I tell Kayani what I am? Will he react like George? Maybe I won't have to admit the whole truth right now. I gather my thoughts, continue slowly.

"Frey is a Keeper of the Secrets. I assume you know that. He is a friend of mine who has helped me through some trying times. I asked him about Sani. He told me where I could find him. Here."

Kayani's eyes flicker. "How do you know about Sani? The shaman's identity is a well-kept secret among the *Dine'é*."

"I respect that. That he was here and what he can do was passed on to me by someone else. I don't know how this person came to know of him."

He isn't pleased with the answer. A scowl darkens his face. "Who else knew that you were looking for Sani?"

"George, no one else." Chael, too, but I can't open that can of worms until I'm ready to admit what I am.

"And he didn't try to talk Sarah out of making the request?"

Knowing how George feels about me, I can imagine he probably did. But since I don't know for sure, I shake my head. "I'm not sure. We didn't discuss it."

"Why would you seek Sani?"

The question I've been dreading. I stall a moment by drawing in a breath and letting it out slowly. The act does nothing to make framing a response easier. "I have a personal reason to seek his council." Ambiguous.

Unsuccessful.

Kayani shifts irritably. "Did you lose someone close to you?"

I should have known he would not accept such a vague response. I know I sure as hell wouldn't. But before I can reply, Kayani adds, "Because if that's the reason you came, you could have saved yourself a trip. Sani does not use his magic to reverse death on a whim. If he did—"

He lets his voice drop and for the first time, a spark of emotion flares through. It's easy to finish his sentence. If Sani reversed death just because he was asked to, Kayani would have already petitioned for Sarah's life to be restored. Wanting something, no matter how badly, is not enough.

It strikes me that Kayani really has no idea that I'm vampire. He's never touched me, even to shake hands, so he's not experienced the marble coldness of my skin. Outwardly, unless I show my vampire face, I look human. A little thin, perhaps, with an unlined face that may make me look younger than my thirty years, but human.

"Have you spoken to George at all?"

Kayani draws himself up, his stoic mask back in place. "No. I expect I'll talk to him later today."

Now I have to decide. I have no doubt George will tell Kayani about me. Would it be better to do it myself now and take my chances?

Kayani drains his cup. "I have to go."

"You can't stay a little longer? I have something to talk with you about."

"No." He rises and crushes the cup in his hand. "I need to prepare. We are burying Sarah this afternoon."

"This afternoon? I thought burial was to be in four days."

"Sarah's parents fear there is black magic at work. They want to bury their daughters today before a curse can be laid." He frowns down at me. "I thought that's why you were here. Frey sent you away until it was over."

Kayani's words stab at me. The man I passed on the way here. Sarah's father come to tell Frey of their plans.

I rise, too, trying to control the uneasiness overwhelming me. If Kayani is right in his assumption, I have to get back to Frey. Because in my gut I know. I remember the expression on the old man's face as he passed me.

Frey is facing Sarah's hostile parent. Alone.

What did Frey say? In their eyes, he deserted Sarah and her son. He'll need support. I should be there.

Kayani and I walk out together, though I'm barely able to restrain the instinct to break and run to the Jeep. I manage to keep the alarm out of my voice long enough to ask, "Will John-John take part in his mother's burial?"

He shakes his head. "No. He will stay with George at the house. It will be a traditional burial. Only Frey, Sarah's parents and I will tend to Sarah and her sister. After, we will come back to the house."

Kayani is parked in a space marked "Police Use." He's still driving the SUV I saw this morning. Rain is coming down harder now. It soaks our clothes and beads in our hair. He glances toward the sky. "Would you like a ride to your vehicle?"

"No. Thank you. I'm not far."

His eyes are still on the sky. "It is a sad day. Even the heavens weep."

CHAPTER 28

I AM STARTLED BY THE SORROW IN HIS EYES. THAT HE
loved Sarah is no longer conjecture. I don't know how
long they had been seeing each other, but I hope she returned his feelings. Maybe it will offer some consolation in
the dark days ahead.

He pulls out of the lot and I sprint to the Jeep, reverse
the course on the GPS and start back.

Why didn't Frey call me when Sarah's parents showed
up to tell me about the burial?

And why did Kayani said he figured Frey sent me away?

I don't like the idea of George being alone with John-
John. It took me about thirty minutes to make it to the
lodge from the house. The only consolation I have is that if
Kayani is just now on his way, too, we should arrive together. I should make it in time to accompany Frey.

I catch up to Kayani quickly. I can see him checking out
the Jeep in his rearview mirror and when he recognizes
me, he signals and pulls over. I do, too.

He strides back to the Jeep. "What are you doing?"

"I'm going back to the house. I want to go with Frey to Sarah's funeral."

He scowls down at me. "It's not a funeral. You are an outsider. Why do you think Frey sent you away?"

I bristle at his tone. "He didn't send me away. I came to the lodge on my own. I wanted to give him time alone with John-John."

"Well, you need to give us all time. You cannot be a part of what is to take place. You could cause irreparable harm. To Frey. To Sarah's parents."

"I respect the idea that the Navajo have customs to honor their dead. I can't see how my observing those customs can lead to harm."

Kayani places both hands on the door of the Jeep and leans toward me. "Listen, Ms. Strong. Sarah's parents are very traditional. They will not have mentioned either of their daughter's names since the accident. Do you want to know why? Because they believe after death, the good part of a person goes on while the bad part stays here as a ghost. Mentioning the name of a dead person calls the ghost. Such a simple thing. But were you to offer condolences, for instance, and in doing so, mention the girls' names, you will have violated a taboo. Do you want that on your conscience?"

He is so serious, so vehement in his argument that I back down. He is right. I have no idea of the intricacies of such long-held beliefs. I would only be a burden on Frey and if I did something wrong, cast a bad reflection on him in a delicate time.

"All right. I'll go back to the lodge. But you have to keep an eye on Frey for me. Make sure no harm comes to him."

Kayani's brow furrows at the request. "What harm could come to him? He has studied the Navajo way."

"Just tell me you will. And on George, too."

His puzzled frown deepens. "I don't understand."

"And if you have time for an explanation, I'll give it to you. If not, please honor *my* request."

He straightens and backs away from the Jeep. "I will." His tone is clipped, formal. "But later, when this day is over, I will come to you for answers."

He waits for my nod of acceptance and leaves me. If George tells him that I'm vampire, he'll no doubt come back armed with Sarah's crossbow and a wooden arrow. A chance I'll have to take.

I watch until the SUV disappears around a bluff, leaving a trail in the muddy red earth. I have two choices.

Forget all I told Kayani and go to the house anyway.

Head back for the lodge and try to locate Chael.

I look around as if divine inspiration might spring from the mighty rain-streaked formations and soaked earth surrounding me. It's Kayani, however, his face, his tone, his willingness to allow parents a chance to grieve in their own way that influences the decision. Another might find such customs archaic. Kayani is a modern cop in an ancient land but he accepts and honors both worlds.

It's a balancing act I understand very well.

It seems the decision has been made. I do a U-turn and head back the way I came. Trying to track Chael down through a psychic connection wasn't very successful. What if I try a simple human way?

Once more in the lobby, I shake rain out of my hair and go directly to the registration desk. A pretty Native American girl greets me with a sunny smile. "Can I help you?"

My turn to put on a perky face. "I hope so. Last night at dinner I thought I saw someone I knew from my college days at UA. He was a foreign student from the Middle East.

I know it's probably my imagination, but if it was Chael, I'd love to say hello. It would be such a happy coincidence is we ran into each other here after all those years. Is it possible for you to check and see if he's registered?"

"Of course. What was the name?"

"Chael. I'm sorry but I don't remember if that was his first or last name. It's spelled C-h-a-e-l."

"No problem. The computer can check both."

Her fingers fly over the keyboard with practiced aplomb. After a few moments, she shakes her head. "I'm sorry. No one on file with that first or last name. Could he be registered with someone else?"

Of course he could. "Try Judith Williams from San Diego. I remember they were great friends."

The fingers do their tap dance once again. This time I'm rewarded with a smile. "Yes, Ms. Williams is registered." She picks up a desk phone. "Would you like me to ring the room?"

"That would ruin the surprise," I reply. "I'll just hang out in the lobby for a while and watch for them." I dig in my pocket for some cash and hand her a five. "Thanks so much for your help."

She accepts the bill. "You are very welcome. If I can do anything else—"

I make my smiling escape, hitting the gift shop first to pick up the *Arizona Highways* magazine before retreating to a strategic spot where I can keep an eye on both the stairs and the elevator. This damn rain may mean they keep to their room. No need to come to the dining room when you don't eat like a human.

Two hours of boredom produce nothing but a sore butt. I relinquish my spot on the couch and pace up and down, stretching leg muscles unused to sitting for such a long period. Reminds me of hours of surveillance with David and that we haven't had to do it in quite some time. Mainly because our new partner has connections to both police departments and bail bondsmen in the Southern California area. Thanks to Tracey, these days jobs find us.

I wonder if I should check in. I've only been gone two days. If David needed me, I'm sure he'd have called. And with Judith Williams here, he's most likely staying out of trouble.

I'm circling back to resume my perch on the couch when a group of four urban-chic bikers arrive in the lobby and make their way to the elevator. They're dressed in form-fitting leathers, talk quietly as if conscious not to attract too much attention, and all have scarves tied loosely around their necks. When one of them, a young woman with long blond hair, slips out of her jacket, her scarf falls to the floor.

She bends to retrieve it.

There are faint bruises just below her right ear, bite marks not quite healed.

I smile as she scrambles to cover them up, looking around to see if anyone noticed.

Oh yeah, chickie.

I noticed.

Chael and Judith sent for takeout.

I toss the magazine onto the stack in the middle of the coffee table and watch them into the elevator. There are only two floors in the lodge. I'm at the stairs and up to the second level before the elevator doors slide open.

The group makes their way down the long hallway. I hang back and watch. They knock at a door near the end. When they've been let inside, I walk down myself and check it out.

Room 230.

It's quiet in the hallway, but too public to risk getting caught with my ear to the door. I move down a few doors and aim vampire hearing into the room. But Chael and Judith are being careful. Nothing comes through. All I get are the soft murmurs of their hosts' voices and the vigorous creak of bedsprings as the people next door in 232 engage in energetic sex.

Well. At least I know where to find Chael. Bursting in now would accomplish nothing except to jeopardize the lives of the hosts.

I glance at my watch. I've been here almost four hours. Would it be safe to return to Sarah's? How long would the burial ceremony last? I should have thought to ask Kayani. I dig my cell phone out of my jacket. I'll call Frey. If he's still with Sarah's parents, I'm sure it will go straight to voice mail.

It does. He's turned it off. I leave a very brief "call me when you can" message and end the call.

A whiff of coppery scent drifts up from beneath the door to 230. Faint but potent as a memory and easily distinguishable to a vampire.

Blood.

It produces a restless surge of adrenaline.

Chael and Judith have started to dine.

CHAPTER 29

T HE BLOOD PULL IS TOO STRONG. I MAKE FOR THE
stairway and retreat downstairs to the lobby. I'll wait
for the hosts to leave before confronting Chael and Judith.

My place on the couch is occupied by a family waiting
for the rain to stop before venturing out. I get a cup of coffee from the coffee bar and find another seat—one with a
partially obstructed view of the elevators but one that will
have to do.

What will I say to Chael? There is no defense he can
offer that would justify his senseless killing of Sarah and
her sister. Especially if it was done just to keep me here.

I don't know what will happen in the next few days. I
suppose it will depend on what Frey decides is best for his
son. He may even choose to stay on the reservation with
John-John. After all, this is the only home the boy has ever
known. The only thing I'm sure of is that he needs to be
with John-John now.

A conclusion I'm sure he's come to himself.

So where does that leave me?

A sense of weariness and despair darkens my thoughts. If I go back to San Diego alone, I go minus one of the constants in my life. Daniel Frey has been with me since the beginning. Besides Culebra, he is the only supernatural I consider a friend.

Worse, the trip will have been for nothing. I would have been the cause of two deaths without being given the opportunity to have my questions answered. Perhaps that's my punishment for coming here with a selfish agenda. I didn't want merely to ask for mortality back, I wanted the shaman to assure me it was the right decision. To answer the how and why of being chosen.

As if life ever grants assurances.

Coffee cup drained, I toss it in the nearest waste receptacle.

I hate this feeling of hopelessness. It's not my nature. I'm much more comfortable with anger. Anger leads to action. Did I always feel that way? I was human much longer than I've been vampire, but the memories of how I felt as a human grow dimmer every day.

Is that a good thing?

The elevator pings open and the four urban-chic bikers step into the lobby. They're a little paler, walk a little slower, leaving a scent of blood and sex in their wake. But they have satisfied smiles on their faces.

I glance at my watch. Two hours. A lot of sex. A lot of blood.

Still they're luckier than many of Judith Williams' hosts. She has a tendency to drain her hosts dry, leaving a disposal problem. Chael must have cautioned her to exercise restraint.

Or threatened to kill her if she didn't.

I wait until they've left the lobby to retrace their steps to Room 230. There is a maid at the door, a housekeeping cart parked to the side. The maid knocks, announces herself, uses her passkey to let herself in when there's no answer.

Curious, I wander down to stand beside the door. The maid is stripping the bed.

"Excuse me?" I point to the bed. "Where is the couple who occupied this room?"

The maid eyes me suspiciously. "Why do you want to know?"

"We had a lunch date. They didn't show. I was concerned something might be wrong."

"Can't help you," she replies, approaching the door with an armful of sheets. "All I know is that a few minutes ago, I got a message that the occupants of this room have checked out."

She dumps the sheets into the hamper and pushes the cart into the room, shutting the door behind her with a decisive click. I'm left in the hall staring at a stupid door and wondering how the hell Chael and Williams managed to get by me.

And where they'd go from here.

I can't believe while I was feeling sorry for myself, Chael managed to slip past me. Had he seen me in the lodge? Maybe when I was having coffee with Kayani? Did he watch me leave with him? Think he was safe to take his time with the hosts?

But how then did he manage to get out while I was sitting in the lobby?

The answers are so simple, I want to thump myself in the head for letting him get away with it. Once he spotted me, he may have asked the receptionist if anyone had asked for him. There was no reason for her to lie. He probably

had the hosts stay in the room while he and his bitch girlfriend slipped out. Told them to wait before leaving. Then
he and Judith took the stairs and made their getaway out
the back.

I fell for it.

Stupid, stupid, stupid.

I don't have a clue where to start looking for them.
They've got to be close. Chael would not miss a chance to
observe the suffering he's wreaked upon my friend and the
consequent pain he's inflicted on me. Otherwise, what
would be the point?

I can't think of a single thing to do now but to go back
to the house. Frey is more familiar with the area than I am.
If there's another lodge or hotel around, he'll know.

On the way back to the Jeep, questions keep popping
into my head.

What if Sarah's parents are still there?

I won't go in. At the sight of their car, I'll park where I
can keep an eye on the house.

I worry at my lower lip. I wonder if Kayani spoke with
George? That one still gives me a bad feeling. The sooner I
tell Frey about George's parting shot to me this morning,
the better. I don't expect Frey to change his mind about
someone he's known longer than me, but he's got to respect
my gut instinct.

It's gotten us out of some hairy situations before.

What happened at the burial today? Frey must be a
wreck. Not only because of John-John, but because he's
surrounded by people who are unlikely to show him much
compassion. Even Kayani must be feeling resentment.

The sky has begun to clear—clouds breaking over
Monument Valley in a patchwork of bright blue and gray.
With the clearing sky, the August heat comes roaring back,

turning scattered pools of runoff into steaming cauldrons of bloodred mud. Vapor rises from the ground in streams like the delicate trains of ghostly gowns.

Even I feel the abrupt temperature change—one moment rain-cooled sixties, the next blast-furnace heat sends people scurrying for icy drinks and sun hats. There's a cavalcade of cars leaving the parking lot to resume day trips interrupted by the summer storm.

I fold back the Jeep's top, already dry by the time I get to the parking space, and tuck it into the boot. One of the advantages of a vampire constitution is the ability to tolerate—even enjoy—temperatures most humans find intolerable. Heat, for instance. The illusion that my body is warm comes only when ambient temperatures near 100— or when I'm feeding or having sex.

I close my eyes, tilt my head back, wait for the first rush of cars out of lot.

For a couple of minutes I take what pleasure I can.

CHAPTER 30

T HE GPS STILL HAS RETURN COORDINATES PRO-
grammed, although when I crank over the engine, I
get the "reprogramming route" message. I hate the tone of
these things—it manages to be mechanical yet condescending at the same time. All systems have it. Some frus-
trated engineer's idea of a joke, I suppose.

The Jeep sloshes through mud and standing puddles as
I make my way out of the parking lot. If it's this bad on a
paved surface, I can only imagine what I'm going to hit
once I get off road.

I find out soon enough.

Once I'm directed to leave the road and head into private land, things get dicey. Hard dirt is now the consistency
of taffy. Sticky fingers pull and suck at the tires, slowing
the Jeep to a crawl. At this rate, I won't make it back to the
house until after dark.

When I get tired of fighting a stubborn steering system
intent on taking the path of least resistance instead of the

direction I need to go, I pull off in the shade of a towering monolith. Waves of heat and gusts of dry desert air scorch the landscape. May as well wait for Mother Nature's blow-dryer to turn the muck back into hardpan.

From where I've parked the Jeep, I see a faint path that snakes around the base of the massive rock under which I've sought shelter. I'm not exactly wearing hiking shoes, but after a day of tedious couch sitting, a walk is a welcome distraction.

I jump down from the Jeep into a puddle of mud, but I've stepped in worse. I shake off as much gunk as I can and glance at my watch. I'll give myself fifteen minutes before getting back on the road.

The path is barely worn but maybe because of the rain, now clearly visible. When I pulled up, I thought I was parked under a single block of towering stone, but I see now it's not solid at all. The path soon takes me into a honey-comb of caves. It's dark and cool inside and smells of freshly turned earth. Filtered light shines in from shafts that allow a glimpse of sky—like fireplace chimneys with open dampers. It's weird and wonderful at the same time.

And it's dry.

I trudge deeper into the catacombs. There is a feeling that I am the first person to have come this way, though I know how unlikely that is. Still, none of the detritus of civilization litters the ground. No broken bottles or soiled diapers. No fast-food containers or cigarette butts. Frey said the Navajo have a respect for the land. Perhaps they take the trouble to police their sacred lands or perhaps those who come here understand what a special place it is.

I've reached a fork in the trail; two paths stretch in op-posite directions. It's darker at this point, but when natural light fades, vampire vision kicks in. I know I've already gone past the spelunking time I allotted myself, but curiosity tempts me to go on.

The question is which way?

I pick up a small, flat rock, scratch one side with a fingernail. Heads I go right, tails left. Flip it into the air, watch it bounce to a halt. The unmarked side seems to gaze back at me impassively.

Left it is.

The air is surprisingly fresh. I calculate I've traveled maybe a half mile into the mountain. The walls of the caves are smooth and warm to the touch. I imagine I hear a pulse beat, faint but distinct. I know I must imagine it because stone has no heart, a mountain no life or spiritual center. Still, a sound like a distant drumbeat echoes in my head.

I put out a hand, touch the stone, as if seeking an anchor in the void. I look around, testing the air with my tongue, breathing in to detect the scent of any other living creature who might be responsible for the sound.

I pick up nothing. Nothing animal, nothing human.

Not even the briny smell of lichen from a dripping pool somewhere out of sight.

Still, the beat is there.

Part of me is unnerved by it, part of me drawn to discover the source. I keep one hand on the stone and move forward. The darkness is complete here, my eyes picking up only the faint glitter of a vein of quartz sparked by my own heightened optic nerves. I trace it with a finger, to mark my path forward. It goes on and on and finally, I stop and drop my hand.

This is useless. The pulse is neither closer nor farther away. I'll ask Frey when I get back. There's bound to be a natural explanation.

I turn, looking to the opposite wall.

Drawings, carved into the sandstone. Animals with round bodies and long, pointed antlers. Others smaller, slimmer, with blunted antlers and cloven hooves. Some kind of bird, wings outstretched to catch the wind. And warriors. With mantles of fur and spears with arrowhead tips.

My own heart jumps, my throat swells. The drawings are so primitive, so beautiful. How long have they been here? How many generations of Navajo come to pay homage to their ancestors in the confines of this sacred place?

A rumble and a gust of cold wind hit simultaneously. The ground under my feet shifts, sending me back against the rocks. I land hard, fight to regain balance. A section of the cave wall straight ahead is opening. Wind whistles around stone, loose rock is kicked as footsteps rustle forward.

I push myself back against the wall of the cave. Someone is coming. The path is too narrow for them not to see me when they pass. So I do what any good vampire would do. I scurry up the wall of the cave and look down at them from the viewpoint of a lizard.

Then they file under me, three men. Two younger, dressed in long buckskin robes, a third, ancient and wizened moving between them. He is dressed in a robe, too, adorned with embroidered symbols, and in his hand, he carries a slender rod.

Suddenly, the old one stops.

And looks up.

Right at me.

His eyes flash in the darkness of the cave. "You have come to seek my council, Anna Strong," he says. "Come down. Join me."

He moves toward the opening in the cave wall, not waiting to see if I follow or not. The two others don't even glance my way.

How did he know where I was? How did he know *who* I was?

I'm so startled, my slide down from the perch is far less graceful than my scramble up.

CHAPTER 31

A S SOON AS I ENTER THE CHAMBER, THE DRUM-beat stops. The elder sits cross-legged on a blanket. The two younger men who preceded him have disappeared. The walls of the chamber look solid and yet the men are gone.

The elder motions for me to sit. I take a place across from him and fold my legs under me. He studies me for a long moment as I do him. His face is bronzed and lined with age. His body is shriveled yet his back is straight, his posture erect.

His eyes catch and hold my gaze. There is so much wisdom reflected in those great, dark eyes that I can't look away—I don't want to.

At last, I find my voice. "You are Sani."

He nods.

"How did you know you would find me here?"

"You found me, did you not?" There is a hint of humor in the deep rumble of his voice. "You are the visitor."

"But I was told you wouldn't see me. That the Navajo fear death above all else. I am the walking dead. I did not believe you would see me."

"I am here now." Sani reaches out a hand and touches my cheek. "You have a question."

His touch sends warmth rushing through me. I want to press that hand against my cheek and hold it there. Instead, I force myself to remain still, hoping if I do, his gentle fingers will remain against my skin.

After a moment, he drops his hand.

The warmth remains, giving me the courage to speak. "I am vampire. I come to seek your counsel. I am told you can restore mortal life to the undead."

"And that is what you wish?"

"Yes. No. I am conflicted. I have a family. A human family. When they are gone, I will be alone in this world. I fear loneliness."

"And yet you are conflicted."

"I am called the Chosen One. Destined to resist dark forces in the vampire community that seek to dominate mankind. If I relinquish that responsibility, I risk subjecting mankind to a terrible end. I don't know why I was chosen to shoulder that burden. I don't know if I'm strong enough to handle it. But as a vampire, I know I have a chance. As a human, I fear I have none."

Sani listens, his expressive eyes seem to penetrate through word and thought and reach into my soul. His face is beautiful in its serenity. I am breathless waiting for him to speak.

"You have a good heart," he says finally. "The heart of a warrior. It is why we meet here. You want to return to the life you knew before. And yet, you are more powerful as vampire and can prevent great evil."

He lifts my chin with gentle fingers to look into my eyes. "You fear the loneliness you will suffer when your family passes on and you are left behind. But is that not the fate of all who are chosen to lead? Perhaps loneliness is the price one must pay for the opportunity to do great deeds."

I am caught in the cadence of his speech, spellbound by the light in his eyes. Even the rhythm of my heartbeat seems to slow in anticipation of his next words.

"Throughout the ages, there have been those given a higher calling. Brave men and women forced to face their fears, to sacrifice their happiness, to choose the greater good over personal desires. You are at a crossroads, Anna. If you choose to return to mortality, can you accept the consequences? Could you live with the consequences?"

I squeeze my eyes shut. I know what he's saying. Can I accept it? Still, there is something else, something darker I need to tell him. "There is another thing I fear. Vampire becomes stronger every day. She senses evil and seeks to destroy it. Sometimes I can control the impulse to kill, sometimes I don't want to." I let my voice drop, ashamed to admit the truth. "Killing has become too easy. Human or otherwise, it doesn't matter."

"You are too critical of yourself," Sani says, brushing the air with a hand. "You have a strong sense of what is right and what is wrong. Trust your instincts." He bends his head closer. "What you must not do is make a hasty decision. You mustn't let emotions overwhelm you."

He sits back, his eyes flashing in the dim light. "But there is something more to consider. There is a steep price to pay if you choose mortality. Your body went through changes when you became vampire. The stress on your organs by the reverse transformation is more severe. You could expect to live no longer than twenty years in a continual state of decline. You will not reach old age. Are you willing to bear that cost as well?"

He gathers his robe around him. "I want you to think hard about what you ask of me. You have many things on your mind now. Your friend needs you. Deal with what you must. Later, when you have had time to reflect, look for the wolf. She will reunite us."

There is a sound behind me and the two robed Navajo who accompanied Sani into the chamber suddenly return. They help him to his feet.

"Go in peace, Anna," Sani says. "We will meet again."

Before I have risen to my feet, he is gone.

I run back to the cave entrance, faster than most animals, a hundred times faster than men, and wait to say my farewell.

I neither passed Sani and his companions on the path nor do they appear at the entrance. Did they take the opposite fork? How were they able to get out without my seeing?

Could what happened have been an illusion?

I stare up at the sky, now bluer than blue, and breathe in the sun-soaked air.

No. I carry Sani's words with me. I feel them like a warm glow in my heart.

I have a decision to make.

But not this minute.

Sani is right.

Frey's face floats to the surface of my thoughts. He's waiting for me at Sarah's home. A friend in need of solace, a child in need of comfort.

This time when I head out, the Jeep has a much easier time of it. The ground no longer feels the need to trap it but cooperates with the crunch of grit under tires that gradually lose their casing of mud.

Sani's work?

Wind still sputters, raising dust devils that whip ahead then fall behind. This afternoon there are many sounds. Birds screeching, fluttering overhead. Predator and prey scurrying behind rocks. The lone bay of a dog.

But there is something missing.

I no longer hear the distant heartbeat of the mountain.

CHAPTER 32

AS DIFFICULT AS IT IS TO GET SANI'S WORDS OUT of my head, his face out of my mind, I focus on Frey as I near the house. I park a quarter of a mile away, beside scrub brush that hides the Jeep from prying eyes. Then I jog closer.

No cars. Not the one I passed with the elderly couple, not Kayani's police SUV. I don't see the van George was driving yesterday, either, so it looks everyone has gone.

Still, I approach cautiously, intending to peek into the window just to be sure the coast is clear.

"I wondered when you'd come back."

Frey's voice from the corner of the porch. In the dusk, I didn't see him shrouded in shadow sitting on the chair Mary occupied when we had our talk. Seems a long time ago now.

I take a seat beside him. His face is drawn, eyes downcast. I detect a whiff of sage and smoke emanating from his clothes. There's a smudge of something dark—ashes maybe—on his right cheek.

For a few moments neither of us speaks. The grief is his and I won't intrude. Nothing I have to say will do anything more than add to the ache he must be feeling.

When at last he breaks the silence, his voice is thick, as if sadness has swelled his throat making speech difficult.

"Kayani said he saw you at the lodge."

I nod.

"He left to find you after—*it* was over. He called a while ago to say you were gone."

Should I tell him of meeting Sani? No. It is Frey's time to talk. I smother the spark of anxiety that flares when I think of what Kayani wished to speak—or confront—me about. Letting only curiosity come through, I ask, "Did he say what he wanted?"

Frey's eyes flash, anger surfacing, the cat close. "Why would you tell him to watch me? To watch George? Why did you go to the lodge in the first place? Who were you looking for?"

I close my eyes, breathe in, search for the strength to tell Frey what I suspect.

When I start to speak, I feel Frey go still and quiet. His eyes bore into me, the concentration of a feline deciding whether the creature he's studying is predator or prey.

It makes the vampire, too, spring to alert. Still, I manage to keep my voice steady, human, and I tell him all. Who I suspect is responsible for the deaths of the sisters, why I believe it, that Chael is here in Monument Valley.

I finish with my suspicions about George, the things he said to me this morning, his anger because I caused Sarah's death. "He thinks she died because of what happened at the council. He wants you to *put an end to me.* His words. I believe he's the one who shot me. He thinks I stand between you and staying here with John-John on the reservation."

Frey stands, moves abruptly to the porch railing; his hands grip the banister. "You told Kayani all this?"

"Of course not. Seeing how Sarah and George reacted to my being vampire, do you think I'd risk it? If he and George talked, though, George may have."

Frey shakes his head. "I don't think they were alone together." He turns to face me, crosses his arms across his chest. "Chael is here? You're sure of it?"

"Yes. Though no longer at the lodge. My mistake." I fill in the details. "I underestimated him. Stupid. I thought maybe you'd know where they might go. Another hotel or lodge in the vicinity?"

"There are a couple of possibilities. I'll check them out tomorrow."

"*You'll* check them out? You don't even know what he looks like."

"But I do know what Judith Williams looks like."

"No, Frey." I jump to his side. "She might recognize you. It's too dangerous."

The pulse in Frey's neck throbs as he clenches his jaw. "No. She won't see me. I'll make sure of that."

"At least let me go with you."

"No. You have to stay with John-John. He likes you. He needs to have a woman near him. It's what he's used to."

That's not the reason he wants me to stay. At least not all of it. "I know what you're thinking but you can't take him on by yourself. He's too old and too powerful. And with Judith on his side, it's two to one. John-John can't lose a father, too."

Frey's anger explodes with a sound half animal, half human. A primal snarl from the panther. "He is responsible for Sarah's death."

I grit my teeth, match his anger with my own. "*I'm*

responsible for Sarah's death." The words linger on the quiet night air, a release of guilt and acknowledgment that's been building inside since we first heard of the *accident*. "Me. I brought this nightmare to you. I won't let you risk your life. I'll stop you. You know I can."

Frey's eyes—the panther's eyes—glow yellow in the dark. "You could try. But I have more to lose than you do. Protecting one's young is a powerful motivator. It makes one stronger, more determined, than simple anger. Or guilt."

He's captured me by the fierceness of his gaze, holds me in a grip of determination and will. He's done this before, when I was newly turned. I thought it was a mind trick. But we have no psychic connection now and I feel as powerless as I did then.

Until I marshal my own strength and fling it back at him.

"Stop it, Frey. Please."

His eyes lose their intenseness, his hold wavers, falls away. He looks ashamed, embarrassed.

I touch his cheek. "I know what you are feeling. But you must let me help."

He shakes his head. "You are my friend, Anna. I respect you more than anyone I've ever known. But you are stubborn. You see your way as the only way. It's your turn to trust me. If you value our friendship at all, you have to trust I know what I'm doing."

"You don't know Chael." I whisper the words.

He passes a hand over his face. When he looks up at me, his eyes are human, full of acceptance and sadness. "Then you will prepare me—tell me all you know about him."

My heart is heavy. I sink back into the chair, collect my thoughts. I remember what happened the first time I met Chael. It was at the gathering that proclaimed me the Chosen One. Frey remains standing at the rail, calm, patient. Waiting for me to begin.

I look into his eyes. "He is a coward," I begin. "And that makes him very dangerous. He will not fight you. Not at first. It's why he has Judith Williams with him. She is a rogue and foolhardy. You must kill her the moment you see her. It's the only way. There may be others, too. If you give me time, I might—"

An abrupt brush of the hand sweeps aside that notion. "Go on."

I don't know what else to tell him. "He is old. He is powerful. He is arrogant. You must catch him unaware. Do not try to extract a confession or engage in a debate. He will choose a vulnerable moment and attack. And he will kill you."

A thought surfaces, an echo of something that came to mind this morning. "Do you know how to use a bow and arrow?"

I do not have to explain; awareness blooms in Frey's eyes. "Yes. Sarah has a crossbow."

"Then use it. Watch for Chael and shoot him the moment you see him. Do it from a safe distance. Aim carefully."

Frey straightens from his slouched position against the porch railing. "Thank you," he says. "Now I think we should we get some sleep. John-John will be up early. I've taken Sarah's room. I moved your things into Mary's."

He doesn't wait for acknowledgment but heads into the house, leaving me staring into the darkness.

Did I tell him enough? Did I tell him too much?

How do you prepare a friend to battle a monster?

CHAPTER 33

IF EITHER OF US GOT ANY SLEEP LAST NIGHT, I'M UN-
aware of it. I could hear Frey pacing in his room the
same way I'm sure he heard me pacing in mine. I didn't
attempt to reach out to him. Everyone prepares for battle in
his own way.

And I had my own battle raging. Deep inside. Sani said
if I chose mortality, I would have only twenty mortal years.
If I were lucky enough to marry, have children, I would
certainly not live to see my grandchildren.

And would any of us survive a vampire uprising? Would
I want to?

It's John-John's sleepy voice and soft footfalls padding
into the kitchen around dawn that draws us out. Frey and I
open our doors at the same time, step into the hall. We're
both wearing the same clothes we had on yesterday. His
still hold that strange aroma. It's not unpleasant—like a
combination of sage and sandalwood. He bobs his head at
me, and I precede him into the kitchen.

John-John has climbed up into his chair at the kitchen table. He looks at us with sad, serious eyes. He holds out his arms to his father and Frey lifts him from the chair, hugging him to his chest.

"Can I fix you something to eat, John-John?" I ask.

He buries his face in his father's shoulder in response. Frey looks toward the refrigerator. "That would be nice, Anna. I think there's a dish in the refrigerator. Sarah's parents brought it for the communal meal last night."

It's the first time he's made reference to her parents or what went on after the burial. This doesn't seem the time to ask for details, though. Instead, I open the refrigerator and withdraw a covered dish. When I peel back the foil, the smell of beans and meat wafts up.

"Can I fix you some, too, Frey?"

He starts to shake his head but I shoot him a warning look. "I'm sure John-John will eat more if you eat with him."

He concedes with a shrug of understanding. "Sure. Fix me a plate."

I spoon two portions onto plates, slip them into the microwave. It's an older model, big and clunky, and it takes me a few minutes to figure out the controls. At last I have the food cooking away.

I join the two at the table. "What would you men like to drink?"

John-John blinks up at me. "You called me a man."

"Well, you are, aren't you?"

He gives a shy smile. "*Amá* used to call me a man."

Frey looks at me over John-John's head. "His mother."

"Well, she was right."

The microwave chimes and I bring the plates to the table. Frey puts John-John in his own chair and they both pick up forks.

"Don't you want to eat?" John-John asks me, all wide-eyed innocence.

Was I ever that young?

I sit down opposite him. "I've already eaten," I tell him. No wide-eyed innocence here.

John-John waits for Frey to take a first bite, then starts in slowly himself. Frey soon is doing nothing more than moving food around his plate, but John-John does manage to eat a fair amount of his. When John-John is finished, I take both plates away before he can notice his father barely touched *his* food.

Frey leans closer to his son. "I have to run an errand this morning. Anna will stay with you. I won't be gone too long. Will you be all right?"

John-John lets no emotion show. "Can I go with you?"

Frey touches his son's shoulder. "Not this time, *Shiye*. I have business to attend to."

"Maybe I could help."

Frey sighs. "Not this time," he says again. He looks over at me. "Anna will play games with you, if you'd like."

I don't miss a beat. "You can show me how to do finger weaving."

A spark of interest. "I could show you how to make a butterfly."

"Deal."

Frey lifts John-John out of his chair. "Okay, then. Go brush your teeth and get dressed. I need to talk to Anna a minute."

John-John heads off for the bedroom. Frey motions me outside and we step onto the porch. Before he starts to speak, he taps the side of his head with a finger. A warning to keep my thoughts cloaked.

"There are two hotels nearby. I'll check them out. I'll call you as soon as I know anything."

"Are you sure you want to do this on your own? I'm scared for you, Frey."

"I have to do this on my own. You, of all people, should understand. My family has been attacked."

I do understand. It's why I'm afraid. "Check in with me. Every hour. Promise?"

John-John joins us and Frey bends down to say his good-bye. John-John has changed into jeans and a T-shirt and scuffed boots. His hair is slicked back.

He's is not projecting his thoughts, nor probing for ours that I can tell. Maybe he's already forgotten that he can. He and his father exchange their good-byes in Navajo and he watches Frey head for the Jeep. I step closer and reach for his hand.

He looks up at me and places his own small palm in my own.

"Before we start the lesson," I say, "we should feed the horses, shouldn't we?"

The Jeep rumbles out of sight. John-John sighs but tugs at my hand, leading me down the steps. I cast a last backward glance.

Come back safely, Frey.

CHAPTER 34

THE HORSES GREET JOHN-JOHN MUCH MORE EA-gerly than they greeted me. He climbs into the corral, petting necks and rumps and getting gentle head bumps that make him smile. I remain outside, safely out of range of those big teeth and restless hooves. After a few minutes he rejoins me and we manage to get the horses fed and fill their water trough with an old-fashioned hand pump before starting back for the house.

"Maybe we can go riding later," John-John says.

"I'd like that, though you'd have to go slow. I've never been on a horse."

His look is one of childish astonishment. "Never? But you're old."

"City girl."

"Oh." He nods with the solemnity of an old soul. "I'd put you on Cochise, then. He's the gentlest."

We climb the porch steps and enter the living room. John-John pauses once in the doorway, looking around and

I wonder if it's his mother that he's looking for. He recovers, squares his shoulders and walks right over to Sarah's loom in the corner. He reaches into a basket beside it and pulls out a skein of yarn. He cuts a length, cuts two, and plops himself on the couch, patting the seat beside him.

"Come on. I'll teach you how to make a butterfly."

I join him, marveling at how composed he is. Even at four, if I'd lost my mother, I'd be an inconsolable mess.

He begins by tying a knot, making the length a loop. He starts it like a cat's cradle. His fingers dip back and forth on the middle string, then manipulate the top and bottom until I'm looking at a creation with the rounded body and wings of a butterfly. By opening his fingers back and forth, the damn wings seem to flutter.

I clap my hands. "That's wonderful. I don't think I can do it, though, you go much too fast."

He hands me the second piece of yarn. "Follow me. I'll go slow."

And we do. I don't succeed the first try. But soon we're fluttering our butterfly wings at each other and laughing.

"How did you learn how to do this?"

John-John pulls his string loose and quickly makes another design, this time a worm that seems to be crawling over and under the two parallel strings. "My mother taught me. But the Spider Woman taught us, the *Dine'é*."

Spider Woman? My thoughts turn immediately to a female cartoon character. "Who is she?"

"Spider Woman taught the Navajo weaving. We learn right thinking and beauty through her gift. She teaches us to concentrate on a task. It is said that if you think well, you will never get into trouble or get lost."

His words belie his young age. Was this one of the lessons his mother taught him? A beautiful, simple fable marrying a child's game with a life lesson? My admiration for Sarah grows.

But suddenly, John-John stops, stares at the string in his hand. "It is also said string weaving should only be done in the winter when spiders hibernate. If you do it in the summer, you may be pulled into Spider Woman's den and you will never get out."

He looks up at me, eyes wide, fingers tightening on the string. "Do you think that's what happened to my mother and Aunt Mary? Do you think Spider Woman is punishing them for breaking her taboo? Will she punish me?"

My rising anger is as powerful as his grief. I hug him, swallowing the fury back, keeping my thoughts and voice under careful restraint. "No, John-John. What happened was an accident. You had nothing to do with it. You have to believe that. Someone who taught you to make such beautiful patterns from string, who taught your mother to weave these incredible rugs is not vindictive. She is kind and good. She would be sad to think you believe otherwise."

John-John's little body shakes against my chest. I reach for a comforter on the back of the couch and wrap it around him. Sorrow is responsible for some of the shaking, but being hugged by an icy undead vampire can't be helping.

He quiets after a while and his breathing becomes deep and regular. He's asleep. I rest my own head against the back of the couch, let my thoughts tumble forth.

I haven't heard from Frey yet. I hate the idea of his hunting on his own. But it's his right. It's his family Chael attacked. I wish I could be there as backup. But I'd never leave John-John alone. Maybe if he doesn't find him today, we can get someone else to watch John-John . . .

My cell phone trills. Shit. I'd left it in the kitchen. I lift John-John carefully and lay him out on the couch. He settles deeper into the blanket, making a small sound like a mewling kitten, but doesn't wake up.

I snatch the phone from the table. "Frey. Where are you?"

"How's John-John?"

Of course that would be his first thought. "He's fine. He's asleep."

"Good. He was restless last night."

"What'd you find?"

"Nothing yet. Went to the hotel that's closest to the reservation. Asked for Chael and Williams at the front desk. Neither registered, though it was long shot that they'd use their real names now. No one seems to have seen a Middle Eastern man, either. I'll hang around another hour or so, see if I pick up any supernatural activity. Then I'll head out."

His voice is ragged with fatigue. "Why don't you come back? Let me look for them."

"No. You stay with John-John."

No hesitation. "Where will you go next?"

"There's one hotel on the res. The View. Maybe I'll have better luck there."

His tone indicates he's ready to end the call. "Be careful," I say after a moment of silence stretches to fill the void. "John-John needs his dad."

All I hear from the other end is a long, slowly released breath.

JOHN-JOHN IS STILL ASLEEP ON THE COUCH. I TAKE A chair opposite him and watch his chest rise and fall. It's remarkable how attached I've become to the kid. I haven't felt like this about anyone since—Trish. My *niece*. She's safe with my parents in France. Who will John-John be safe with? Frey is the logical choice. But that means up-rooting him unless Frey decides to stay here.

And then I will lose them both.

I should be used to the feeling.

I shake off the gloom. My feelings don't count in this situation.

The sound of a car approaching brings me out of the chair and to the door. I step out onto the porch, closing the door softly behind me. Kayani's police vehicle is winding its dusty way toward the house.

He climbs the steps to meet me. His face still bears the marks of sorrow, grief pulling at the corners of his eyes and mouth.

"I'm sorry." I can't think of another thing to say.

He bobs his head. Once. "John-John?"

"Inside. Asleep. I don't want to leave him alone too long."

"I thought I'd spend some time with him."

"I think it's a good idea."

I hold open the door and we go inside, walking quietly into the kitchen. "Can I offer you some tea?"

He shakes his head, the hint of a smile flickering for the instant it takes him to say, "I can't stand the stuff. I tried to get Sarah to keep coffee around, but—"

We stare at each other. Finally, I motion to the chairs around the table. "Want to sit?"

He sinks into the chair as if his body weight is suddenly too heavy for his frame. He lays his car keys on the table. He's in civilian clothes. Jeans, a long-sleeved shirt, boots.

"Day off?"

"Week off," he replies. "I took personal time. In case I'm needed here."

"You will be." Should I ask about yesterday? I don't

know anything about what happened. "If you don't want to talk about it, I understand. But where were Sarah and Mary buried? Is there a Navajo cemetery? Frey mentioned a communal meal. Is that part of the ritual?"

At first I think Kayani is not going to answer. His eyes grow dim and introspective. But he recovers. "There is a cemetery. But most don't use it. The Navajo have a real fear of ghosts. If one does have relatives in the cemetery, he often doesn't know exactly where they're buried."

He speaks slowly, thoughtfully, as if translating his people's beliefs from his native tongue to English as he goes.

"Sarah and Mary were buried in a secret spot in the desert. They were buried in Navajo dress; one of Sarah's blankets was placed in each coffin. They were buried with trinkets of their life. The purification rites were performed, then we, the parents and I, returned to the house each following a different path. So the dead could not follow."

"And Frey?"

"Frey destroyed the tools used for the burial and took care of obliterating all footprints left behind. When we returned here, another cleansing ritual was performed. This time by a medicine man to bless the house and make it a place of peace and happiness again. After, we shared a meal, to assure the success of the ceremony."

He challenges me with serious eyes. "Does that sound foolish to you?"

If only he knew. I have experienced more than my share of ancient rituals. None of which made as much sense to me or were as benevolent as these beautifully simple ones. "No. Not foolish. I wish I had such beliefs."

He gives me another searching glance. "You are not a religious woman?"

"You say it as if surprised."

"I am. You have an energy that radiates strength. Most often that comes from strong religious beliefs."

Or from being vampire.

I pick up a sound from the living room. "John-John is waking up."

We rise as one. Before we join him, I tell Kayani, "Thank you for explaining your customs. It's important to me to understand."

"It is important for *all* to understand." He pauses. "When the time is right, I expect you to show me the same courtesy."

With that not-so-cryptic remark, Kayani follows me into the living room.

CHAPTER 35

JOHN-JOHN IS HAPPY TO SEE KAYANI. THE TWO TALK quietly in Navajo, giving me the opportunity to slip back into the kitchen and consider my next move.

Would Kayani stay here with John-John while I joined Frey? I'm pretty sure he would. But I don't have a clue where this View Hotel is, and if I ask Kayani, it's bound to spark questions. I could check for an address in a telephone book if I could find one.

I start in looking, opening and shutting each cupboard and drawer carefully and quietly. Sarah's cupboards are all, as I suspected they would be, neat, clean and organized. It dawns on me after I go through them all that I'm looking in the wrong place. A phone book would be in her desk, of course. I don't remember seeing one when I searched for the address book, but then I didn't have to go through all the drawers before I found what I was looking for.

When I pass through the living room, Kayani and John-John look up.

"We're going riding," Kayani says. "Would you like to join us?"

"You go ahead. A city slicker like me would just slow you down."

John-John says to Kayani, "Do you believe? She's never been on a horse."

Kayani gives me a sly once-over. "I believe it. We'll take her another time."

John-John scoots off the couch. "I'll get my hat."

Kayani rises, too. "Will you be all right by yourself?"

"Of course. I think taking John-John riding is a great idea."

John-John is back in a flash. He has a round-crowned hat on his head and is shrugging into a lightweight denim jacket.

"It's awfully hot out there. Do you think you need a jacket?"

"We're used to the heat," Kayani explains. "And the sun is pretty fierce. Skin cancer, you know. Better to be protected." He looks at John-John. "Did you use sunscreen?"

John-John nods, and I find myself smiling.

It's seems such a dichotomy—Kayani spouting modern thoughts about protecting against skin cancer and a few minutes before, explaining burial rituals that include protection against ghosts.

"Okay then, we're off." Kayani says. "See you in a while."

I watch the two down the steps and until they disappear around the back of the house. Then I'm back in Mary's room. I find the phone book, one skinny little thing compared to the voluminous tomes we get in San Diego. There is a full-page ad for the View Hotel. But no real address or directions. When I call the hotel, I'm once again given GPS coordinates that I'm sure would help if I had a car with a GPS.

I can't even ask for directions from the house specifically because I don't know where exactly we are. I program
the number into my cell phone and hang up.

My eyes wander out the living room window.

Kayani's vehicle I'm sure has GPS.

And his keys are on the table.

I snatch them up and head for the car, pausing only to
make sure John-John and Kayani have started on their ride.
I see them in the distance, moving at a brisk pace, little
clouds of red dust marking their trail.

So far so good.

As soon as I get to the car, though, I realize my great
idea has a serious shortcoming. There's a keypad entry system. Pressing every button on the remote does nothing except set off an alarm, which luckily I'm able to squelch. I
suppose it makes sense. No cop would want his car stolen.

Shit.

I could break a window, but that's not only impractical,
it's stupid. How would I explain it?

The ad said the hotel was located near the visitor's center and about five miles from the lodge. Could I retrace my
steps from yesterday on foot? Once I get to the lodge, how
hard would it be to get directions to the hotel?

I've run across desert before, with Frey. The night he
mentioned when the two of us were sitting in the Jeep,
watching the sky, waiting for the sunrise. Was that only a
couple of days ago? It seems another lifetime. So much has
changed. So much has been lost.

Frey showed me the way then. Just as he has so many
other times in our short acquaintance. He's always there for
me. And what have I done for him in return? Caused him
misery and brought death. I can't believe he can stand to
look at me.

Well. The least I can do now is find him. Help him track down the two who orchestrated this last horror. I'll use animal instinct. I know I'll pick up Frey's scent once I get close.

I leave my jacket and Kayani's car keys on the porch. Drawing my thoughts, I center on calling the vampire. She comes willingly, flexing muscles in preparation for our trek. She's happy to be free, happy to be hunting. It doesn't happen often. Like the domesticated cat that seldom tastes freedom except in dreams of her primal ancestors, she relishes the prospect.

And so we run. I follow the Jeep's tracks in the dusty earth. We retrace yesterday's journey until the point where a fresher trail presents itself. Frey this morning. I'm tempted to follow it. But instinct says, keep on to the lodge. If I lose Frey at the first hotel because of traffic and false scents, I've wasted precious time.

And so we run. Senses full of the perfume of the desert, dazzled by the color and texture of the earth underfoot, distracted here and there by the growl of another predator. A warning, but halfhearted. Even the cougar and wolf know they are no match for vampire.

And so we run. Familiar terrain now, I pass the monolith that gave me shelter yesterday. A flicker of human thought. A decision to make. Can I give up this sense of freedom? Do I want to?

The lodge rises up in the distance. I slow my pace. Slow my heart. I need to be human when I approach. It takes some minutes. Vampire is not ready to relinquish her hold.

Patience. Your time will come again. Soon.

Then you will have your reward.

You will have blood.

Chael's blood.

CHAPTER 36

THE LOBBY IS ONCE AGAIN FULL OF TOURISTS EI-
ther just back or about to depart on a tour. Excitement
and anticipation color the air.

I approach the concierge desk. A bronze-skinned Navajo in a long-sleeved shirt and intricate bolo of beaten silver looks up at my approach. He's handsome, young, dark
hair polished to a sheen as it falls around his shoulders. I'll
bet it's soft.

I'm tempted to reach out and touch it.

I resist, opting instead to smile and ask, "Can you give
me directions to the View Hotel?"

He looks at me with eyebrows raised in shock. "You
aren't thinking of staying with our competition instead of
here, are you?"

It takes me a beat to realize he's teasing. I hold up both
hands. "Never. I'm just supposed to meet someone there."

While I'm talking, he's pulled a map from a rack on the
corner of the desk. He's smiling when he looks up and I

imagine that thousand-watt smile coupled with that begs-to-be-touched hair have been the downfall of many a maiden.

It stirs vampire lust, and not for blood.

I ratchet down the hormones and concentrate on the directions he's tracing on the map. "It's only about four miles east on Monument Valley Road."

An easy run. I thank him and leave. There are four young college-age girls behind me, all big eyes and blond hair and sexy innocence, and I wonder what kind of personal instruction in the Navajo way he offers besides directions.

I run parallel to the road, out of sight of cars, but close enough to hear the wind rush of traffic. Vampire chastises me for thoughts of the handsome boy. Her thoughts are on finding our friend. Then we kill our enemies. Carnal pleasure comes after.

I'm there in minutes. The hotel is surrounded by pinnacles of rock, mesa and sand and framed by clouds. Shadows roam and dance over the desert floor. For a minute, human Anna enjoys the view, then she's called back by vampire.

First, find Frey's Jeep in the parking lot. I don't see it. Is it possible I beat him here?

The lots are full. It's a combination of sight and scent that lead me to the Jeep.

A hand on the hood. Warm. The smell and gurgle of fluids cooling tells me he hasn't been here long.

I hang back, out of sight, of the entrance. There is no artificial landscape here—the ground is barren of plants so I must find a spot in the only shade available—a corner of the building itself—and press back out of the light.

I open the conduit cautiously. Not to transmit, but to

receive what I might. Even expecting it, I am disappointed that nothing comes through.

A grim thought. Has Frey already confronted Chael? Is he lying wounded, or worse, nearby? How many times have I beaten myself up for breaking the psychic connection between us? It leaves Frey helpless to reach out to me for help and me powerless to find him on my own.

Shit. I can't wait here. It's possible Chael and Judith have already moved on. Maybe I wasn't giving them the show they expected. If this attempt is a bust, I'm sure Chael will come up with something else.

I return to the Jeep. I'll ride back with Frey.

A shuffle of feet from the front of the hotel—as if people were running to get away. Frightened voices call for security. I smell fear and anger.

Fear from the humans escaping from inside.

Anger from Frey.

I buck the tide of people moving out to fight my way in. I see Frey, alone in the back of the lobby, crossbow drawn taut. He has a handkerchief over the lower part of his face. I hear Judith Williams' thoughts now, as she begs for her life. I can't hear Frey's response but I know what I want to tell him.

Don't listen.

In a heartbeat, I'm beside him. "Shoot her."

She turns eyes filled with horror in my direction. "Anna. We are vampire family. Don't let him do this."

"Frey, if you don't shoot her, I will," is my snarling response. "If she's here, Chael is close."

"Do we need her to find him?" Frey asks me, voice devoid of all emotion.

"No."

The arrow sings across space in a whisper. Judith Williams holds up her hands. The arrow pierces the right one and pins it to the middle of her chest. She has time to glance down once before her body crumbles into red ash.

"We have to go."

Frey points with the crossbow to a stairway in the back of the lobby. Behind us, there is the sound of footsteps running our way. Either security or the police or some brave or curious soul wanting to see what has happened.

Frey and I don't check behind us to find out. He pauses once to snatch up the arrow and we are behind the stairwell door and out the back before they reach the pile of ash that was Judith. I wish we had time to clean up. In a culture with skinwalkers who practice curse magic, I'm afraid some innocent might be blamed for what happened.

On the other hand, someone who practices curse magic is hardly innocent. I have experience. As far as I can remember, Frey's identity was hidden behind the handkerchief and no one rushing to get out paused long enough to take note of the woman running in. There's nothing left to identify as remains. Most likely, witnesses will describe a kidnapping. Process of elimination of the hotel guests may turn up Judith Williams as the "victim." Even if that happened, Chael would most likely lie about his roommate being missing.

We're at the Jeep and out of the lot before the alarm spreads. Only when Frey has taken us off the main road does he pull over and turn to me.

"Who is with John-John?" No recrimination in his tone, only a father's interest.

"Kayani."

"Good. How did you get away?"

"He and John-John went riding."

"He lent you his car?"

"No. I didn't tell him what I was doing. I tried to steal it, but it has pretty good security."

He lets a grin touch the corners of his mouth even as he's shaking his head. "You tried to steal a cop's car?"

"But I didn't. No harm, no foul."

"You hoofed it across the desert?"

"Felt good, actually. To let vampire have her head."

"I understand. Well, what now? No sign of Chael, but if Judith Williams was there, he must be, too. Do you think he'll give up and leave? He hasn't succeeded in getting rid of you and I don't know what else he can try."

I let my gaze stretch out over the landscape. "I don't know. He's crafty. But he's not good at working without someone to throw under the bus when things get rough. How did you find Judith anyway?"

He taps a forefinger against his head. "She was leading a host out of the hotel. Telling the girl she was taking her somewhere more private. She was taking her behind the mesa to kill her. It was there in her thoughts. I got there in time."

"Why didn't you follow her? You took a chance taking her down in the lobby."

"She picked up on me too soon. As it was, she threatened to kill the girl as soon as she read my intentions. I managed to scare the girl into bolting. But Judith wasn't about to go outside quietly. I remembered what you said."

"Kill her on sight. Good decision."

"So what do we do now?"

I consider for a minute. "Let's watch the road leading from the hotel. I do think Chael will try to leave. As soon as he can. Unless he has some contact here on the reservation, with Judith gone, he's by himself."

Frey puts the Jeep in reverse and swings back toward

the road. Luckily, there is only one way in and out of the hotel parking lot. We find a place to park the Jeep behind some desert scrub and crouch down to watch the road.

One car enters the lot, a big Lincoln Navigator with tinted windows and a set of oversized tires designed to leave as big a carbon imprint as possible. It's closely followed by a parade of police vehicles, both civilian and Navajo, screaming in with flashing lights and sirens shrieking. The driver of the Navigator pulls over and jumps out, hand on chest. He's a blue hair, probably a year or two closer to the big one after thinking he was the object of pursuit.

Frey and I know better. We watch the cops head for the entrance of the hotel, some rush inside, others set up a perimeter with crime scene tape.

They're going to have a tough time analyzing that crime scene. If they even think it a crime scene. What's left? A pile of fine ash and little else. I remember Detective Harris and his visit to me a few days ago about Williams. But in that case, there was tangible physical evidence. Just enough to confuse things. Here there is no body. Only witness accounts that they saw a standoff between a woman and a masked man with a bow. Both are now gone. If for some reason, they run DNA on this ash, it might come back human, but at least the age of the deceased will be in acceptable human range.

Not long after the police arrive, the lot is blocked off by a Navajo Police vehicle. An officer steps out and begins flagging down approaching tourists and telling them they have to turn around, that the hotel is temporarily closed. He's greeted with a lot of unhappy grumbling, but all comply and make lazy U-turns, wondering out loud what has happened.

Frey looks over at me. "What now?"

"You should go home," I say after a moment's consideration. "The police probably think Judith Williams was kidnapped. Somebody may describe what you're wearing even if they couldn't see your face. I'll stay here and watch for Chael to make his move. He's old and powerful, but I doubt he's had to fend for himself against humans very often. His minions take care of the dirty work. He may be looking for a way out. I think I'll give him one."

Frey narrows his eyes. "What do you mean?"

"He'll need help to escape." I spread my arms. "Here it is."

Frey nods his understanding. "Where will you take him?"

I tell Frey about the cave I explored yesterday. I leave Sani out of it—one problem at a time—but behind those rocks seems a perfect place to take care of a villain like Chael.

Frey frowns. "Those caves are sacred. What you propose would desecrate what they represent. No. I think I have a better idea."

Frey describes a mesa, here, in back of the hotel. There's an opening in the rock, hard to see from the desert floor, but an easy climb to reach. "Get him there and you'll have all the privacy you need."

I realize Frey is offering to let me take care of Chael and my spidey sense starts to tingle. "You'll go home? Let me handle Chael?"

He lowers his eyes. "You were right last night. I can't risk John-John losing both his parents. Killing Judith Williams was too easy. I know Chael won't go down without a fight and you are the stronger between us. I trust you to take revenge for Sarah's death just as I trust you with the life of my son."

His words raise gooseflesh on my arms. Partly because

they're said with so much sincerity, partly because the lowered eyes are a tell. He's spouting crap. One thing I know about Frey, he's a fighter. His pretty speech would have been pitch-perfect had he not added the part about trusting me with the life of his son. It sounded like a codicil to his will.

He's up to something.

But I haven't the time to challenge him. I wave him off. "Okay, get going. I'll get back to Sarah's as soon as I can."

He gets back into the Jeep, cranks it over, and heads in the direction of Sarah's house, all without another word or backward glance.

Oh yeah. He's definitely up to something.

CHAPTER 37

T HE POLICE HAVE HERDED EVERYONE INTO THE
lobby. They're taking the witnesses at their word that a
crime has been committed. They begin going down the list
of guests, checking each name as it is read off and the
guest is identified and separated from the rest.

I know this because I've scurried like a lizard up the
back wall and can see down through windows too high to
cause anyone to look up. Chael is not among the mingling
masses.

Nor is he emitting any telepathic trail for me to follow.

Which means, I have to find him the hard way.

I slip onto a third-floor balcony and start peering into
windows. I figure Chael would be staying in one of the best
rooms and since the rooms on this floor have big windows
with magnificent views, this is where he's likely to be.

I find him on the fifth try. He's on his cell phone, talking
softly, a slightly hysterical tone to his voice. He's desperate
to get out of the hotel before his name is called and the

police come looking for him. He's dressed, as always, like a dandy—pleated slacks, tailored shirt, leather loafers. He has a cream-colored sweater thrown over his shoulders, sleeves knotted over his chest.

I watch for a moment—deciding. Should I kill him now? It's what I told Frey to do.

And yet.

There is someone helping him here on the reservation. Has to be. Is it George? Whoever it is could be another threat to Frey and his son even with Chael gone. Better to find out.

Vampire growls in frustration. She looks forward to the kill.

Patience.

The slider is unlocked and I slip inside. Seems appropriate somehow since it's the way he intruded on me.

He's not aware of my presence until I pick up á lamp from a table and let it fall with a clatter to the carpet. He drops the cell phone and whirls around with a flash of teeth and fist. The human Anna is obviously the last person he expected to see.

Anna? What are you doing here?

He's emitting more fear than threat.

I learned not too long ago that Chael is like a lot of old-soul vampires who have lost the edge that makes them truly dangerous. For centuries, they have relied on others to do their fighting and when cornered, resort to threats and promises to tide them over before they can call their minions. Then they stand back and watch the carnage, taking full credit, of course.

I make it a point to look around the room, ignoring his question and countering with one of my own. *Where is your whore?* I ask innocently.

His mouth droops into a frown. *Someone killed her. Right here in the hotel. Shot her with an arrow. It wasn't you?*

No. All I offered was encouragement. I feign shock. *How did you find out about it? Were you there, too?*

Chael acts like he's going to ignore the question, but then he says with an angry sweep of his hand, *Stupid, stupid woman. I told her indulging herself was too risky. But just feeding was not satisfying enough for her. She needed the kill. The host got away. Came up here. Told me some man made her run away from Judith, that he was going to kill her. When I heard the commotion in the lobby, saw the ash, I knew it was true.*

What happened to the host?

I don't know. I don't care. I told her if I saw her again, I'd kill her. She's gone.

His eyes narrow. *How did you know I was here?*

I pause the length of a heartbeat. *I came to the hotel to meet my friend and his son. I got here right after—it happened. Suspected it was Judith when I heard a witness describe the victim and that somebody had her at arrow point.* Now it's my turn. *What are you doing here? Did you follow me?*

There's a moment's hesitation while he processes what I said. He knew I was at the lodge because he saw me. He can't be sure though, that I saw him. He lets go of uncertainty and launches into his story. *I was concerned about you. I heard there were skinwalkers on the reservation at war with the vampire. I came to warn you.*

How noble. You weren't afraid those same skinwalkers would hunt you?

My expression must reflect the skepticism churning the acid in my stomach because he ignores the question and follows with, *Then when I got here I heard about the terrible accident that took the life of Frey's wife and sister-in-*

law. I thought you had enough on your mind. I'd wait until a better time to tell you. It must have been a skinwalker that got Judith. I told her she was foolish to venture out of the room. It must have been a skinwalker.

Must have been. I've never seen Chael project insecurity before—anxious, rambling, filling his thoughts with empty words in a desperate attempt to persuade or distract me.

Until?

Someone must be on the way to help him.

Time to move things along before he thinks to ask again why I'm here or worse, how I found him.

Well, we'd better get you out of here. The police are taking roll downstairs and you are going to be missed. You and the late Judith Williams. I have a place for you to hide until we can decide what to do.

He backs away. *No. I feel safer here. I have a contact on the Navajo police. I've been trying to reach him but all I get is his voice mail.*

That's probably because he's downstairs with the rest. And as long as there are others present, he's not going to be able to help you. Come on. I know a way we can climb down over the wall in back and sneak away.

His face draws up. His thoughts are cloaked, but I can feel the intensity of the battle he's waging. He doesn't trust me, but he's alone and so am I. In his arrogance, he is sure he can handle anything I throw at him.

All right. I'll go with you.

I turn my back and start toward the slider at the same time there's a knock on the guestroom door.

"Police, Mr. Sidhu. Open up."

Chael pushes against me in an effort to propel us forward faster. The grin that lights my face is hidden by the fact that I'm out the slider and headed for the corner of the building so fast, all Chael sees is the blur of my back.

He's as dexterous as I am and we shimmy down the building like two reptiles fleeing the talons of a raptor. Once on the ground, we move too quickly to be noticed by the police officers posted at the back door to the lodge. Then we're off across the desert floor, headed for the mesa a mile away.

Chael is fast, almost faster than I. At one point, he slows and sends a message. *Where are we going?*

It's not far now, I reply. *I have a vehicle hidden in the mouth of a cave.*

The answer satisfies him. He was not looking forward to a long trek on foot. Even vampires have their limits.

I have to scan the area Frey mentioned before I find the opening about twelve feet up a dirt and loose rock pathway. I point. *There.*

Chael shields his eyes with a hand. *I don't see a vehicle.*

It's back inside. Come on. We'd better take cover before we're spotted.

He's looking up at the rock strewn path with distaste. *Why don't you get the car? I'll wait for you here.*

Afraid to scuff your loafers? I let the sarcasm drip. *Get over it. It's too soon to be trekking across the desert leaving a plume of dust anyone can follow. We'll hole up for a while, until it's clear.*

He doesn't like the idea, but the reasoning is sound so he gives in with a shrug. He follows close behind me, slipping on rock and gravel his smooth-soled loafers were never meant to travel. The legs of his dark trousers are powdered with dust. I'm sure the idea that he'd be trekking through the desert with me was the last thing on his mind when he got dressed this morning.

When we reach the mouth of the cave, he peers inside. This cave is far different from the one I explored yesterday. The floor is littered with guano dust and animal scat. The smell of rotting vegetation and stale air gusts out at us.

Chael wrinkles his elegant nose. *How far back is the car?*

A ways.

He lets the barrier slip from his thoughts. His eyes turn hard. *What are you playing at, Anna Strong?*

We're facing each other, the pretense of civility falling away like shattered glass.

Oh, I'm not playing at anything, Chael. I brought you here to answer for Sarah and Mary. You took innocent lives to what purpose? To keep me here? I want to know one thing before I kill you. Who is the skinwalker helping you?

He draws himself up, a flicker of anger tenses muscles, fists clench and unclench at his side. *Again, you show your arrogance, your ignorance. What do you think will happen if you kill me? Do you think my death will go unavenged? I am a leader of one of the Thirteen Tribes. I have followers who are even now on their way to help me. They will hunt you down and everyone close to you and no one will be spared. You will have sparked a war that will destroy the very things you argued so eloquently to protect at council.*

Pretty words, Chael. I take a step closer, baring teeth that ache to tear out his throat. *Perhaps you should have thought of that before you sent me on this fool's errand. I was turned down by the council. You knew I'd not be allowed to see the shaman. Was the plan to let skinwalker curse magic destroy me?*

That I saw Sani anyway I keep buried.

A smile draws the corners of his mouth into a humorless grin. *Turned down by the council? You really don't have a clue, do you?* He pauses, as if savoring what will come next.

Your request was not turned down. Sarah never got the chance make her plea to the council.

He watches me, enjoying the flashes of emotion that flicker through my thoughts. Anger that he lies so blatantly, fury that he thinks I'll fall for it . . . curiosity because I don't know why he'd throw out such an outlandish lie. George told me I'd been turned down. Insinuated that Sarah's death was my fault because she was killed coming back from the council meeting where she pled my case.

George lied. Chael's shoulders drop, as if he knows he's hooked me and he can release some of the tension gripping his body. *Sarah was never allowed to speak at council.*

None of the tension has drained from my body, however. I lower my head and growl at him. *How do you know this?*

I know a member of the council. He had been well paid to see that your request was considered. He came to me after, to tell me what had transpired. A problem had been brought by the elders to the council's attention and it occupied the entire meeting. Sarah was told to come back next week.

I turn away from Chael—not completely. I would never be so foolish as to turn my back to him. I step close to the rock wall of the cave so I can gather my thoughts. Privately. I allow nothing to come through that he might pick up.

If Chael is telling the truth, George purposely led me to believe Sarah had spoken to the council. There was no misunderstanding. He told me my request had been turned down. I remember how he looked sitting at the kitchen table, the way he swept an arm and said, *All this was for nothing.*

I recall every word Sani said. He never told me how he knew I was seeking his council, did he?

But why should I believe Chael? How can I know?

I can do but one thing. Chael offers his thoughts in response to my own. *Take you to the elder who is on my payroll. He will verify that what I say is true.*

An elder on your payroll? I can trust someone whose loyalty is for sale? You must offer me something more than testimony that's been bought and paid for.

Chael retreats into his own thoughts a moment. Then his eyes spark with an answer. *The man I saw with you at the lodge yesterday? He is a policeman, is he not?*

Yes.

Then ask him. By now he will have been apprised of the problem.

He hadn't been as of yesterday.

Oh, but he will be now. This is something that threatens the economy of the entire Navajo nation.

And what is this problem?

Chael spreads his hands. *Someone is flooding the market with fake artifacts from the sacred caves. They are wonderful fakes, hewn from the original rock, but fakes nonetheless. The originals are sacred to the Navajo. Only a few are ever sold and then they must be displayed in the proper way in Native American museums. Tracking down the counterfeiters has become top priority for the locals. They are sure the thieves are working from the reservation. Here.*

I close my eyes, picturing the beautiful drawings in the cave.

Do you know something? Chael asks, jumping at my hesitation. *If you do, you will certainly make the elders look more favorably on your request for an audience with Sani.*

My thoughts are scattered. I know nothing of counterfeiters. But if Chael's story is true, was it just a horrific accident that killed Sarah and Mary?

Did I urge Frey to kill Judith Williams for nothing?

I slump back against the wall of the cave, ignoring the dampness seeping from the rock, pressing fingers against my eyes. Finally, I raise my eyes to Chael. *Why have you stayed on? Did you intend to wait the week and see what transpired?*

I told you. I heard about the skinwalkers.

I let a snicker rumble from the back of my throat. *And you were going to warn me? When? Hate to break it to you, but you're too late. I already had a taste of curse magic. I figured it was someone on your payroll, too.*

He shakes his head. *No. Skinwalkers are tricky bastards. There's no loyalty in them to anyone but those initiated with them into the witchery way.*

But I'm sure you wouldn't have minded if I'd met my end at the hands of one.

Chael's expression shifts to irritation. *I told you. I don't want you dead. I want you removed from the position of the Chosen One.*

And you want it done in a way that cannot be traced back to you.

That is preferable, yes.

At least that's something I can believe. Dying at the hand of a skinwalker would certainly meet the criteria.

What do I do now?

I was so sure it had been Chael behind Sarah's death, I never considered the possibility that the car accident had been just that—an accident.

My stomach knots with indecision. Chael is still an enemy. I could kill him here in this place and dispose of his body so that it would never be found.

Vampire thinks that is a good idea. Chael is no match for my anger and strength.

The human Anna is not so sure. I watched Judith Williams dissolve into ash and felt nothing. She was not a friend, but now I find she may not have been the enemy I imagined. Oh, she would have proved herself worthy of death eventually. Her lack of restraint would have been her undoing. Realistically, killing her saved the lives of unsuspecting hosts.

So easy to rationalize. What was it that Chael said to me at the cottage—when the time comes, I'd kill her for him.

And I did.

Chael stirs beside me, anxiety beginning to bloom in his thoughts. Does he suspect the decision I'm wrestling with?

Let me go, Anna, and you will have a powerful friend.

I should not hesitate this minute to tear out Chael's throat. Sani's words echo again in my head. Would killing Chael assure the safety of mankind? Would it guarantee my return to mortality could be achieved with no disastrous consequences?

I peer at Chael. He is nervous, an insect squirming on a pin. He is but one of a growing legion who are tired of vampires being kept in the shadows. Killing him might spur his followers on to escalate the violence against those they see as their subjugators.

Friend? Never. But making him a martyr would not be smart, either. And there's still that nagging question of why I don't feel the evil in Chael. Why I don't feel the powerful need to kill him. It is a riddle to be solved.

I open my thoughts. *Go. We will never be friends. But today, we are not enemies.*

His relief is palpable, he draws himself up, squares his shoulders. *You will not regret this.*

Make sure I don't. Leave the valley. I will check your story. If you have been lying, I will find you.

He reaches into a pocket. I look down at what he holds out to me.

A business card. Like we are two traveling salesman exchanging numbers. He's holding out a fucking business card.

This number will reach me no matter where I am.

I'm too dumbstruck by the sheer idiocy of the scenario to do more than take it and stare.

He makes his exit head held high, aloof as departing royalty. The only thing that mars his departure is the very ungraceful fall he takes as his feet slip on loose rock. He lands on his ass, recovers quickly, and glances back to see if I noticed.

I let him know that I did.

CHAPTER 38

A S SOON AS CHAEL IS OUT OF SIGHT, FLEEING BACK toward the hotel, I turn and trek farther back into the cave.

"Okay, Frey," I call out. "You can come out now."

At first there is no sound—just water dripping from somewhere out of sight. Then shuffling. Frey's scent, soap and shampoo, tickles my nose before his form materializes from the gloom. He's rigid with anger.

"You let him go. You didn't kill him."

We retrace our steps to the mouth of the cave.

I hunker down, squatting on my heels. Frey joins me. I know he couldn't pick up my thoughts, but he would have been able to pick up Chael's. "You heard that Sarah didn't address the council?"

He nods stiffly. "That will be easy enough to check. What about the other things? Do you really believe he had nothing to do with the skinwalker attack on you?"

"Yes. I think it's time we looked at this from another

angle. George lied to me. He lied to you, too. He made it clear he would like to see me dead. I think he knows more than he is letting on. You must, too, or panther would have made quick work of Chael."

Frey picks up a rock and tosses it outside. "Judith Williams," he says, regret softening his tone. "I killed her, and she was an innocent."

"Not exactly an innocent. Remember how she killed those two hosts in Mexico? It's taken months for Culebra to win back the trust of both host and vampire. She had a taste for killing. You said yourself, she intended to kill the young girl she was taking from the hotel when you found her. That girl was the innocent. Not Judith Williams."

I pause. "And you did it at my bidding. I am as much to blame as you."

Frey peers out toward the hotel. "I can't believe George attacked you. He'd have no reason. Sarah was to speak to the council; he must have known there was a good chance your request would be turned down. With Sarah dead, he could lie about it, he did lie about it, and the logical assumption would be that you and I would be gone before we knew any different. Attacking you made no sense."

Ah. "So you believe he may be a skinwalker."

He doesn't meet my eyes, not ready to make the concession. His words come slowly. "It's such an inconceivable notion. George is Navajo. He leads tourists and tells them of the connection between the people and the land. He is a respected member of the community. How could he commit such an onerous cultural taboo? And why?"

I can think of one reason. The smugglers Chael mentioned. Is he in league with them?

Doesn't explain why he attacked me, though. I knew

nothing about the counterfeiting operation until a few minutes ago.

Maybe George just doesn't like vampires.

Imagine that, vampire growls.

I sense Frey's eyes boring into my head. "What are you thinking? Do you know something?"

Not really. If Frey is having a hard time believing his friend could be a skinwalker, how will he react when I tell him he may also be a smuggler?

Especially since I have no proof.

"Let's get back to the house. Kayani will know about the counterfeiters. At least that's one part of Chael's story we can check out."

We push to our feet. "Where's the Jeep?" I ask.

Frey makes a vague sweeping motion with his hand. "Off the road, about a half mile back."

And then we're off, jogging across the desert floor like two friends out for a little run. Under a midday desert sun. In ninety-plus-degree temperatures. Fully clothed.

Business as usual.

THE DRIVE BACK IS QUIET, NEITHER FREY NOR I WILL-ing to share our thoughts. I have a question for Kayani that I think will do more to persuade Frey that George is not the good guy he thinks he is.

And to let Chael off the hook.

For Sarah's death anyway.

Still, that her accident might have been caused by a moment's inattention or carelessness rings false. The worm of doubt slithering around my gut is fast turning into a python.

It could just as easily been a skinwalker that frightened her off the road as a vampire.

Where was George the night of the council meeting?

THE HORSES ARE BACK IN THE CORRAL WHEN FREY and I arrive at the house. Kayani and John-John are on the porch, drinking out of plastic tumblers. Kayani's feet are on the railing, his chair tipped back. John-John mimics Kayani, but his feet are too short to reach the railing so his rest on a small table, his chair tilted back against the house.

I don't usually react to cute, but this makes me wish I had a camera.

John-John squeals when he sees his father, lets his chair bang forward and rushes down the steps. Kayani rises, too, and the smile he has at John-John's delight increases my estimation of him a hundredfold. There is not even a shadow of jealousy on his face.

Frey scoops John-John into his arms and turns to me. "John-John is going to tell me all about his ride. Why don't you visit with Kayani and we'll go inside."

He doesn't wink or give me a nudge. Doesn't have to. I get it. I touch the top of John-John's head. "I'll want to hear about your ride, too, later, okay?"

The two disappear inside. Kayani watches me as I climb the steps and join him. He holds up his glass.

"Want some? Ice tea. This stuff is not nearly so bad cold with lemon and sugar."

I hold up a hand. "No, thanks. I'll take your word that it's good."

Kayani motions to John-John's chair and I take it. For a

minute I wonder how to broach the subject of the counterfeiters. A minute. Kayani doesn't seem the type to require
subtlety.

"Frey and I heard a rumor today. Counterfeiters smuggling fake artifacts off the reservation. I hear it's become
top priority for all law enforcement."

Kayani doesn't register surprise or feign indiffer-
ence. "Yes."

"That was the subject at tribal council?"

He finishes his tea and places the tumbler on the table.
"Yes. It's of great concern. There is already too much *au-
thentic* Native American jewelry and rugs peddled everywhere from the local Wal-Mart to eBay. We can't do much
about it. But to counterfeit petroglyphs and the works of
ancients and have them displayed as real is a desecration to
the honor of our ancestors. That it may be done here by
members of our tribe is unforgivable."

"I saw some of those petroglyphs. They are beautiful in
their simplicity and elegance. I understand why you would
want to protect them."

"You've been to Canyon de Chelly?"

I shake my head. "No. I saw them not far from here. In
a cave."

Kayani's demeanor changes so fast, it almost gives me
whiplash. His face loses its friendliness and becomes hard.
"What do you mean?"

His tone is as harsh and accusatory as his expression. I
raise my eyebrows. "I don't understand. Did I do something wrong?"

"Who took you to the cave?"

The cave? "No one. I found it by accident. Coming home
the storm had turned sand to mud. The Jeep was having a

tough time slogging through it. I pulled over to wait until it dried."

Kayani doesn't look satisfied with the explanation. "And you decided to do a little exploring?"

"I saw a faint path. I followed it to the cave. Kayani, I disturbed nothing." Just had a secret meeting with the most sacred member of the tribe.

"Did you see anyone?"

Since I assume he means anyone up to no good, I can answer honestly.

"No. I only know two people here on the reservation. You and George Long Whiskers."

There's a moment's hesitation before Kayani says, "You told me to keep an eye on him at Sarah's burial. Why?"

Perfect segue. "I don't trust him. He's said—" Shit. How do I put this? "He's said some pretty harsh things to me. In fact, he lied about what went on at the council."

"What did he say?"

"Can I ask you a question before I answer that?"

Kayani bobs his head once.

"Was George at the council meeting?"

"No. He is not an elder."

"I know you weren't at the meeting, either, but I assume you know where the meetings are held?"

"The lodge. What difference does that make?"

"Were you around there that night?"

Another quick bob of the head. "Sarah and Mary and I had dinner before Sarah had to leave for the meeting. I left Mary to go back to the station not long after."

"Did you see George that night?"

A reflective pause. "Yes. He was at a table on the deck

with two men." He draws a quick, sharp breath. "I didn't recognize them."

Kayani and I both retreat into our thoughts. Can it be this easy? The cynic in me says no, the pragmatist says sometimes things *are* just what they seem.

Still a long way from connecting George to the deaths of the sisters. Could Mary have overheard a snatch of conversation that might have made her suspicious? Could George have suspected that she did?

"Kayani, how much money can be made from selling counterfeit artifacts?"

"Thousands, maybe hundreds of thousands. There's a thriving market both legitimate and black market for Native American art. Especially the art of the ancients."

Well, there's motive. If George was meeting with the two strangers to talk business, and Mary heard something incriminating, George could easily have arranged that accident.

Kayani snatches his car keys from the table. "Let's take a ride. Copies of art from that cave are the newest ones to show up on the black market. If you show me how you gained access, maybe I can find out how the counterfeiters are doing it."

He opens the screen door and tells Frey that we'll be right back. We're down the stairs and at the car before Frey can offer a reply.

CHAPTER 39

W E'VE ARRIVED AT THE CAVE. KAYANI PULLS OVER in the same spot I had twenty-four hours before. Now that the ground has fully dried, I realize the path would be invisible to the naked eye. We climb out and Kayani stops to grab a large flashlight from the back of the van. Then he motions me ahead. "Show me."

It isn't difficult to retrace my steps. I recognize my own scent still lingering in the quiet air. When I come to the fork, I point to the left. I look back to see Kayani frowning at me.

"What?"

"I can't believe you wandered in here. This area is off-limits. Not even tour guides are allowed here without permission."

"And I can't believe you're acting like I'm the only one to ever discover these caves. Surely, any hiker could stumble on them."

"How?" Kayani's tone rings with accusation. "Did you

notice any other tracks? We are very careful to limit access to certain areas of the tribal park. If you'd been caught here, the penalties would have been stiff."

"So, what now? Are you going to arrest me for trespassing?"

Grudgingly, he does the "go on" motion again with the flashlight. As I turn to lead him deeper inside, I catch another whiff of scent. This comes from the right fork. It's the unmistakable odor of men, hanging in the air the same way mine does.

"Where does that fork lead?" I pause to ask Kayani.

"It goes deeper into the mountain. Exits about a mile to the east. Comes out close to the hogan where you and Frey spent the night."

Sarah must have told him. The subtle emphasis he puts on the words "spent the night" makes it obvious he's still not sure Frey and I are just friends.

As soon as we start out, he clicks on the flashlight. The powerful beam almost disorients me with its glare. I'd have done better without it, but he wouldn't have. I let my eyes adjust and keep going.

I also listen. No telltale beat of the drum today.

We come to the wall with the petroglyphs. Kayani lays a respectful hand against the rock. "My ancestors left these to mark their passing. It angers me to see them desecrated."

"At least they weren't taken from the cave," I offer as some measure of consolation.

He doesn't look consoled. He flashes the light on the ground. Nothing. But once again, I detect a scent. There have been men here. Not Sani and his two companions, I realize with a start. There is nothing of their scent that lingers.

I move back into the cave. I let my fingers trace the rock.

Is there some kind of entrance to the chamber where I met with Sani? I close my eyes and let my sense of touch take over.

"What are you doing?" Kayani asks.

"Just wondering if there was another way out of this cave."

"Not here. Why would you ask?"

I shrug in a noncommittal response.

"Do you think there might be another entrance?" He's beside me, running his hands along the wall the same way I did. He feels nothing.

When our hands accidentally come in contact, he says, "Your skin is like ice. Do you want my jacket?"

"No. Thanks. I'm fine."

His eyes turn back to the wall. In the glare of the flashlight, an angry scowl shadow paints his face into a contorted grimace. "Nowhere to hide. No way of knowing how often they visit the place. Shit."

First time I've heard a curse pass those stoic lips. "So what do you want to do?"

"What I'd like to do is find George and beat some answers out of him."

I'm beginning to like Kayani more and more. For once, I'm not the one suggesting brute force to solve a problem.

"Does George work today?"

I may as well have asked if mud tastes like taffy. He blinks at me. "What?"

"Does George work today?"

"I think so. Why?"

"What about his wife?"

"She works in the lodge gift shop."

"Any kids?"

"What does that have to do with anything?"

"Are there any kids at home?" I enunciate each word as if talking to a slow first grader.

Awareness blooms. "No. Are you suggesting a little breaking and entering?"

"Not if it's going to get me arrested."

He stares at me. "I can't help."

"Don't expect you to."

"You can do this?"

"Did Frey mention what I do in San Diego?"

A shake of the head.

"I'm a fugitive apprehension officer. I can pick any lock made."

That sly look crosses his face. "Except maybe keypad locks, huh?"

So he noticed, did he? "How'd you know?"

"Heard the alarm. Since it shut off pretty quickly, I figured I didn't need to come back. Were you planning to take the car for a joyride?"

"Just needed the GPS."

"Right." He starts to lead the way out of the cave. "No need to test your expertise. Nobody locks their doors around here."

When we come to the fork, I once again pick up the scent of men—the same scent I detected in the cave. "I think you should watch the entryway near the hogan."

"Why?"

How do I put this delicately? Because I picked up a *scent*?

Why not? "I smell—men. Walked here recently. I smelled them in the cave, too."

That brings a raised eyebrow. "You *smelled* them?"

I tap the side of my nose. "Exceptional olfactory powers."

"That must be hell in a crowd."

No kidding. Especially the scent of menstrual blood in a hot room. I shrug.

Kayani's response is to raise an eyebrow.

We trek our way back to the car. Kayani does radio ahead and asks for air patrols to keep a particular eye on the area near the hogan. He isn't specific as to why he's making the request, but with the recent revelation concerning fake artifacts, he doesn't have to be. A suggestion that trespassers might have been spotted on private land is all it takes.

Once we're in the car, I ask, "Are there other sites like this?"

"Several. I only hope this is the only one being defiled."

His use of words like "desecrate" and "defiled" makes me aware of how important protecting his heritage is to Kayani. He doesn't look at what's being done as merely illegal, he looks at it as a personal attack.

Frey will, too, if there's a connection between George and the accident. Still no clear-cut proof of that. If I can be alone with George for a few minutes, though, I'm pretty sure vampire can get him to connect the dots.

Her powers of persuasion are legendary.

CHAPTER 40

G EORGE LIVES IN A SIMPLE CLAPBOARD HOUSE
about five miles from Sarah. Like Sarah's, there's no
landscaping to speak of, just a simple fence of low juniper
that snakes around the property. Unlike Sarah's, the paint
is sun-blistered and peeling, a porch holds two rocking
chairs and a battered couch that face out toward the yard.
The house projects a feeling of neglect.

Kayani stops a half mile away and takes out a pair of
binoculars. George's tour bus is not in sight. Neither is any
other vehicle.

Kayani holds the binoculars out to me. I take them for
form's sake, but I see everything I need to without them. I
hand them back after a few seconds.

"What are you going to be looking for?" Kayani asks.

"Well, I suppose it would be too much to hope for a
workshop with a petroglyph assembly line."

Kayani grunts.

"Pictures of the cave walls, maybe? Paint? Whatever

might connect him to the smugglers." What I don't add is that I also plan to be on the lookout for a blowgun. I wish I knew other signs of a skinwalker's presence, but I'm not sure Kayani would be any more receptive to the idea that George practices curse magic than Frey is.

I climb out of the passenger seat, lean back in to ask, "Are you going to stay here?"

A weird expression passes over his face. A hint of humor mixed with a bit of concern and a healthy dose of knowing it's "cover your ass" time. "I'll take a little drive. Better if you get caught for me to answer the call legitimately instead of trying to explain why I happened to be lurking nearby."

I ignore the "if you get caught" part. "Aren't you supposed to be off this week?"

A shrug. "If we catch the counterfeiters, no one is going to care. Besides, I'm a cop. We're on duty even when we're not."

I push the door shut. "Give me fifteen minutes. Won't take longer to search a place that small."

"Meet you right back here."

He pulls away. Refreshing to be set loose without the usual admonitions to be careful or watch your back. Kayani takes it for granted that I can handle myself. And he thinks I'm human.

I turn to study the house. It's set on the top of a gently sloping piece of land. Take away the background of that magnificent mesa, and it could be any other remote cabin far removed from civilization. No neighbors within my line of sight. Not even the hum of traffic or buzz of an airplane breaks the silence. "Lonely" and "isolated" are words that spring to mind.

Perfect if you're up to no good.

Frey had a different take, though. What did he say? The Navajo have a close connection with the land.

So why would George choose to break it?

There's no cover between where I stand and the house. I have no choice but to sprint the distance, moving faster than a human is capable of moving and hoping Kayani hasn't pulled over somewhere to watch me through his binoculars.

Once I reach the house, I don't head for the front door, but race around to the rear where I expect to find a back way in. There's no door, only a couple of windows. Still, that's no problem. The windows are open and without screens.

However, the lack of security makes the possibility of my finding something incriminating highly unlikely.

But I'm here and all is quiet inside. No sight or sound to indicate anyone's home. I climb in.

The room is a small bedroom. Unfurnished except for a couple of boxes. When I peek inside, the musty smell of old blankets wrinkles my nose. The closet is empty, too.

The door of that room leads to a short hallway, then a bigger bedroom and a bathroom. The bed is made, a beautiful handwoven blanket thrown over it like a spread. The room is clean; the furniture smells like beeswax. The feeling of neglect I experienced outside does not reach into the interior of the house.

Once again, nothing in the closets except what one would expect. Jeans, skirts, vests, boots, blouses. There are a couple of beaded outfits under plastic, resplendent with feathers and colorful headdresses. Nothing to implicate George in a crime or in the practice of curse magic. Nothing to suggest anything other than a traditional Navajo couple.

The living room and kitchen are as neat and clean as the bedroom. I make quick work of opening cupboards, peeking in drawers. Like Sarah, George's wife has a loom and on it, a half-finished rug awaits completion. A basket of yarn lies beside it.

The living room furniture, a couch and two chairs, is old but spot free. The tables and chairs gleam with polish. A hardwood floor has been swept and waxed. There are no pictures on the walls or on the table surfaces. Only a paperback, another Tony Hillerman novel, adorns the squat table near a reading lamp.

I blow out a breath and look around.

Nothing.

A glance at my watch says I've wasted ten minutes.

I go out through the same window I came in. When my feet touch the ground, I look around. George doesn't seem to have horses or livestock of any kind but there is a small lean-to some distance from the house. I'm there in an eyeblink.

The lean-to is more substantial upon closer inspection. Made of wood, recently constructed judging from the feel and smell of it, and about twelve feet by twenty.

The door is heavy and has a good-sized padlock securing it.

Thank you, George. Most people don't realize that if they need to keep something secure, size does matter. The smaller the lock the better. A large padlock, like this one, is easy to pick because there's more key space to work with and bigger pins.

Now, to find what I need. A quick trip back to the kitchen and a revisit to the ubiquitous junk drawer. Something to use as a torsion wrench. A long, thin screwdriver. Something to use as a pick tool. A paperclip.

Now, as a vampire, I could pull that lock apart and not break a sweat. But if there's something important inside, it'd be a good thing to have Kayani and his deputies open it officially instead of trying to explain how it got broken. Better, too, not to alert George that someone broke into his shed.

Besides, the human in me wants to see if I still have the touch.

I do. The point of the screwdriver slips easily into the bottom of the lock. The straightened paperclip fits into the top. A little pressure on the screwdriver, a little pressure on the paperclip, and I get the satisfying click of an opened padlock.

Less than three seconds.

A new personal best.

David couldn't have done it faster.

No time to gloat. I push open the door, slip inside, close the door behind me.

The first thing I'm greeted with is the strong musk of animal. It's dark and close inside. Vampire smells predator and springs to the surface. With a growl, I crouch and peer around.

The pelts of a bear, coyote and wolf are splayed on a table in the back of the shed. Vampire retreats when she realizes there is no threat. She stays close, though.

On the side wall, a blowgun hangs from a leather thong. Beneath it, another table. This one holds small, rounded beads in one pottery jar and a white powder in another. I recognize the beads. Bone charms, Frey called them, as he pulled one from my arm.

Next to the jars, pieces of broken pottery. One has something wrapped around it. I bend close. Pick it up. Hair, soft, smelling of grass and sunshine. My heart jumps. I recognize the scent.

It's John-John's hair.

What are they planning to do with it?

Nothing. Now.

I stick it into the pocket of my jeans. I will take this with me and the threat of discovery be damned.

A sound from outside. A car pulling up to the house.

Kayani? Why would he come to the house? I still have a few minutes left.

I peek through the door. An old sedan, gray from sun and weather, is parked at the side of the house. A woman stands beside it, midfifties, dressed in a long velveteen skirt and cotton smock. Her waist is cinched by a conch belt of large silver disks each with a stone of turquoise and agate in the center. She wears a squash blossom necklace and bangles of silver. Her face is soft, rounded with age but her back is straight and she stands tall, commanding respect.

She looks toward the shed.

George's wife? Can she see the door slightly ajar from where she's standing?

She takes a step in my direction. Then stops, turns back toward the house. The sound of another car approaching has drawn her attention.

Kayani's police vehicle pulls behind her car.

She and Kayani exchange greetings. I don't waste a second. I take another quick look around the shed, recording to memory what I see. The screwdriver and paperclip are shoved into another pocket. Then I close the door softly behind me, relock the padlock, and slip like any other desert creature into the bright midday sun.

CHAPTER 41

I WAIT FOR KAYANI TO RETURN TO THE SPOT WHERE
we planned to meet. I watch as he chats with the woman a
few minutes, then climbs back into his vehicle and drives off.
The woman looks again toward the shed, sees nothing amiss,
gives her head a little shake and retreats into the house.

I jump in as soon as Kayani pulls up.

"Well?"

"First, thanks for distracting her so I could get away. Is
that George's wife?"

"Yes. When I saw her pull up, I figured you might need a
little help. Lucky you were in that shed instead of the house."

I pull the screwdriver out of my pocket, wipe it with the
tail of my blouse and let it fall to the floor of the cab. Kayani glances at it but doesn't ask what I used it for. Plausible
deniability.

"Might want to throw that into the nearest Dumpster," I
suggest with a tight smile.

He looks at it again, distastefully, but chooses to pursue

more important matters. "What did you find?" he asks, heading away from George's.

"Not what I expected." I dig into the other pocket and pull out the pottery shard wrapped with John-John's hair.

When Kayani sees it, he slams on the brakes so hard, my seat belt snaps taut, my head whip lashing forward and back.

"Ouch."

He reaches over and snatches the thing out of my hand.

"You found this in the shed?"

"Do you know what it is?"

I can tell by his expression that he does, but he barks, "What else did you find?"

I tell him. The pelts, the blowgun, the bone charms. I pause a beat when I'm finished to ask, "He is a skinwalker, isn't he?"

His dark eyes pierce mine. "You know of such things?"

"Only what Frey told me. But that—" I point to the charm in his hand. "That I don't know about. It's John-John's hair. What did he intend to do with it?"

Kayani peers at me again, searching my face for something . . . Wrestling maybe with how much he can confide to this outsider. I can't come clean with everything, but if I tell him I've had personal experience with a skinwalker, perhaps that will gain me some measure of trust.

"I was shot with a bone charm. I'm pretty sure now it was George who did it."

Kayani's eyes widen. "What? When?"

"The night of the accident. The night Frey and I spent in the hogan."

"You should be dead."

"Frey recognized what it was right away. He got it out of

me in time to prevent the poison from working." That and the fact that I'm vampire and my body could heal itself once the charm was removed.

My shoulders tighten, waiting for Kayani to ask why George would target me, a question I'm dreading. I may have to tell him what I am.

While I wait, Kayani is silent. Then, "Why didn't Frey tell me?"

"I suppose he wasn't sure you'd believe it." Flimsy but plausible. I don't give him time to think about it, either. Relief, impatience and concern for John-John make me cut off any chance for more questions. "What were they going to do with John-John's hair?"

His eyes refocus. "How did you know it was John-John's?"

He keeps answering my questions with questions of his own, but I'll give him this one. I already laid the ground-work. "I told you—good sense of smell. Try it yourself. You've been around John-John a lot. His hair smells like a little boy who spends a lot of time outside."

He raises the charm warily to his nose, closes his eyes, inhales. "I guess my nose isn't as sensitive as yours." He touches the hair, examines it. "It's the right color and tex-ture, though."

He bangs his hand against the dashboard with so much force, I jump. "Why would he be after John-John?"

I choose this moment to advance another theory. "I think maybe he caused the accident that killed Sarah and Mary, too."

I say it softly, then brace myself, expecting heated de-nial and unequivocal rebuttal to blow with gale force my way. Instead, I get more silence so I forge ahead.

"Could Mary and Sarah have heard something the night of the meeting? Maybe a conversation between George and the men he was sitting with on the deck?"

Kayani presses the palms of his hands against his eyes. "Did you find anything to connect George with the counterfeiters?"

"No."

"Then they might have been tourists he took out that day. We need something concrete to connect them."

I touch the charm. "If George goes looking for this, he'll know someone has been in his shed. He'll know someone recognizes what he is. How do you think he'll react?"

"Skinwalkers are reviled in Navajo society. He'll want his secret protected."

"How does one become a skinwalker? Frey said it had to do with desecrating the body of a loved one. He didn't believe George could ever do that."

"Well, it looks like he was wrong, doesn't it?" Anger flares in his voice. "It is said that if a Navajo pronounces the full name of a *yee naaldlooshii*, a skinwalker, that person will die for the wrongs they have committed."

He draws in a breath, a look of purpose tightening the lines around his eyes and mouth.

I put a hand on his arm. "No. Don't. If you speak George's name and it works, we may never find out if he is behind the counterfeiting. Or who is working with him. Protecting the good of your people is important, isn't it?"

Kayani breathes out. His eyes narrow a bit as he looks at me. I suppose he's wondering why I, a stranger to the Navajo, so easily accepts that he could kill with the invoking of a name.

But he doesn't ask.

Wordlessly, he takes the charm from my hand, opens the car door, steps onto the desert floor. He throws the charm down, crushes it with the heel of his boot. Then he picks up the strands of hair and lets them gust away on the breeze.

"Let's get back to Daniel," he says. "He must be warned."

CHAPTER 42

FREY IS WAITING FOR US ON THE PORCH WHEN WE arrive back.

"Where's John-John?" Kayani asks the minute we've jumped out of the truck.

"Inside. He's already asleep. The poor kid is dead tired." He looks from Kayani's face to mine and back again. "What's going on?"

There's so much Frey doesn't know about our afternoon excursion that it takes both of us several minutes to bring him up to date. His reaction is predictable.

He directs his anger first at Kayani and me. "You two went off without letting me know what you were doing. What if you'd gotten caught? What if George had decided to shoot you again with a bone charm? Or you, Kayani? John-John would be next and I would have known nothing about it."

Kayani accepts Frey's wrath. "You are right. It was stupid not to let you now where we were going. But at the time, we thought we were hunting smugglers, not a *yee naaldlooshii*. It wasn't until Anna found the proof in George's shed that we realized John-John was in trouble."

"Did you destroy the charm?"

"Of course, my friend."

"Then it is time I pay George a visit."

Kayani nods in understanding. "It was my first reaction, too. But Anna reminded me we don't yet have proof that he is behind the counterfeiters. We must be sure one way or another before we act. There is a greater good to consider."

"Not to me there isn't." Frey is on his feet, ready to sweep any obstacle out of his path. "I won't give him an opportunity to harm my son."

"I love John-John, too," Kayani says quietly. "I have known him since he was a baby. I will die before I let harm befall him. We must come up with a way to protect John-John while pursuing the truth of the other matter."

"And how do you propose to do that? Do you have a plan?"

"Maybe," Kayani replies. "We will take turns tailing George round the clock. At least one of us will always be here with John-John. We will make sure no one, especially George, gets close to him."

"And how do we tail him when he's out on one of his tours?" Frey's voice is tight with frustration. "There's no way to follow him in a car. He'd spot that in a minute."

"I'll take care of that," Kayani says. "On horseback. I know the land as well as George. I know where he takes the tourists. If he makes any unplanned spots, speaks with anyone not part of a group, I will see it. He will not spot me, I can promise you that."

Frey is not ready to let go of his rage toward George. "I will give you twenty-four hours," he says. "Not a minute more. If you find nothing you can use to stop the counterfeiters in twenty-four hours, I will go after George on my own. I will make him talk."

I don't know if Sarah told Kayani that Frey was a shapeshifter, or if he is aware that Frey's other form is panther. The look that passes between the two men, however, makes me suspect that Kayani knows what Frey is capable of.

Kayani checks his watch. "George will be returning home from the lodge. Daniel, you will watch the house tonight. I will stay here with Anna. If you see anything suspicious, call on the cell."

"No," I interrupt. "I should take the night watch. Frey should stay here with John-John. You both should."

Kayani looks ready to argue but Frey is looking at me.

In the same way Kayani knows what Frey can do, Frey knows what I'm capable of. He knows I'll do whatever's necessary to keep George from coming anywhere near John-John. More important, he wants to stay close to his son. "I agree with Anna," he says. "She should take the night watch."

Kayani's expression reflects skepticism and surprise. "Anna, do you even remember how to find George's place?"

"I do. I have become more adept at noting geographical points. His home is close to a mesa. I'm sure I can find it again."

"Hunt's Mesa," Kayani says. "Let me show you on a map."

He trots out to his car and returns with a map. This is not the typical tourist map, though, it's a map that marks all residences in the tribal park. There are well over a hundred, spaced far apart with no paved roads connecting them.

"I had no idea there were so many homes in the valley."

Frey presses close to look. "Where is George's?"

Kayani traces the route from Sarah's to George's. He is—was—actually her closest neighbor.

Frey's anger resurfaces. "He had John-John the night of the accident. He said he was taking him to Sarah. I never thought to ask when he showed up at the hogan why John-John was at his house. I was too relieved that he hadn't been in the truck."

Self-recrimination rings through his voice.

"Doesn't matter, Frey. John-John is safe. We'll keep him that way." I hold out my hand. "Do you have the keys to the Jeep?"

He digs into a pocket of his jeans and withdraws the keys. Places them in the palm of my hand.

"I'd better get going. We've missed trailing him after he dropped off his afternoon group. Let's hope he heads straight home and doesn't make a stop anywhere else. I'd hate to think we missed our only opportunity to catch him with those men again."

Kayani refolds the map. "I'll head for the lodge, just in case. If he's already left, I'll call you. It should take him forty minutes or so to get home. I'll retrace his route, then come back here."

Frey walks with us to the porch steps. "Keep a sharp eye out, Anna. George can take animal shape. You saw the pelts. Any of those are formidable opponents."

His voice is calm, but his eyes telegraph a more urgent message.

Bear. Coyote. Wolf.

I nod my understanding. But I have vampire inside.

There is no more formidable opponent.

* * *

IT'S MIDNIGHT AND I AM SO BORED, MY TEETH GRIND with impatience. George arrived home a little after six. From the time, Kayani confirmed that he wouldn't have had time to stop anywhere and, backtracking his route just to be sure, came across no one unfamiliar on the way. He returned to join Frey.

The house is quiet, but not dark. Lights shine in the living room and kitchen. Shadowy figures pass in front of drapes pulled across front windows. Odd since there are no neighbors to see inside.

Finally, the lights are extinguished and I settle back on the seat. I expect George and his wife are retiring for the night.

The sound of the front door jerks me back to attention. George and his wife stand quietly on the porch. They glance around furtively, as if assuring themselves that they are alone.

Then they walk quickly down the steps, sticking to the shadows, and head for the back.

I follow. Vampire is in her element at night. I am a shadow among shadows in the light of a crescent moon.

I'm at the back of the shed just as they approach the front. They are speaking in Navajo. The wife must have said something about thinking she saw the door open this afternoon because George is examining the lock.

He finds nothing because there is nothing to find. His response to her is condescending and sharp in tone.

That changes when they have been inside for only a moment. They had to have noticed the missing charm. Both voices escalate in anger and accusation. Questions are thrown back and forth, reproachful replies flung like stones. I'd give anything this minute to understand Navajo.

It grows quiet.

George leaves, comes back with a red plastic can. A gas can. The sharp smell of gasoline being splashed on surfaces wrinkles my nose.

He and his wife back out of the shed; he's still dribbling gas in his path. Then the scratch of a match, a flare of light, and the shed goes up in a great whoosh and burst that turns night into day.

CHAPTER 43

N O.
    I need to do something—to save something from the shed to prove that George was a skinwalker. If only they would move away, but they stand watching.

I grab my cell phone. Call Frey. Whisper to send Kayani and the fire department.

Does the Navajo Nation have a fire department?

I guess I'll find out.

I need a distraction. I can pull out some boards in back but I can't do it quietly.

A siren. Good.

Kayani only five miles away must be screeching toward us. George and his wife exchange astonished glances. Not hard to read their expressions. How could anyone get here so quickly?

George runs back to the car with the gas can. His wife stares at the shed as if willing it to burn faster. I don't wait any longer. I remember where the blowgun hung from the wall. I find the place, rip out the boards with my hands and fingernails. A section comes away. The blowgun still hangs from its nail. I snatch it and the bone charms in their pottery jar. The one that held ash has already burst from the heat.

I glance up to find George's wife staring at me. She raises a hand and waves some kind of feather stick at me, shrieking.

But vampire has already taken over. To the woman, I become a blur, too fast for her to follow, even with her eyes.

Her shriek continues to follow me. It hangs in the air until it's cut off abruptly. I watch from the Jeep. Kayani has arrived at the house. He grabs a garden hose but the hole I tore in the side of the shed has only accelerated the burning. The meager trickle of water from the hose does nothing. Finally, he drops it on the ground and the three stand helplessly as the shed burns to the ground.

Only the eyes of George's wife are not on the shed. They scan the dark, try to penetrate the shadows. She searches for me.

MY CELL PHONE TRILLS. I SNATCH IT OUT OF MY pocket.

"Gus." It's Kayani. "Cancel the fire call. It was a shed on George Long Whiskers's property. It's gone. No need to waste water. Send everyone home."

He clicks off. I watch as he leads George and his wife into the house. Lights go on, and I take the hint. I start the Jeep and head back to Frey's.

* * *

IT'S TWO HOURS BEFORE KAYANI REJOINS US AT Frey's. His first words to me are, "Please tell me you got something out of the shed."

We're on the porch. I reach to the floor and pick up the blowgun and pottery jar.

His shoulders drop with relief. He picks up the blowgun gingerly by the end and uses a plastic evidence bag he took from a jacket pocket to handle the jar. "I'll lock these in the car."

We wait for him to rejoin us. He lifts his nose. "Is that coffee I smell?"

Frey and I both lift mugs. "John-John and I had time on our hands this afternoon," Frey says, his tone as pointed as a jabbing finger. "We went shopping at the trading post. There's a pot on the stove."

Kayani wastes no time helping himself.

Frey waits for him to lean his butt against the railing and take an appreciative pull before jumping in. "What now?"

I shake my head. "I wish I could say I got away with the blowgun clean, but George's wife saw me. She shrieked like a banshee and waved some feather thing at me."

Kayani puts his mug down on the rail. "She did?"

"Does that mean something?"

Excitement lights his eyes. "It means she's probably a witch, an 'ánt'įįhnii. She may be the one who initiated George into the witchery way. It is thought only childless women become witches, and she is childless."

"Is she powerful?"

"Together they could be formidable."

Frey stirs impatiently, "So where does that leave us?"

"If she describes Anna to George and he connects you to Frey and John-John—"

"Which I'm sure she will. George knows I'm a v—"

I catch myself. Kayani frowns. "You're a what?"

I look over at Frey. He gives me an "it's your decision" raise of the eyebrows.

I lean back in the porch chair, putting a little more distance between Kayani and myself. "I'm a vampire."

Kayani snickers the kind of snicker that usually precedes, "You're kidding, right?"

But the seriousness in my face stops him. That and the fact that Frey has not challenged the claim.

I see the doubt and suspicion build in his eyes. Trust and comradeship evaporate. He glares at Frey. "You knew she was a vampire? You brought her to your son's home?"

An echo of Sarah's condemnation. Frey replies in the same heated way with many of the same words. I tune it out. Kayani will have to come to his own conclusions. I rise abruptly, "I'll be inside when you decide what to do."

I pour myself another cup of coffee, glance at the clock. It's almost dawn. Frey has only given us twenty-four hours to solve the smuggling problem and we are not any closer to a solution than we were twelve hours ago.

Maybe going to George and letting vampire convince him to come clean is the best plan after all. It would keep Kayani and Frey clear and John-John safe.

And if George isn't involved in the counterfeiting, what then? He still has the deaths of Sarah and Mary to answer for.

Kayani will just have to pursue the criminal investigation on his own.

Without George, who will most likely be dead.

CHAPTER 44

JOHN-JOHN'S SHRILL SCREAM MAKES THE MUG SLIP from my hand, but before it crashes to the floor, I'm in his room.

John-John is sitting up in bed, his eyes wide, his body trembling. I gather him into my arms, hug him close, rock him. Frey is beside me then, and I slip away to let him take over. He talks to his son in Navajo, soft crooning, words whose meaning come through even without the benefit of literal translation.

He is consoling his son, telling him he is all right, assuring him his father will never leave him.

Kayani has come into the room, too. He avoids my eyes, but something he picks up in John-John's replies to his father makes him cross to the window. He parts the curtains and looks out.

I join him and whisper, "What is it?"

"John-John says he *felt* something watching him. A red eye. When he woke, it disappeared."

"A nightmare?"

"Some legends speak of skinwalkers carrying red lights."

"You think George was here? In John-John's bedroom?"

Frey has picked up John-John, blankets wrapped tightly around his little frame. "I'm taking John-John in the kitchen for some warm milk."

We watch until he's out of sight. I'm shaking with outrage. "How could he get in without our seeing him?"

"He may not have." His eyes are troubled. "What John-John saw might be part of a curse."

"But we destroyed the charm, didn't we?"

"One, at least."

"There could have been more?" Each word fans the anger boiling in my blood until I think I will burst into flame. "I need to get to George and his wife. I can make them talk."

"You or vampire?" Kayani's words are sharp.

"Does it matter?" I snap back.

He surprises me by not rising to the bait. To the contrary, his tone softens. "Daniel has great faith in you," he says simply. "Your kind are not known for their humanity, but I have seen nothing of an evil side to your nature. I have watched you with John-John. He would not respond to you if he sensed danger. You may be the best hope we have to rid ourselves of this curse."

"Then I will go. Now."

"We need to talk to Daniel first."

"No. He will want to come with me. He is too angry. Do you know about Frey's other form?"

Kayani nods. "Sarah told me. She was afraid John-John might have inherited his father's curse. It terrified her."

"It is not a curse. It is a gift to be managed and contained and can be used for good. Frey has helped me too many times to count." I wave a hand toward John-John's bed. "What people like George and his wife do, skinwalkers and witches who work black magic against innocents, they are a curse."

"And still, you don't want Daniel to go with you?"

"If it was a matter of stopping them from attacking John-John, I would send Frey by himself. He deserves revenge. But if George is also behind the counterfeiters, I am in a better position to extract information in a more—" I hesitate, choosing the word. "*Restrained* manner."

A smile touches the corners of his mouth. "You must be careful. Of both George and his wife. We can't be sure who is the most powerful." He dips a hand into his pocket. "Do you want to take my car? A police vehicle may catch them off guard."

"No. I can cover ground faster on my own." I head for the window, slide it open. "Stay in here as long as you can. Frey will think we are still talking. Once he knows the truth, it will be hard to convince him not to follow."

I climb out, stretch, call vampire. Kayani is saying something, but we're already off, racing the wind, racing toward evil. His words fade like shadows before the approaching sunrise. Freedom, excitement and anticipation send the flush of bloodlust to warm cold limbs.

Vampire looks forward to this meeting. Vampire will show what it is to be feared.

CHAPTER 45

THEY ARE TALKING QUIETLY INSIDE, GEORGE AND his wife. I hear the words, but it is in a language unfamiliar to me. I wish they were vampire or shape-shifter so I could understand.

I crouch beneath a window, straighten to look up. They are in the kitchen and they have a wreath of something on the table that they are taking apart and reforming into smaller bundles.

My gut twists. Garlic. They are making talismans of it. They are expecting me.

I back away, watch, sniff. The odor comes only from here. They have not yet polluted the rest of the house with the one substance my system cannot abide.

I need to get them to come outside.

I find a rock. Hurl it through the front window. Then another. I slide under the porch and wait for the front door to open.

George's feet clump above my head. His angry words

frighten a flock of birds into screeching flight. He yells in English and Navajo, not sure if the rocks were thrown by tourists who have wandered far from the public lands, or neighborhood boys looking to make trouble. Before the echo of his words bounce off the mesa, I've punched through the wooden decking and grabbed his ankle. One good pull, and he is tumbling down the steps, a startled cry punctuating his fall.

His wife comes to the door to see what has happened. What she sees is vampire, holding her husband by the neck, teeth bared and yellow eyes flashing.

She runs back inside, comes out with one of those foul wreaths clutched to her chest. "Let him go, devil." She shakes the garlic at me. "You cannot hurt us."

My answer is to nuzzle George's neck, my teeth gently biting. The sound of his blood rushing with fear under that thin, fragile layer of skin makes my own heart pound with excitement.

George smells of panic. He feels my teeth at his neck, he is afraid to pull away. He says something in Navajo to his wife.

She takes a step closer. "No. She cannot hurt us. We are more powerful."

She needs to be convinced that vampire is serious. I worry at his neck, not deep enough to reach the source, just deep enough to cause blood to leak from a small wound. And to cause pain. While he squirms and squeals, I lick at his blood with glee, savoring the texture, the unfamiliar taste of his blood. It is delicious. I taste earth and sun and history stretching back through time.

I want more.

George's screams interrupt my pleasure.

His wife looks at me with more respect now. "What do you want from us?"

It is difficult to pull vampire back, to let the human Anna come forth to ask the questions that must be asked. I relinquish my awareness reluctantly but not my hold on George.

"Why John-John?" I ask in a guttural voice.

George and his woman exchange looks. I take another nip, lap another trickle of blood before it stains his shirt. He cries out. "Tell her."

The woman breathes out the words. "We had nothing against the child. We meant only to frighten him. Get his father to take him away. We were afraid Mary might have told him our secret."

"*Our* secret? You two and Mary?"

She nods.

"What secret?"

"The artifacts." The words at first come hesitantly, then more quickly as the woman spins her tale. "It was Mary's idea. Make them. Sell them on the black market. She had connections in the city."

Even hearing it, vampire has trouble grasping that Mary would conceive of such an idea. "Why would she do it?"

The woman looks surprised I'd ask such a question. "For the money. Mary wanted money to get off the reservation. She had no intention of coming back after college the way her sister had."

"Then why kill her?"

George finds his voice. "We didn't plan to kill her. She found out what was to be discussed at the council meeting. She was afraid *we* would betray *her*, so she decided to betray us first. She had a meeting with the two men who were helping us. She didn't know I was joining them. When I appeared, she acted like everything was fine. But I could tell. She was hiding something."

George's wife tosses the wreath of garlic behind her. A show of good faith, I suppose. Vampire is still leery. "When we found out that an investigation was about to be launched, we went to speak again to the men working with us. They told us they already knew. That Mary said we should stop until things quieted down. But we could tell they were holding back."

She pauses, her expression tells me she's gauging what she should say next. "We persuaded them to tell us the rest. Mary planned to turn George and I in as the smugglers. If we didn't agree to take the blame, she'd reveal that we were skinwalkers. She had proof for both, the rock from the cave and some of our charms. After a time, she could start the operation up again, sell only overseas. Safer that way."

"And where are the men who told you this?"

Another pause. "Gone."

I'll bet. Dead, more likely.

"How did you cause the accident?"

"I appeared as bear," George says. "I could see that Sarah and Mary were arguing. Sarah tried to stop in time, but she was going too fast. When the car rolled, they both were thrown into the road." A sharp intake of breath. "You have to believe me. I didn't mean to kill Mary. Only scare her into keeping quiet."

I think of Mary. College student. Her whole life ahead of her. "Did Sarah know what Mary was doing?"

George shakes his head, carefully, aware that my teeth are still within tearing range. "No. Maybe. It could be what they were arguing about in the truck. Mary may have said something to make Sarah suspicious. Or Sarah might have found the cash Mary kept hidden in her room and made the connection on her own after she heard what the elders were to discuss. Sarah had respect for our ways."

"Who shot me with the bone charm?" I ask the question, part of me dreading the answer.

"Mary." George is quick to distance himself from the act. "She didn't want a stranger hanging around. She knew you were vampire, knew it would make you so sick, Frey was likely to take you away."

"So Mary was a skinwalker, too?"

"Why do you ask?"

"Because I saw no one near when I was shot. She couldn't have gotten away so quickly on foot or by car."

"She would use the cave," George said. "She knew them well."

The cave. The one branch that came out close to the hogan. Mary would know it well.

I have only one more question. "Why did you lie to me about what was discussed at council?"

I address the question to George, but it is his wife who replies. "To get rid of you." The woman holds out her hand in supplication. "We wanted you and Frey and John-John to leave us in peace. We have committed many wrongs, but we are ready to atone for them now."

Vampire takes a firmer hold on George. "So," my human voice says, "you are willing to come with me to Kayani. Tell him all you've told me."

The woman nods solemnly. But the flash of disdain in her eyes belies her intention. Her hand dips into the pocket of her skirt, pulls something small and shiny that she points at us.

No magic here. A little revolver.

George's body goes rigid under my hands. He snaps out something in Navajo.

She answers in English. "Solving problems," she says. "First one."

The bullet hits George in the throat. He sags against me. "Then the other."

Vampire is not afraid of the old woman with the little gun. She prepares to toss the man aside, even though his blood is enticingly close.

But vampire is surprised by a blur of motion that springs from the earth and knocks the woman backward with a force that sends her sprawling.

The woman's eyes widen as panther crouches, circles, growls until she shrieks with fear.

It is the last sound she makes.

CHAPTER 46

WE LEAVE THE BODIES. PANTHER AND VAMPIRE
run back into the desert, the sun turning sand and
rock golden.

It reminds me of other times, other deserts, and I am
happy to be with my friend.

When we reach the house, panther bounds through John-
John's window, heads for Sarah's bedroom. I follow. Quickly,
vampire fades and the human Anna, the human me, is back.
I glance down at my clothes to make sure there is no blood
staining them, and for a minute, vampire reasserts herself,
jealous that panther fed and she had only a taste.

But reason chases petty consideration away, and I go out
to find Kayani and John-John.

They are down at the corral, brushing the horses with big,
flat brushes. John-John stands on a wooden crate to reach his
horse's back. He and Kayani are talking softly in Navajo.
The expressions on their faces are identical—serious, intent.
I marvel at how mature John-John is—four going on forty.

Kayani spies me first. He raises an eyebrow. "Daniel?"

"He'll be down in a minute."

I place a foot on the lowest rail of the corral and boost myself up. "How are you two doing?"

John-John is grinning. "Want to help? We haven't brushed Geronimo yet."

He points with the brush to the big buckskin, watching in the corner while his two compatriots practically swoon with delight as the brushes scratch and tickle their hides. Geronimo looks a little resentful to me.

"Maybe another time. I'll just watch."

John-John giggles. He knew I'd say that. His laugh says "silly city girl."

Frey joins us then, freshly showered, his skin smelling of soap. "Kayani, can I speak to you a minute?"

I release a breath. "You go ahead. I guess I can help John-John brush the horses."

Kayani ducks through the fence and hands me the tool—it's not really a *brush*. It has teeth.

"Currycomb," Kayani says in response to my puzzled inspection. "Always brush in the direction of the hair." He demonstrates with a sweep of his hand. "And by all means, avoid those back hooves. Good way to get kicked."

Great.

John-John is giggling again behind his hand.

"Thanks a lot for the tip," I call out to Kayani's retreating back. He waves a hand and keeps walking.

John-John is watching so I gather my courage and step over the fence. John-John shows me how to guide the currycomb over the horse's back. I expect the animal to shy away and bare his teeth at me.

To my surprise, he rolls his eyes once, dances a little against his tether, then settles down to let me go to work.

I grin at John-John. "Not bad, huh?"

John-John grins back. "Not bad at all."

WHEN WE FINISH WITH THE HORSES, I SMELL OF sweat and horse shit. The look on John-John's face, though, is worth the olfactory assault. He thinks I did a good job. We hose our faces and hands and head back to the house.

Frey is on the porch. Alone.

"Kayani?"

"Gone to take care of some business."

John-John plops himself down beside his father. "Why didn't you join us at the corral?"

Frey slips an arm around his son's shoulders. "You and Anna looked like you were having so much fun, I didn't want to interrupt."

He leans his head against his father's chest. "What is going to happen now? Will you be going away?"

Much as I want to know the answer myself, I take that as a hint to leave the two alone. "I'll be inside. Showering."

On the way to the bathroom, I stop in Mary's bedroom to pick up fresh clothes and underwear. Her laptop is gone from the desk.

Kayani took it, I'm sure. Maybe there's something on it to confirm George's story. Maybe there's nothing and Mary was never working with them at all.

But there is one other thing.

I look around. What is it that George said? Mary kept cash hidden in her room. Where would she have hidden it? Sarah didn't strike me as the suspicious type. Mary's "hiding place" is most likely in plain sight.

I start with the drawers—desk and wardrobe. Pull each one out and look top and bottom. Nothing.

The closet? Clothes hung in no particular order. Nothing on the shelves.

I get down on my knees and look under the bed. A small suitcase. I pull it out and open it.

Three stacks of one-hundred-dollar bills held together with rubber bands. I fan one but don't bother to count it. A small envelope holds a bone charm and a piece of rock. A note:

> *Your cut from the last batch. Buyers want more. Meet me at the lodge tonight.*
>
> *G.*

I imagine handwriting analysis will make it easy to verify that George wrote the note.

Here's the proof. All together in one neat package. I'll give it to Kayani the next time I see him.

But does it matter?

There's no left one to face justice. Everyone's dead.

Only the ancient drawings prevailed, saved from further exploitation.

Perhaps that's enough.

I close the suitcase, shove it back where I found it.

Then I do what I started to do—head for the shower.

CHAPTER 47

SHOWERED AND RID OF MY PUNGENT JEANS (I HOPE the smell of horse comes out in the laundry), I'm ready to rejoin the world. Frey and John-John have moved into the living room. I make a pot of coffee and sit myself down at the kitchen table, still unwilling to intrude on father and son.

The events of the last few days flood over me. My heart is heavy with guilt. My presence precipitated all that happened. There's no denying or rationalizing that fact.

And what have I accomplished?

Frey and John-John appear at the door. "We're going to make breakfast. Care to join us?"

But instinct tells me they have more to discuss. John-John's eyes are red-rimmed. Did Frey tell him that he lost another friend—George? Or that he was leaving? My heart breaks for the boy.

I pick up my coffee mug and push away from the table. "You two eat. I'll be on the porch."

Frey gives me a weak smile, and I know it was the right decision.

I take the same old porch chair that I've occupied how many times since we arrived? Each time I sit here, it seems there's a new question to puzzle out.

This time I'm the puzzle. Sani said I would see him again. I am no closer to a resolution now, though, than I was twenty-four hours ago.

Sani *said* I would see him again. If Sarah never presented my petition, how did he seek me out? *Why* did he?

The sun rises higher in the sky, reminding me of the first time Frey and I saw the house and Mary Yellow Bird. I thought her an Indian princess. Now she and her sister are dead. No storybook ending here. Greed and disrespect for her own heritage brought about Mary's death. Nothing supernatural or otherworldly about it.

So, could I have found the answer if I'd been mortal? Or would the bone charm have ended my life the first night I was here?

Everything that's happened since I became vampire, everything I've accomplished, everyone I've saved or harmed, has been because I am no longer human.

But the price. My family living across the ocean. My business partner put in danger twice. No chance of a relationship that lasts longer than it takes to have sex or feed.

Stephen. Too soon yet to see if we can make it work. And if we did—

Twenty mortal years.

If I married, could I bear a child? Or would the stress on my body from the transformation back to mortal make it impossible? Certainly, if I were able to conceive, I would not live to see my grandchildren. Would my enemies in the vampire universe launch their attack on the mortal world knowing I was no longer able to confront them? Would they seek revenge on my family?

What legacy would I leave?

A world of terror? No less crime or injustice? A world still threatened by Chael's lust for power?

Sani said there have always been those asked to sacrifice personal happiness for the greater good. Could I really be one of those? I know my shortcomings. I'm rash, impulsive, quick to judge. I lack the wisdom of the shaman. I'm not pure of heart. I stumble through each crisis blindly. One step at a time. If not for my family, for my friends, Frey and David and Tracey, I doubt I would have survived this last year.

But if not for me, if not for vampire, they might not have survived, either.

It comes in a flash of insight.

Vampire and I complement each other. When I need strength and courage, she is there. When she needs compassion and restraint, I am there. We are two halves of a whole.

I gaze out over the land, now dazzling under a blinding summer sky.

Sani said it—I have been wrong to worry I cannot serve as a protector and live life as a mortal. Isn't that what I've done this past year? I've walked the tightrope between two worlds and hopefully, both are better for it. Oh, there are problems that still need resolving. David and his flickering memories of a night under the spell of a vampire. Harris and his blossoming curiosity about me.

But when did problems ever disappear completely?

My family is safe. I have friends like Daniel Frey who

know and accept the vampire. Human friends who know and accept Anna Strong. And now, Stephen.

There is only one way I can protect them all.

And perhaps make up for some of the damage I have caused.

I have my decision.

CHAPTER 48

THERE IS MOVEMENT AT THE EDGE OF THE PROP-
erty. A soft blur of gray moves behind rocks. Then the
blur takes shape and steps into the open.

A wolf looks up at me with calm, intelligent eyes.

A thrill of eagerness, of anticipation courses through
me. Sani's messenger.

Wolf comes closer. Not threatening. Her eyes shine into
mine. She stops at the edge of the porch, waiting. I come
down to meet her. She brushes under my hand until it rests
on her back.

The ground tips and begins to spin.

A vortex of sight but no sound. A sensory barrage of
color without shape. A rainbow gone mad.

Colors fade. The spinning slows, stops. Wolf is gone.

I'm standing in the middle of a circle. Alone.

Vision clears.

Not alone.

All around me, twelve ancients sit, their solemn faces

reflecting wisdom, understanding, *knowing*. They are naked except for loincloths of leather, beaded and tied with thongs. Their faces and bodies are old, creased with age, but exuding vitality and warmth. They each hold a long, slender stick carved with symbols—a tree, a mountain, a stream. Others I don't recognize in my ignorance.

For I am more aware of my ignorance than I have ever been. I am humbled to be in the presence of such power. We are not in the cave. I don't know where we are. It's open ground and all I see around us is earth and sky.

In the center, Sani. He rises, takes a step into the circle, squats back down, motioning for me to do the same.

As before, I follow his example, folding my legs under me.

"You have made a decision," he says.

My heart thuds with sudden fear. Not for what I am about to ask, but because I have so little right to ask it.

"What is it?" His gentle face reassures me.

"I will not ask for mortality to be restored. Not for me."

He catches the subtle nuance of my last words. "What are you asking?"

"I ask that Sarah be returned to her son. She is dead because of me. I can face any challenge. I am adult and vampire. There is a little boy who lost his mother and aunt. If I can lessen his pain, I will bear the consequences."

"The consequences?"

"Grant me twenty years. I will do all in my power during that time to rid the world of those vampires who would destroy it. I will make sure my successor is like me—a protector. I ask nothing else."

Sani is silent. Probing his heart—or mine? I can't tell. He lets nothing show in his expression.

Finally, he says, "It is always sad when young ones die.

Mary betrayed her sister and tradition. Her alliance with George Long Whiskers led to their deaths. Whether or not you were here, they would still both be dead."

"No. They would be alive if I hadn't persuaded Frey to bring me here."

"Can you be sure?"

"Does it matter? I am sick that John-John is alone."

Sani takes my hands in his. "I cannot grant your request. Sarah has been buried in the Navajo way. She has traveled this path. That you would ask in her name is a tribute to your spirit. I know your fears for the boy, but he will not be alone."

I close my eyes for a moment, sadness overwhelming me. I wanted to give John-John his mother back. I failed. In my heart, I suppose I knew I would. I square my shoulders and raise my face to meet Sani's gaze.

"Then I have made the only decision I can. I will remain vampire, protector. I only hope someday to be wise enough to know what is right and to have the courage to fight for what is right."

Sani's eyes shine into mine. "Follow your heart in all things and you will not go astray."

His grip on my hands loosens, but I don't let go. "Tell me," I ask. "Why did you agree to meet with me?"

He smiles, patting my hand. "You have respect for the Navajo. For the old ways. There is too little of it, even among our own people."

He rises, takes my hand, pulls me to my feet. "You are a soldier—a guardian. Don't fight your nature. Embrace it, learn from it. You have an important role to play. You've just begun to understand how important. You seek love, for yourself and others. It is understandable. But seek knowledge, too, and through it, understanding. There are many factions, many battles ahead. You will be the ambassador to bring all sides together. That is the gift of the Chosen One."

He lays a hand on my head, a blessing.

And a farewell.

Just like before, I don't have time to process his words or respond. Sani is gone. The scene around me melts into a blur.

The next moment, I'm back on the porch.

CHAPTER 49

I HEAR FREY CALLING ME FROM THE KITCHEN BUT I'M too disoriented to get up right away. I'm not sure my legs will support me.

What happened wasn't a dream. Was it?

The last few minutes replay in my head as vividly as a movie. Sani's words are imprinted in my brain, there for me to call up when I falter.

The thought fills me with warmth.

It's as if I have a little of Sani's spirit inside.

When I walk into the kitchen, Frey and John-John are seated around the table. Frey tilts his head, peers at me. "Are you all right?"

"Sure. What's going on?"

Frey motions for me to take a seat. "I have to tell you something."

I slide in next to John-John. He looks a little happier, his eyes clearer. He holds out a hand to me and I blow into his palm. He grins.

Frey isn't so happy. "I've made a decision."

I beat him to the punch. "You're staying here with John-John."

He looks startled, as if I've pulled a chicken from behind John-John's ear. "Don't look so surprised." I muss the child's hair. "It wasn't so hard to figure out. I knew before you did."

Sani's words, the boy will not be alone.

And Frey's admonition: magic always exacts a price. The bigger the magic, the bigger the price. Isn't that what he said?

This is my price to pay. Life without my friend. Even if the magic didn't work the way I hoped it might.

This is my price to pay.

"You could stay with us," John-John is saying. "I could teach you to ride and speak Navajo."

"I wish I could. But I need to get back to work. I'll come visit, though. I think it's time I learned to ride a horse, don't you?"

He is smiling. I touch his hair, softly, and stand up. I don't know how long I can pretend to be upbeat about Frey's decision, even though I know it's the right one. The only one. Sadness is so close to the surface, I'm afraid it will overwhelm me. How will I get along without my friend?

"Besides," I say through the huge lump in my throat. "I've been thinking about my own family. I think it's time I paid them a visit. Trish has been scolding me for staying away so long."

With a side trip to New York. I missed Stephen's debut network appearance. Maybe I can catch the next one in person.

I can tell by the look in Frey's eyes, he approves. I wish

I could communicate how much I'm going to miss him. Maybe it's better that I can't.

"He knows," John-John pipes up. "He's going to miss you, too."

Frey and I laugh. "I forgot how smart you are." I hug John-John to my chest. "You take care of your dad."

I let John-John go, fighting back tears. "I'd better call my pilot and have him pick me up in— Ah, where would be the closest airport?"

John-John's eyes get big. "You have a plane?" he asks before Frey can answer.

For just a moment, excitement and wonder sweep the cloud of sadness from his eyes.

I bend down so our faces are close. "I sure do. Tell me, John-John, how would you like to take a ride on a private jet?"